THE RISE OF THE BLACK WOLF

GREY GRIFFINS BOOK 2

THE RISE OF THE

BLACK WOLF

Derek Benz
& J. S. Lewis

Orchard Books
NEW YORK
AN IMPRINT OF
SCHOLASTIC INC.

Library of Congress Cataloging-in-Publication Data
Benz, Derek. Lewis, J. S.
The rise of the Black Wolf / Derek Benz and
J. S. Lewis. — 1st Scholastic ed.
p. cm.
"Grey Griffins."
Summary: Aided by the Knights Templar, the four young
Grey Griffins face a host of evil forces, including Morgan LaFey's
Black Wolves, who kidnap Max's father while the quartet
is spending what at first seemed a fairytale Christmas
break at the Sumner's castle in Scotland
ISBN 13: 978-0-439-83774-3, ISBN 10: 0-439-83774-X
[1. Magic—Fiction.   2. Monsters—Fiction.
3. Scotland—Fiction.]   I. Lewis, J. S. (Jon S.)   II. Title.
PZ7.B44795Ris 2007
[Fic]—dc22
2006013716
10 9 8 7 6 5 4 3 2 1   07 08 09 10 11 12

Printed in the U. S. A.
Reinforced Binding for Library Use
First edition, January 2007
Text type set in 10.25-point Res Publica
Display type set in Skreech and Stinkymovement
Book design by Richard Amari

In loving memory of my hero, Thomas K. Crawford.
You will never be forgotten.
— Jon

For Ioulia, my солнышко. May your light burn ever-bright.
And to my parents, Arlen and Bonnie, who have walked along
this path with me since my very first steps.
— Derek

To Nancy Coffey for setting us on this wild adventure. And to
Lisa Sandell, Rachel Coun, Stephanie Nooney, Suzanne Murphy,
Tracy Van Straaten, Richard Amari, Marijka Kostiw, Ken Geist,
and the entire Scholastic team. Not only are you the best
in the business, you are and always will be official members
of the secret Order of the Grey Griffins.
— Derek and Jon

Contents

THE RISE OF THE BLACK WOLF

GREY GRIFFINS BOOK 2

PROLOGUE

DARKNESS SPILLED into eleven-year-old Max Sumner's bedroom as he rubbed his eyes and looked around. It was happening again . . . something was coming for him.

Max slid his hand under his pillow only to find that the *Codex Spiritus,* the magical book that could save his life, was nowhere to be found. His heart raced in panic and his skin began to crawl as Max realized how helpless he was. When the monster came for him, there would be nothing he could do.

Suddenly the window burst open with a crash, hurling snow and sleet that stung Max's face and whipped frantically through the air. Then came a rush of beating wings and the deafening cry that Max recognized instantly as bats — hundreds of them.

His eyes frozen shut, Max opened his mouth to scream, but the wind sucked away his breath and numbed his ears until all he could hear was the pounding of his own heartbeat. He was lost in a fury of blizzard and bat wings, drowning and senseless.

Then, suddenly, the wind stopped and the room grew quiet.

Max managed to slowly open his eyes, and as his vision cleared, he could see a tall figure standing before him, wrapped in the swirling shadows of a long and tattered cape.

As their eyes met, Max began to shiver. It wasn't the interloper's smoldering eyes that frightened him. Nor was it the shining sword held in the stranger's gloved grip. There was but one single feature about this man that scared Max more than anything else: his smile, wherein lay the unmistakable fangs of a vampire.

"No!" Max shouted, as he sat up in his bed, sweat beading on his forehead as he took shallow breaths. But there was no vampire, and his window was shut and locked tight.

The nightmares had returned.

The Beginnings of a Creepy Christmas

AVALON, MINNESOTA, lay in the snowy plains of Middle America. A fresh winter rain had swept across the land, covering every tree limb, street sign, and electrical wire with a wrapper of gleaming ice. And when the sun managed to poke through the clouds, the entire town seemed to sparkle.

The Grey Griffins, a secret club made up of four best friends from King's Elementary School, walked beneath the branches of the woods with smiles upon their faces. They were returning home after searching for the perfect Christmas tree, and with winter break near, the air was bursting with anticipation.

"We should be careful, though," Ernie Tweeny mumbled through the long rainbow scarf that was wrapped around his head like a python. Between that and his stocking cap, all that could be seen of his face was Ernie's ample nose and horn-rimmed glasses that were fogged over in the frosty air. "There are still monsters creeping around in here, you know."

"Cheer up," encouraged Natalia Romanov, her long red braids bouncing with each step. Despite her diminutive stature, Natalia was tough as nails and twice as sharp. She always kept her wits, which was the sign of a good sleuth — and Natalia was the best in town, even at eleven years of age. "There aren't any monsters out here anymore," she claimed. "Or at least not that many."

"But . . ."

"Come on," Harley Eisenstein added with a reassuring pat on Ernie's shoulder. "Don't be such a chicken. It's almost Christmas. What could possibly go wrong?" Harley was standing ankle deep in the snow, wearing nothing more than a hooded sweatshirt, a jean jacket, and fingerless gloves. He was big for his age, a head taller than most of his friends. And brave. If Harley ever got scared, no one knew about it. Ernie, on the other hand, was pretty much afraid of his own shadow.

"Fine," Ernie said, sighing, as he looked about, pushing down his scarf to take a deep pull from his asthma inhaler — cold air and nerves were bad for his condition. But luckily, the sun was bright and shadows were scarce. "Just don't say I didn't warn you. I know I saw something move in the trees back there . . . something's been following us."

Only a few months earlier, the woods surrounding the town of Avalon had been teeming with goblins, Spriggans, pixies, and other unspeakable nasties that had jumped out of the darkest pages of fairy tales. At first it had only been a mistake. Harley had been tricked into releasing the monsters that had been locked up in Max's magical book, but events took a turn for the worse when Morgan LaFey, an immortal witch, showed up in town one day. She set out to use Max and his book for something far worse: to open Oberon's Gate, a portal to a dark world. If she had succeeded, Oberon, King of the Shadowlands of Faerie, would have marched through with an army of goblins, putting an end to their quiet town — and then the rest of the world. But the Griffins, working side by side with the fabled Knights Templar, had foiled the plot. It was, admittedly, more difficult than it sounds, but as Natalia was happy to point out, all's well that ends well.

Ernie, however, continued to remind the other Griffins that their terrible adventure was probably only the beginning of something far more dreadful. His theory was that happy endings only ever came true in books. This was real life.

"We'll be fine," Grayson Maximillian Sumner III, or Max as he preferred to be called, assured Ernie. "I know these woods inside and out. Besides, we're almost home."

Max was the leader of the secret Order of the Grey Griffins. His sun-streaked hair had darkened dramatically with the start of winter. Apart from his storm-gray eyes, which changed color with the weather, there was little else that stood out about Max. He was neither short nor tall; he wasn't picked first when they played sports — though never last; and while he managed to get good grades in school, his marks were nowhere near Natalia's. All in all, Max was pretty much like most boys his age, except for two points: His recently divorced parents were billionaires, and he possessed one of the most powerful magical artifacts ever created, the *Codex Spiritus*.

"I just want to know how Harley plans to put a tree like this in a trailer so small," Natalia remarked, pointing to the tall spruce that Harley was dragging behind him — a gift for his mother. Natalia wasn't trying to be rude. She just approved of straight talk. After all, it was no secret that Harley *did* live in a run-down trailer on the outskirts of town, with barely enough room inside to open the refrigerator door.

"It'll fit," said Harley, snorting. What the Eisenstein household lacked in creature comforts, they more than made up for in love. Max only dreamed that his parents cared about him half as much, especially since the divorce.

The Griffins trudged through the snow, Natalia and Max at the front while Harley trailed behind with the trunk of the Christmas tree swung over his shoulder. Ernie, because he knew very well that monsters only attacked kids in the front or end of a line, had placed himself safely in the middle, quietly munching on a carrot stick. Ernie's father was an orthodontist, and in a small town like Avalon, riddled with gossips and busybodies, family members with dental issues were notably poor for business. When a cavity had been discovered, Ernie was barred from his beloved junk food and a strict diet was enforced.

"Hey, look," Harley called, suddenly dropping the tree as he ran off the path. "Footprints."

"From a dog," Natalia replied. "What's the big deal?"

Harley shook his head as Max drew near. "Close. It's a wolf, and a big one, too."

"A wolf?" Ernie exclaimed nervously, looking over his shoulder.

"Ah, don't worry so much," Harley replied, slapping Ernie on the shoulder. "They're more scared of us than we are of them. Come on. Let's follow the tracks and see where they go."

Ernie's face turned pale. It wasn't so simple to convince him — especially after he had nearly been eaten by a werewolf just a few months before. That wasn't easy to get over.

"It looks like they're leading toward my house," Max said. "And we're going there anyway. We'll be fine."

Ernie shook his head. "Those tracks lead straight toward Lethe Creek Bridge. I don't care if it's on our way home or not. That bridge is bad news. In case you forgot, there *is* a reason that we never go that way anymore."

"Because you never let us," reminded Harley.

"No," Ernie argued. "It's because something nasty lives below it."

Harley smiled and picked up his tree. "You can go your own way. We're following the tracks. Who knows, maybe we'll even find its den."

"That's what I'm afraid of," Ernie pointed out.

As they marched along, they began to hear howling and snarling just ahead. The Grey Griffins had expected that the wolves were far away, but when the four friends broke out of the thickets near the Lethe Creek Bridge, they quickly realized Ernie had been right — the wolves were directly in front of them.

Ernie gasped and started to run off as Harley grabbed his coat, pulling him back toward the thick bramble. "Don't move a muscle," he whispered. "They haven't seen us yet, and if you run away, you're going to draw their attention . . . which means you're gonna end up as a snack."

But the wolves weren't paying attention to the Griffins at the moment. Instead, the six snarling canines were snapping and howling at something else. They had completely surrounded a tiny animal and were moving in for the kill.

"Oh, my," Natalia whispered. "We have to do something . . . the poor little thing."

"Better it than us," offered Ernie sensibly.

"Wait," Max said. "That's a faerie."

"Really?" asked Harley.

"Yes. I see it now," Natalia breathed as quietly as she could. "I think it's a pixie. . . ."

In fact it was, and a beautiful pixie at that. Though fully faerie, she looked like a young girl, perhaps about Natalia's age, though no taller than a finger. She had lovely red hair that spiraled down her back in waves, flowing past her wings of gossamer that fluttered nervously as the wolves drew near. "They're going to kill her," Natalia cried, covering her eyes.

"We have to do something," urged Ernie as a rush of bravery filled his chest, though where it had come from was anyone's guess.

Max looked around, doubting there was much the Griffins could do to save the pixie. Undeniably, Max was getting pretty good at defeating magical creatures like goblins and other dark monsters, but wolves were another matter entirely. They didn't have faerie blood, which meant the *Codex* wasn't going to be much help. Outside of getting the wolves angry, Max didn't think there was much they could do. Besides, the wolves were huge and they looked hungry. It was probably best to leave well enough alone and make a quiet, if not hasty, retreat.

But just as one of the wolves leapt at the pixie with its slavering jaws opened wide, Max realized that it wasn't the faerie who was in trouble at all; it was the wolves. With an explosion of fire, the pixie shot into the air and began to burn so intensely that the Griffins had to shield their eyes. A wave of heat rolled through the forest as the sound of billowing flames echoed in their ears. All at once the snowy landscape evaporated as the little faerie let loose a maelstrom of fireballs upon the wolves, who were backing away into the deep recesses of the woods. Angry snarls had turned into cowardly yelps, and within seconds, there wasn't a wolf left in sight.

"It's a Fireball Pixie," Natalia said, jotting down a quick note in her *Book of Clues,* a pink spiral notebook weathered from use that was liberally decorated with unicorn stickers. She stored in it all the clues that her detective mind thought important. "I never would have believed it if I hadn't seen it with my own two eyes." Then, in her wonder and delight, Natalia began to move toward the little creature with the same gentle care as she would have approached a lost puppy.

"Just because she looks sweet, it doesn't mean that she is. You saw what that thing did to those wolves," warned Harley.

Natalia sighed in disappointment, but her spirits quickly rose when she caught sight of the little faerie looking over at her curiously.

"Isn't she beautiful?" Natalia smiled.

"She's a flying fireball," Harley pointed out skeptically. "And that's not the kind of pet you'd keep in your room or bring for show-and-tell. Just be careful."

The red-headed creature watched the Griffins with curiosity for a long while, before finally taking a step forward. She seemed hesitant, not entirely sure what the Griffins might be or — more important — what their intentions were. But as the winged beauty drew closer, a flickering flame began to roll up and down her limbs.

"I've never seen anything so beautiful in my whole life," Ernie breathed in wonder as he took a cautious step toward her. "Do you think she grants wishes?" Not waiting for a response, he held out his hand toward her. "Hi there," Ernie offered. The pixie tilted her head in curiosity as her halo of fire began to grow.

"Um . . . I don't think that's such a good idea," Harley urged. The air around the Griffins began to heat up, and suddenly, the faerie leapt into the air, her wings a blur of motion as she hovered.

Ernie's smile faded. Had he done something wrong?

As the pixie regarded the skinny Griffin, she seemed to be wavering between laughter and anger. Then, just as Ernie began to inch back toward his friends, the fiery creature's countenance fell in doubt, which in turn faded to suspicion, and finally rage.

"She's gonna blow," Max exclaimed, backing away. Even Natalia, who previously had been just as enamored with the pretty wings and sparkling eyes as Ernie, was beginning to agree.

"Let's get out of here!" she shouted as she turned and raced back down the path from where they had come. Max and Harley were right behind, with Ernie in tow.

The Fireball Pixie burned fiercely as she flew after the Grey Griffins. To survive, the fleeing friends tried to zigzag through the trees, dive under fallen trees, and even run around in circles. Yet no matter where they went, the pixie was never far behind. Soon, they found themselves speeding back into the very clearing where they first found the faerie, their boots splashing in puddles of melted snow.

"Max," Natalia shouted as her braids flew in the air behind her. "Your book! You've gotta use it!"

She was right. There was only one way to stop a runaway faerie: the *Codex Spiritus*. As Max raced toward Lethe Creek Bridge, he whipped off his backpack and fumbled a bit with the straps before finally pulling out the magic book. At the same time, he could feel heat from the Fireball Pixie scorching the back of his neck. They only had seconds left before they'd be cooked.

Max raced ahead, waiting for the magic words to come; and when the voice inside his head answered, he cried aloud, *"Lunestarë."* The book opened in a flash. Suddenly, a shimmering ball of blue fire flew out of the pages, shooting over Max's head as it raced to meet the fiery pixie. Too late, the faerie realized her danger, as the glowing ball enveloped her in a crackling cage of energy. The tiny figure let out a frustrated shriek, as the enclosure shrank around her, before rocketing back into the book and disappearing with a poof of blue mist.

Exhausted but relieved, the Griffins slowed to catch their breath, as Harley patted Max on the back. "Good work. I thought we were goners, for sure."

"I want to see her picture before you close the book," Ernie exclaimed, moving in to get a closer look.

Such was the power of the *Codex.* It held within its pages a menagerie of monsters, which could be let loose upon the world with a single word. Yet those that escaped from its grasp could likewise be ensnared once again with another magical utterance. Only Max knew what words to say. And even he didn't know how he knew. The words were just sort of whispered into his mind by a strange voice. But that voice was now growing fainter as Max used the magic book more and more. Now, more often than not, the words were falling from his lips without a single prompt from the mysterious voice.

As the Griffins crowded around Max's book, they could see that there, on the page titled FIREBALL PIXIE, was a painting of the little faerie that had nearly scorched them to death only moments before. She now stood in a field of wildflowers, her doe eyes staring back at them mischievously.

Max snapped the *Codex* shut, and Ernie sighed. "That was too close," Max said, looking over at Natalia, who leaned down to pick up something off the bridge where they were now standing. Whatever it was, she was holding it in the palm of her hand, studying it intently.

"What are you doing now?" asked Harley, as he watched Natalia pull out her *Book of Clues* again.

"What does it look like I'm doing?" she replied as she handed Ernie the object, positioning his hand so she could see it. "Please don't move," Natalia requested as she began to sketch the mysterious artifact. Natalia took copious notes on just about anything unusual, from bizarre insects to obscure poems.

"What is it?" asked Ernie, always wary of picking up anything off the ground. He wasn't fond of germs. Yet no matter how many times he washed his hands, Ernie seemed to collect sick days at school like others collected baseball cards.

"It's a cufflink," Max said, walking over to take a look for himself. "My dad wears 'em with his dress shirts." It was silver, shaped like an oval, and carved about the outer edge was a series of strange symbols with a sword pointing downward in the center. Max had seen symbols like these before. They were called runes, a type of ancient writing, but he couldn't read them.

"Look over there," Harley pointed, walking across the bridge. "There are some tire tracks up ahead." Max followed him, but Ernie stayed right where he was as Natalia continued to sketch. He knew better than to move before he was given leave.

"They aren't very old," Harley proclaimed, as he knelt down for a closer look. He was an exceptional outdoorsman and could tell a wren from a sparrow a mile off. "A few hours at the most, I bet. And it looks like there were at least three guys walking around here, too . . . and they were all pretty big, judging by how deep the footprints are."

"Looks like one of the wolves was over here," Max noted, pointing toward a familiar set of tracks.

"Yeah," agreed Harley. "It was probably sniffing them out."

"There," Natalia said, satisfied with her drawing as she plucked the cufflink from Ernie's hand, placing it, along with the tablet and pen, back into her coat pocket.

"But why would anyone drive this far into the woods?" Harley murmured, scratching his head. It didn't make any sense. "Besides, isn't this private property?"

"I guess," Max said, shrugging as Harley jogged back to the far side of the clearing.

"At least," Harley called, picking up his abandoned Christmas tree, "things can't get any worse."

That was when the Griffins heard the howling of wolves behind them, and without another word, they bundled up their coats and raced home.

2

Tidings of Discomfort
and Ploys

DOWNTOWN AVALON was decked out for the holidays. The street lamps were tied with giant red bows and wrapped in fresh holly, evergreen wreaths were hanging on all the doors, and a river of lights illuminated the eaves. In the heart of the town square stood a towering Norwegian spruce, topped with a bright shining star. It had been donated to the city by the Sumner family and was meticulously decorated with thousands of the finest ornaments imported from distant lands.

"Isn't it just breathtaking?" Natalia exclaimed, as she gazed at the tree with her hood drawn up to keep out the chill. Since capturing the Fireball Pixie that morning, Natalia had found herself in a perfectly grand mood in which everything felt possible.

"Not bad at all," added Max. Christmas was his favorite holiday, and he had helped pick the tree for the town square.

"You guys wanna see something really amazing?" asked Ernie, ignoring the conversation as he walked over and plastered his face against the front window of the Spider's Web, Avalon's one and only comic book shop. "Check this out . . . *Uncanny X-Men* number one. Do you think Santa has any of those in the North Pole with my name on it?"

Just then three chattering girls from King's Elementary approached, skates slung over their shoulders as they headed toward the park. When they caught sight of Natalia, one turned and whispered something to the other two, and they all started to laugh. Natalia turned and pretended not to notice.

For her entire life, Natalia had struggled to fit in with other girls. Over the years they had made fun of her for everything from her red hair and freckles to her pink banana-seat bike with the unicorn flag. Of course she had tried to sit by them at lunch, or talk with them in line. But nothing seemed to work. Even the girls who were nice one day would be rude the next. Eventually, Natalia gave up and began to spend time exclusively with Max, Harley, and Ernie, who, despite being boys, accepted her, no questions asked. And sometimes, they'd even stand up for her. Like now.

With a whack, a snowball exploded as it struck the lead girl's forehead, sending her hat flying into the air. With a collective shriek, the three gossips ran off.

Natalia turned and found Harley smiling, with another snow-ball at the ready.

"Thanks, Harley," Natalia offered in discomfort, clearing her throat. "You didn't have to do that. Anyway, they'll be twice as mean on Monday."

"Not if I'm around," he answered, waving her off. "If you pick on one Griffin, you pick on all of us."

"That's right!" Ernie seconded, who knew only too well what it was like to be picked on. Harley, of course, was too big to bully. And Max was too, well, Max Sumnerish: It was hard to pick on someone whose family could buy him a professional football team for Christmas.

"Come on, guys," Max called, heading off down the sidewalk. "I still need to get something for my mom, and it's getting late."

"You're gonna buy your mom a Christmas present?" asked Harley incredulously, trying to keep from laughing. "From a store in Avalon? Yeah, right."

Finding the right gift for Annika Sumner was no small task. Annika spared no expense lavishing herself with all of life's most unconventional luxuries — shopping sprees in Milan, precious gems from London, and a bevy of designer gowns from New York.

So what exactly were you supposed to buy someone who had everything? Max had no idea. But he knew that he had to think of something fast. There were only a few shopping days left before Christmas Day.

"I suppose I could have ordered something out of a catalog, but . . . ," he said as he pondered a blue dress in a store window. Max generally had good taste but not in the women's clothing department. That was completely foreign to him.

"That's *exactly* what you should have done," Natalia scolded. "Why men procrastinate when it comes to giving gifts, I'll never know. It's just not logical. They always wait for the last minute, then end up buying whatever is left hanging on the racks right before the stores close on Christmas Eve."

"Well, maybe your mom has a boyfriend by now," Ernie suggested, trying to be helpful. "If she does, then you might be off the hook. I bet he'll buy her a really fancy present."

Max stopped dead in his tracks, grinding his teeth as he glared at Ernie. A boyfriend? If his mom even thought about that, Max was prepared to pack his things and move to Grandma Caliburn's house. He only had one father, and that's the way it was going to stay.

"You're such a nitwit," Natalia said. "Can't you go one minute without sticking your foot in your mouth? You think Max wants to hear that sort of thing? Besides, I am sure it's not true."

"What did I say?" Ernie asked in bewilderment. "I'm just thinking maybe he doesn't have to buy a present, that's all."

"Hey, who's that guy over there?" asked Harley, staring into the alley across the street. "Does he look familiar to any of you?"

The other three spun around, but could see no one. Harley shrugged. "I guess he took off."

"What did he look like?" Natalia prompted, as she took out her *Book of Clues* and readied her pink pen. "Was he a faerie or a human?"

"Human," Harley replied with a nod. "Definitely. He was wearing a black trench coat with a white scarf and an old-fashioned hat."

Natalia nodded as she took down the description, complete with a drawing based on Harley's description.

"Well, he's gone now," Max pointed out. "Anyway, maybe we're just a little paranoid after what happened last fall with Morgan. I mean, why would some strange guy in a hat stare at us anyway? Maybe he just happened to be looking in our direction."

"Whoa, look at this!" called Ernie suddenly as the Griffins approached a lonely telephone pole at the corner of the street.

There, stapled between tattered flyers promoting piano lessons and weight loss programs, was a photocopied picture of Ray Fisher, their notorious classmate and self-professed nemesis from King's

Elementary. Ray had gone missing about the same time as the faerie invasion a few months back, and there was now a hefty reward for information leading to his safe return. Unfortunately, the Grey Griffins were the only people who knew what had happened to Ray — and they weren't talking. Even if they did, no one would believe them. What were they supposed to say? That Ray, who had betrayed not only the Griffins but all of humanity, had turned into a freakish blue monster with shining yellow eyes? That he had last been seen disappearing into a magical portal? No, that story was best kept quiet. At least, for now.

"That sure is a lot of money." Ernie whistled. "Do you know how many comic books I could buy with ten thousand dollars?"

"Is that all you can think about?" asked Natalia in disgust. "What about Ray's parents, for goodness' sake? Their only child has disappeared, and for all they know they'll never see him again. It has to be a horrible time for them. Especially during Christmas. Don't you feel even a little sympathy for them?"

Ernie shrugged. He tried to feel bad, but whenever he did, he kept remembering that Ray had tried to set him on fire, and that was hard to get over.

"It's my fault," Max said in a wavering voice. "If I hadn't found the *Codex* in my grandma's attic to begin with, none of this would have happened."

"No, Max. It's not your fault," argued Natalia. "We've been through this at least a dozen times. It was Ray's choice to turn into a monster, not yours. Remember that you're the one who tried to help him . . . to turn him back. So stop beating yourself up. Besides, if it wasn't for you, Avalon . . . and maybe even the whole world would be destroyed by now."

"I'm afraid the Lady Romanov is quite correct," came a sonorous voice, startling the Griffins.

Max turned to see Olaf Iverson, whom everyone referred to as Iver. The old gentleman gave a slight bow and tipped his black derby. Dressed in a greatcoat and wingtip shoes, Iver stood in the chilly winter air with an enormous smile on his face. He was a giant of a man, but intimidating only when need be (which wasn't often). His thin silvery hair framed a wise and thoughtful face that could have passed for anywhere between sixty and six hundred years old. Yet it was his frosty white beard and cheery blue eyes, more than anything else, that made many children not-so-secretly speculate that the eccentric proprietor of the Shoppe of Antiquities might in fact be Santa Claus.

What most people *didn't* realize, however, was that Iver was actually a Templar Knight. The Templars were the most honorable and heroic soldiers the world had ever known — just like Max's grandpa Caliburn had been, and perhaps one day, Max himself might be. What's more, since Grandpa Caliburn's mysterious death, Iver had been given the task of instructing Max in the ways of the Templars. Yet, in the process, Iver had become something of a sur-rogate grandfather to not only Max, but the other Griffins as well. Above all things, Iver was one of the best friends the Griffins had.

"Hey, where'd you get that, Iver?" Ernie asked, pointing to an umbrella that the old man had pressed beneath his arm.

Iver was not a typical sort of man, and therefore, rarely did he possess typical things. Case in point, the umbrella Iver carried with him had a head shaped like a gargoyle, intricately carved and frighteningly realistic. This by itself was hardly worthy of note, because what had caught Ernie's eye was that the gargoyle had just winked at him. Umbrellas weren't supposed to wink.

"What? This old thing?" Iver asked, a broad grin sliding across his face as he tapped it on the ground. "Oh, it's been with me for quite some time. Handy in bad weather, you know."

"But there's not a cloud in the sky," Natalia pointed out aptly.

"Some clouds are not so easily seen," Iver replied crisply as he tucked the umbrella back under his arm, signaling the conversation had come to an end. "Now I hate to seem discourteous," Iver continued, "but I wonder if I might have a moment alone with Master Sumner."

The Griffins looked at one another and shrugged.

"Okay by me," answered Harley.

"Yeah," Ernie agreed. Iver's talks tended to be a bit long-winded and filled with lots of complicated words. Besides, Ernie had other things on his mind. "We want to go look at some comics, anyway."

Harley nodded. All three boys were voracious comic book fans. They spent nearly as much time in the Spider's Web as they did in Iver's Shoppe of Antiquities. In fact the owner, Monti, was one of Ernie's idols. He had the scoop on all the latest news in the comic world, and he even wrote and penciled his own underground comic book.

"We *could* go to the library, you know," Natalia said as Harley and Ernie raced through the door, leaving her talking to herself outside. With a sigh, she followed. But despite her protests to the educationally barren world of colorful cartoons and caped heroes, she could be glimpsed, at times, reading a discarded comic when she thought no one was looking.

"Let's walk," suggested Iver as he led Max down the snowy brick street.

"What's going on?"

"I've been meaning to talk with you for quite some time," Iver said slowly, measuring his words with care. "I want you to know how impressed I've been with your progress."

"Thanks," Max mumbled, blushing slightly as his boots crunched in the snow.

"Don't be modest," countered Iver with a proud smile. "The knowledge you've gained and the skills you've mastered over these past few months are nothing short of extraordinary. Your emerging abilities are greater than even our most conservative hopes."

"Wow" was all Max could manage to say as he thought back to everything that had happened since he and the Griffins had defeated the Shadow King. It was one thing to be a billionaire's son, but it was quite another for Max to realize that he was a part of magical legacy that positioned him to act as a protector of the world. Not to mention, there was still quite a lot of cleanup work to do in Avalon itself. Max had mistakenly assumed that the battle at Faerie Hill a few months back had resulted in the automatic recapturing of all the evil faeries back into the *Codex*. Sadly, this wasn't even remotely the case.

"You are quite welcome," Iver replied, reaching into his coat for a pipe. "But Spriggans in lockers, leprechauns in milk barns, and Fireball Pixies in the forest are only the beginning, I'm afraid."

Max remained silent. How Iver had known about the Fireball Pixie at Lethe Creek Bridge was a mystery, but Iver always seemed to know things others didn't.

The old man paused, tamping some tobacco into the bowl of his pipe. "This task you've been given by the Templar is no small thing, Master Sumner. You must know now that we can only delay the Shadow King for a time or pray he no longer finds us interesting. But a reckoning will come and we must prepare for that day."

Max answered with a reluctant nod. "But at least we don't have to worry about Morgan LaFey anymore. Or Ray, either."

Iver responded with an arched eyebrow when Max called the Black Witch by name. "Actually, Ray is the reason I wished to talk with you." There was something in Iver's tone that filled Max's heart with dread. "You see, he's been found."

"Ray's alive?"

Iver nodded, glancing up at the wintry sun as if he were gauging the time. "Very much alive."

"Well, I guess that's good . . . isn't it?" Max replied uncertainly, finding it hard to hide his disappointment. "His parents will be happy, at least."

Iver shook his head. "I'm afraid he won't be coming home any time soon."

"Why not?

"Because it was LaFey who found him."

All at once, a cold wind filled the air around Max, and his eyes grew wide in dismay. Morgan LaFey, the Black Witch? What could she want with Ray? Whatever it was, it wouldn't be good.

"What about Sprig?" Max asked in sudden hope. Even though the little faerie had gotten him into a lot of trouble, he would never stop thinking of her — or the fact that she had sacrificed her life for him. As far as Max knew, she had died while protecting him from Ray. But he had never known for sure. . . .

"I've not heard," Iver said with a look of sadness. "She was terribly wounded before she disappeared, and now that Ray has resurfaced, I can only assume the worst for Sprig. Still, she loved you. And where there is love, there is always hope."

Max nodded solemnly, then looked up at Iver. "Morgan probably hates me now — especially after we stopped her from releasing the Shadow King."

Iver said nothing.

"Do you think she wants revenge?" Max had to admit it had been a fear of his for months now.

"Perhaps," Iver said. "Yet we have to consider the possibility that it may not have been her intent to actually release the Shadow King to begin with."

"What are you saying?" Max exclaimed.

"I'm not certain," Iver replied as he chewed at his pipe stem. "I am only now beginning to understand it myself. But in the meantime, you must be on watch . . . for anything. And I urge you to be brave, for in my absence I want you to take extra care of yourself . . . and your friends."

"Where are you going?" Max asked in disbelief. How could Iver leave Max and the Griffins alone after news like this?

"There are matters that need looking into. But don't worry," Iver assured. "I will see you and your Griffins before Christmas, if I can. Obey Logan, and stay close. And don't let the *Codex* out of your sight . . . not for one moment."

Max nodded reluctantly. Talking Iver out of leaving, let alone anything else, would be impossible, so he didn't even try.

"And your grandfather's necklace . . . ," Iver continued, his intense eyes scanning Max's. "Do you still wear it?"

Max nodded again, patting his chest where it hung. He never parted with it.

"Excellent. See that you don't lose it." Then, with a tip of his hat, the old man walked away, disappearing around the corner without another word.

Max's jaw sagged. Iver had delivered the worst news he could have imagined, and then just walked off — and right before Christmas, too.

Suddenly, a Land Rover pulled up to the curb, its exhaust pipe rumbling. The door opened and a man dressed in black from his leather boots to his limo-tint sunglasses stepped out. The man's raven hair was cropped short, and a slender, nearly invisible scar ran along his cheekbone. Every step was confident, and though his steely eyes were hidden beneath the sunglasses, there lurked a rare power as he approached. This was a man who seemed to be aware of everyone and everything around him — every thought and every movement. He was someone to fear. That was, if he didn't work for you.

"Hey, Logan," called Max as he rushed over to his family's bodyguard. All billionaire kids have bodyguards — at least that's what Max's dad had told him. But none were more qualified than Logan, who was a martial arts expert (with more black belts than one could count on ten fingers), a stunt man (who had credits in no less than a dozen blockbuster action movies), a champion race-car driver (with a choice collection of exotic sports cars), and who could make a seriously mean peanut butter and jelly sandwich. "I thought you weren't picking me up until later?"

Logan shook his head and removed his glasses, revealing piercing eyes. "I'm afraid not," he said in his Scottish accent. "We've had a change of plans. There's a message waiting for you back at the house. Your father . . ."

3

Receiving a Note and Checking It Twice

MAX RUSHED THROUGH the front door, skidded across the marble floor, and shot into the kitchen where Rosa, his mother's housekeeper, was busily scrubbing the countertops. Max couldn't contain the excitement, as he thought about the letter that had finally arrived after months of painful silence. What could the note say? What did he want? Was he coming back?

"Where's Dad's message?" Max shouted, nearly out of breath as he dug through a deep stack of mail, spilling a pile onto the floor.

"It's upstairs on your bed," Rosa replied, looking at Max with a smile. Rosa knew how much Max loved his father. But she was also all too aware of how much Max's mother hated the man. Because of that, Rosa kept her joy for Max under wraps.

Max whooped and ran off, only to turn around and walk back to the kitchen with trepidation. "Rosa?"

"What is it, Max?" Rosa replied in her melodic Spanish accent.

"Does Mom know about the letter?"

"She will," Rosa said gravely. It wasn't a threat. It's just the way things worked in the Sumner household.

Max frowned. He had wanted to keep the secret to himself, because he knew that his mother's wrath awaited. Nothing got past Annika Sumner, but for the moment, Max was going to bask in the delight of his father's correspondence.

Excitement welling, Max raced through the door, rounded the corner, jumped over the cat, and ducked beneath a passing servant whose arms were full of silver dinner platters. An instant later Max shot up the stairs and into his room, slamming the door shut behind him.

There it was. Near the edge of his bed lay a yellow envelope, unopened. A telegram. Greedily, Max tore it open and read the short message:

Maximus . . . miss you. . . . Come to Scotland for Christmas. . . . Will be like old times. . . . Plane waiting for you and the Grey Griffins on Wednesday. . . . Logan will take care of the details. . . . See you soon . . . Dad.

Max read the note five more times, hardly able to breathe. His father wanted him to come to Scotland for Christmas? It simply had to be true. The letter was right there in his hands. Now, no matter what his mother said, Max knew his dad hadn't forgotten about him. Finally, it would be like old times — or as close as it was ever going to get after the divorce. But that was good enough for Max.

Smiling broadly, Max grasped the letter to his chest and fell back onto his bed, the news of Ray and Morgan LaFey dissipating from his mind like a bad dream, only to be replaced by the fantasies of a sumptuous winter holiday in Scotland with the man who meant more to Max than anyone. Things were decidedly looking up.

Despite the bone-chilling temperatures outside, Max, Harley, Natalia, and Ernie huddled together in Max's expansive tree fort, the official headquarters of the secret Order of the Grey Griffins. They had lost their haven a few months before when the tree it stood in shot up into the sky like a magic beanstalk, giant branches tearing down most of the walls. But with Oberon's defeat, everything seemed to go back to exactly the way it was before. The high towers, swinging bridges, and even the slide were back to normal, as though nothing had ever happened.

Their headquarters sat amid the shadows of a forest that had once been haunted by hordes of goblins and other monsters, but successes like their defeat of the Fireball Pixie were helping build the Griffins' confidence.

Each member of the team had a special role. For Max, besides his prestigious responsibility as Guardian of the *Codex* for the Knights Templar, he was also the Master of the Order for the Grey Griffins — after all, he did own their secret hideout. As Guardian, he was getting greater command of the *Codex* every day, able to defeat creatures he would have never dreamed possible. And as the leader of the Griffins, he was the glue that held them together. But Max wasn't the only one with an important job.

Harley was the Griffins' Warden, which meant he enforced the law. He was also becoming an excellent battle tactician whenever the four of them faced trouble. The duty of Marshal had been awarded to Natalia, who was also a dead-eye when it came to throwing iron nails with precision aim. This was particularly handy when fighting evil faeries, who were deathly afraid of iron. Begrudgingly, Ernie accepted the mantle of Steward, which he knew implied that he was the secretary and had to take notes. But to his credit, he was growing braver every day. And whereas before, he might have just fainted dead away when confronted by a monster, nowadays he had grown into an ally that the other Griffins could rely on. Not to mention, his uncanny nose for danger could sniff out trouble better than anyone else's.

A state-of-the-art central heating system kept their tree house warm in the winter months, and the four friends found themselves sitting snugly at a table with stacks of colorful Round Table trading cards at their fingertips. While the game was immensely fun, it also came with a mysterious legacy. According to Iver, the Templar Knights had used Round Table cards as a secret form of communication after their exile a thousand years ago, and even today it remained a critical tool used by Iver in Max's training as he grew into his role as Guardian of the *Codex*. But as the Griffins played, they weren't thinking of the history or the lessons they might learn. Their minds were firmly attached to the fact that it was the most amazing game they had ever seen.

"I can't believe your dad invited us all to Scotland for Christmas," Harley said in disbelief. He'd never been out of Minnesota himself, let alone traveled to Europe onboard a private jet.

"Pretty cool, huh?" Max smiled at his friends, who, miraculously, were all allowed to go with him. Of course, getting Harley's mom to let him go had been the simple part. She had to work a double shift at the diner on Christmas Day. If it wasn't for Max's generous offer, Harley was going to have to spend Christmas alone. But what was more remarkable was that Natalia's and Ernie's parents had also agreed. If Natalia's parents were strict, Ernie's were just plain militant about knowing where their son was and if he had gotten himself into trouble. Yet for reasons only they knew, both the Romanovs and the Tweenys gave their permission without question. Now all that was left was Max, but he knew good and well that the odds weren't stacked in his favor. Annika Sumner wasn't a fan of Max's father. Still, Iver said when love is involved, there's always hope, and Max knew his mom truly loved her son, even if she struggled to show it since the divorce.

"Are we really gonna fly in one of your dad's private jets?" Ernie asked, his mouth hanging open. Like Harley, Ernie had never been on a plane, either. "Is there a kitchen onboard? How about a television? There has to be something. It's a long flight, I think. Or is it? Mom said we're flying forward in time. That has to be weird. . . ."

Max shrugged, barely paying attention to Ernie's nervous chattering. At the moment, he was locked in Round Table combat with Natalia, who had challenged him to a duel, attacking Max's vampire. Shaking his ten-sided knucklebones, Max let them fly across the table, hoping against hope he'd beat her this time.

Max closed his eyes and sighed in disappointment as the knucklebones came to a rest.

"That's an eighty-six," Natalia noted with a sigh of relief. "Not enough to beat my werewolf. You needed a ninety-one . . . at least."

"Where'd that werewolf card come from anyway?" asked Ernie, eyeing it suspiciously. "Maybe you should throw it away. It kinda brings up some bad memories."

"Don't be silly," Natalia replied with a wave of her hand. "It's one of the most powerful cards in the deck. I'm not going to toss it out just because you might have a nightmare."

"It's your turn, Ernie," Harley called out. "Speed it up." Harley enjoyed Round Table, but only when things moved along at a brisk pace. Ernie was notorious for stalling when he didn't have a good card to play.

Ernie wiped his nose on his sleeve and then smiled devilishly at Natalia before flipping over a card that showed a fierce-looking Frost Dragon. Everyone's eyes grew wide — a dragon of any kind was nearly indestructible. With a confident smirk, Ernie picked up the dice and pointed at Natalia's werewolf. While her card was generally hard to beat, it was nothing compared with a dragon. All Ernie needed to roll was a 4 or higher. Without even looking down at the table, he let the dice drop as he kept his eyes on Natalia — just waiting to savor the moment of victory that was all but assured.

"A zero-one," Harley exclaimed in disbelief. "You fumbled!"

"I did?" Ernie cried, thunderstruck. It was virtually impossible. He looked on in dismay as Natalia quickly removed his dragon from the playing field, tucking it into her own deck before snatching another card from Ernie's hand. Unfortunately, a fumble meant that instead of losing just one card, Ernie lost two. He was out of the game.

Yet on the game went, as the three remaining players battled back and forth. Natalia eventually trounced the other two boys and was soon sorting through her newly captured treasures with glee. But even as she did, she placed the werewolf and vampire at the bottom of the deck. Despite their value, something about them made her uncomfortable, and though she didn't admit it, she had nightmares herself. She knew very well that sometimes these cards seemed to have minds of their own.

"So I did a little research down at the library to check on the cufflink that we found by the bridge," Natalia mentioned as she finished sorting through her cards, making sure that Ernie's dragon was accounted for.

"And?" prodded Harley.

"And I couldn't find anything."

"No way," replied Ernie, who wasn't used to Natalia coming away empty-handed in her research.

"I *do* believe it's Norse, though," Natalia added quickly, trying to prove her research hadn't been in vain. "You know, like the Vikings."

"I love the hats Vikings wear," Ernie stated, holding up a finger on either side of his head like two horns. "I drew a superhero like that once called Grim the Gory."

Natalia rolled her eyes.

"Do you know what the runes say?" Max asked curiously.

"Not a clue," Natalia replied, laying out her next few cards on the table in perfect alignment. "I tried to translate them the best I could, but I don't think the words are in English."

"What are they?"

"German, I think," Natalia answered, thoughtfully. "At least, that's what Mr. Nichols, the head librarian said."

"Maybe I could ask Monti; he knows all kinds of stuff."

"This isn't a comic book, Ernest," Natalia reminded him. "And besides, we're all sworn to secrecy. That means no mention of the cufflink, Templars, faeries, or anything of the sort. Remember?"

"I still can't figure out why we're the only people who can see faeries," Max wondered aloud, as he pushed away from the game table and looked out the window where a soft blanket of snow was falling. "Well, besides Iver and Logan, anyway." It was an interesting point that stumped the Griffins every day. One moment they might be sitting in the cafeteria quietly munching on sandwiches, and the next, a small faerie would appear out of a classmate's lunch box, steal a potato chip, and disappear through a crack in the wall. And none of the other students would see a thing.

"I bet it has something to do with the *Codex*," Natalia offered. "Maybe some of its magic rubbed off on us. Or maybe we're the only ones meant to see them?"

"What does that mean?" asked Ernie, taking a bite out of an apple.

"And don't forget that Dr. Blackstone can see 'em, too," Harley pointed out. At the very mention of King's Elementary School's chief disciplinarian, the room seemed to grow dark. "Remember, he was in on the plot to kill Iver and was working side by side with those Kobolds."

"You're right," Natalia said, shuddering at the painful memory.

"But Dr. Blackstone hasn't said a thing since Morgan disappeared. Do you think he knows where she's gone to?"

"Probably," commented Harley. "But why is he back at school teaching instead of in jail where he belongs?"

"That's where they should put Ray, too," Ernie added. Since he first heard about their classmate's mysterious return, Ernie had been looking over his shoulder nervously. Ray was definitely on top of the list of things that scared Ernie.

"Maybe he's changed since we last saw him," Natalia pointed out. "It has been awhile. Maybe he's sorry for what he did?"

Ernie shook his head defiantly. "Ray was a bully way before he ever changed into a monster. Besides, even if all of his blue scales fall out and those horns and teeth disappear, he'll still be a jerk. Remember, he tried to kill us. I don't think I will ever get over that, thank you very much."

"Good point," Harley added. "So you should be happy that we're going to Scotland for Christmas and leaving Ray far behind."

"I hope you're right," Max grumbled. But he could easily imagine Ray stowing away in the cargo bin of his father's plane, just waiting to wrap his blue hands around Max's neck.

"You're not going, and that's final," ordered Annika Sumner as she strode about the kitchen, waving her arms in the air with such passion and purpose that one might think she was an accomplished stage actress.

Upon receiving word of his father's invitation, Max's mother had chartered a plane from New York City and flown back to

Avalon. As soon as she walked through the door, she sliced through the niceties.

"But everyone else can go . . . ," Max argued for the umpteenth time. "How can you do this to me? I see you every day, but I haven't seen Dad forever. It isn't fair."

"No, it isn't," Annika replied coldly. "Life isn't fair. But, like me, sometimes you just have to learn to live with it. Besides, I know what's best for you. You don't, otherwise you'd be in charge." Annika had worked herself into such a fury that her neck had become blotchy and red. "If that man was any sort of a father, do you think he would have waited this long to see you . . . or call you, for good-ness' sake? How hard is it to pick up a phone, Max? Don't they have phones in Scotland?" Annika Sumner's words cut through her son's heart. "This is just another one of his mind games. You can never trust him. Never! Do you hear me?"

Max looked at his mother, torn between hurt and rage. He wanted to shout and cry at the same time. In all his life, Max only knew his father to be kind and generous, and he recalled longingly the times they had gone on adventures in the woods, to football games and movies, and done tons of other fun stuff that fathers and sons like to do. But that had all ended suddenly. The morning of their last day together, Max and his father had been playing catch, and a few hours later, Max was waving good-bye from the front steps as his father drove off, disappearing from Max's life for good. He'd never seen it coming.

"Aren't you going to say anything?" Annika asked, a wildness lingering in her eyes.

What was he supposed to say? But something deep within Max told him that his father would work it out. He just had to.

Monday morning dawned, signaling the start of the school week, and soon the yellow school bus rattled up to Max's front gate. Logan could have driven him to school in a stretch limousine, but Max just wanted to be with his classmates. Besides, Max assumed that Logan was secretly trailing them anyway (though he never could prove it). Max often thought Logan was too obsessed with his safety, but then again, with the likes of a thousand-year-old witch, an overlord bent on world domination, and an army full of ghastly goblins hunting him down, Max reconsidered. Maybe Logan had a point.

The next stop on the route was Brooke Lundgren's house, which was almost as big as Max's own home. Brooke's family had been close to the Sumners for many years before the divorce, yet Max didn't know her father well. Though a kind man and adoring father, Dr. Lundgren was something of a recluse, which set him up as a delicious target for the town gossips. And despite his wife's membership on the school board and impeccably tuned social calendar, rumors about their family persisted. It certainly didn't help matters that the Lundgren home was full of mysterious artifacts from all over the world and that Dr. Lundgren was rumored to dabble in the "dark" sciences. Max thought the whole idea ridiculous. But if there was one thing Max didn't like about Brooke's father, it was that his own father wasn't more like him. At least, not anymore.

Brakes screeching, the bus jerked as the stop sign swung out.

*   *   *

The front gate of the Lundgren estate had been wrought from iron, and sitting atop the columns were two frightening gargoyles, each grasping shields with a mysterious sign emblazoned upon them. Just beyond, a cobblestone path snaked toward the Gothic mansion that seemed, no matter the weather, to be wrapped in ominous clouds. It looked rather out of place in the quaint little town. But the sprawling manor had its own particular charm.

Brooke waved when she saw Max staring out the window, but he was distracted and didn't notice. There was something fluttering about her lunchbox that had caught his eye . . . a glimmering spark.

It was a pixie, no bigger than a finger, with long graceful limbs and lashes. Max had seen the gossamer-winged faerie before. She had become Brooke's shadow over the last few months, following her everywhere, though Brooke seemed not to have noticed. Max had set his mind on capturing the faerie and putting her back in the *Codex*, just in case it meant Brooke any harm. But whenever Max came too close, the faerie would disappear without a trace.

"Hey, Brooke," Max greeted, as she walked over. The prettiest girl in the fifth grade, Brooke had chocolate brown hair and luminous eyes that sparkled with laughter.

"Good morning, Max," she replied, sitting down in the seat across from him. The pixie was, as usual, nowhere to be found. "Aren't you excited?" she asked. "We only have three days of school left before winter break."

"Are you going anywhere for vacation?" Max offered casually, squinting as he tried to catch sight of the elusive pixie — had she turned invisible or just flown off? Then he caught Brooke looking at him, and blushed. Growing up, he and Brooke had been the best of friends. Yet age, circumstance, and the strange butterflies in Max's stomach had forced a sort of distance between them.

"Dad's taking me skiing in the Swiss Alps," Brooke offered a moment later, "and he said I could bring a friend, so I'm taking Emmy with me. Isn't that cool?"

"Sounds fun," agreed Max, though he really didn't like to ski. Fighting goblins was one thing, but flying down a hill with no brakes seemed crazy. However, if there was anyone in the world who could make him try, it was Brooke.

"So what are you doing over Christmas?" Brooke asked as she leaned toward him.

"I'm supposed to go visit my dad in Scotland," Max replied as casually as he could manage, though he left out the part about his mom saying no.

"Your dad? Really?" Brooke asked, her eyes lighting up. "Well, I bet you're going to have a great time. Your dad is so wonderful, and I bet he misses you a lot. I mean, I would if I were him." Then, realizing what she had said, Brooke quickly fell silent and blushed.

Nobody saw that the pixie in her jacket pocket blushed as well.

4

MAX SWUNG into an ink-stained desk beside Harley and set his books down with a thud. Yawning, he shuffled through his homework, then looked up as he noticed Natalia standing in front of him, looking at her usual front row seat, which was now surrounded by the very same three girls who had been the target of Harley's snowball only a few days before. The three of them were sitting and gossiping about something that sounded terribly important when Natalia took in a breath of courage and walked over to them. Their conversation halted and their eyes narrowed as Natalia approached and took her seat next to the girls. But just as Natalia sat down, she jumped back up with a cry. She had sat on a tack.

The girls broke into sudden laughter, then got up and walked to the back of the room just as the bell rang, leaving Natalia sitting all by herself — as usual. Protectively, Max gathered up his books and took a seat beside her.

Today, like most days, Ernie arrived after the bell, skidding into their homeroom, his arms overflowing with ragged books, chewed pencils, and an assortment of superhero erasers.

"Why are you still wearing your coat?" Max asked as Ernie accidentally dropped his favorite pencil, which quickly vanished. "You look like an orange marshmallow."

Ernie just shrugged, though by the look on his face, Max knew he was hiding something. Then, as Ernie bent down to pick up his pencil, Max, and the rest of the class, discovered Ernie's secret. A small animal, long, thin, and covered in fur, jumped from the inside of Ernie's winter coat and raced across the floor. Ernie practically knocked over his desk as he crawled after it, spilling everything to the floor. All the boys in class laughed as Ernie slithered between the desks on his belly, trying to catch the animal, while most of the girls had climbed to the tops of their chairs, shrieking in fright.

"Ernest Tweeny, what is that thing?" Natalia asked in disgust. She was sitting cross-legged in her chair, her feet safely up off the floor.

"My parents gave me an early Christmas present," Ernie huffed, as he dove after the animal, though his effort came up short. "I really wanted contacts so I can get rid of my glasses, but they got me a ferret instead. I actually think she's kinda cool, though. Her name's Winifred."

"Well, it looks like a weasel, and I suggest you get it out of here this instant," demanded Natalia, "before Dr. Blackstone hears about it. You'll get detention for sure."

At mention of Dr. Blackstone's name, Ernie grew scared.

Like an acrobat, Winifred jumped up onto a girl's desk, then hopped from table to table through a forest of shrieking girls. She then leapt over to the aquarium, eyeing the fish hungrily. That's when Harley reached out and grabbed the ferret by the back of her neck. Winifred hissed at him, revealing a row of razor-sharp teeth. Harley generally had a way with animals, but this one was obviously an exception. Quickly, he handed her to Ernie, pulling back his fingers before the ferret had a chance to bite them. "Nice pet, Tweeny."

"She *is* nice," Ernie defended, stroking the ferret on the head. "You just scared her."

"Well, you better find a place to hide her before someone comes looking," suggested Max. "Like your locker."

"You're just lucky Mrs. Bone is late again today," Natalia offered, keeping her distance from Ernie and his pet.

"Whatever," dismissed Ernie, who stuffed Winifred back into his coat, zipping it up as far as it would go.

Admittedly, school had not been the same since the disappearance of their favorite homeroom teacher, Ms. Heen. While Rhiannon Heen had only led the class for a few short months, the Grey Griffins had found themselves spellbound by her seemingly magical qualities. She would show up when least expected, and just in the nick of time. Ms. Heen also seemed to even know the hidden thoughts of each and every one of her students, but that was nothing compared to the realization that she was much more than an ordinary schoolteacher. At the battle on Faerie Hill, right before their eyes, Ms. Heen had transformed into a figure of shimmering light and terrific power, stopping the Black Witch single-handedly. Unfortunately, she had disappeared before the kids had been able to solve the mystery of her true identity.

By contrast, Ms. Heen's replacement, a seemingly ancient woman with steel gray hair and powdery pale skin, accented by just a touch too much rouge, was a kind and gentle woman, though chronically late.

"Ahem . . . ," came a frightfully familiar voice. The Griffins didn't need to turn around to recognize who was standing in the doorway. Ernie sat up straight and spun to face forward, hoping to keep Winifred hidden.

"Where is Mrs. Bone? Late again, I presume?" Dr. Diamonte Blackstone asked rhetorically from the back of the room. His eyes flicked about the room, from student to student, as if he were picking out a feeder guppy to throw to his pet piranha.

The students remained deathly quiet. No one wanted to be called upon, especially the four Grey Griffins who had, admittedly, a rather checkered past with Dr. Blackstone.

"Mr. Sumner," Blackstone growled. "Please see me in the hall. I would like to have a word with you."

Max slowly rose to his feet, head hanging down as he followed Dr. Blackstone out the door. The other children watched him with wide eyes, not so secretly expecting the worse.

Dark hair slicked back with oil, and eyebrows lowered in concentration, the teacher's penetrating eyes scoured Max as though he were searching for something. "Mr. Sumner, rumor has it that you are traveling across the Atlantic over winter break."

Max remained silent, looking at the floor.

"Well, I hope," Dr. Blackstone continued, forcing what he might have thought was a charming smile, "that your trip is most agreeable. I can only assume you are going to see your father. I am sure he misses you very much."

Max raised his eyes and looked at Dr. Blackstone incredulously. Was it possible he was trying to be nice? It didn't make any sense. Diamonte Blackstone was *never* nice.

". . . and I'm sure you miss him, as well," the teacher continued. "Scotland is quite a magical place. I've had the privilege of studying there myself. It was in Edinburgh, to be precise. In fact, I hold Scotland very dear to my heart."

Max studied the assistant principal suspiciously, wondering where the conversation was leading, though he said nothing.

"At any rate, I wish you a bon voyage, as they say. I can assure you your holiday will be one you will always remember," he said, with just a hint of sneer crossing his lips. "Good day."

And with that, the scariest man at King's Elementary turned on his heels, his black overcoat fluttering about him like a throng of bats, as he disappeared down the hall.

"I wish you'd stop sulking," Annika Sumner said to Max while she gazed at herself in a gold-leafed mirror. "It's not going to do you a bit of good."

"But . . . ," Max started.

"I'm trying to protect you, Max," his mother maintained as she applied another layer of lipstick. "The sooner you understand that, the sooner we can start getting along again. You have no idea who your father really is."

Max glared up at his mom as she brushed past him to put on her cashmere coat. She was off to another society event, leaving Max and his sister alone with the servants. Annika was always gone. And in Max's opinion, her absence was more noticeable than his father's; his dad at least had the excuse of being thousands of miles away. "At least Dad wants to spend time with me . . . ," he mumbled.

"What did you say?" she asked, stopping in her tracks as her voice chilled over like frost. Max swore he could feel the temperature of the room drop when his mother was angry.

"It's not like you're ever around," Max complained, his voice growing stronger with his rising resentment. "You don't want to see me or Hannah, anyway. I don't even know why you had kids to begin with. We might as well have never been born!" Annika stood there, wide-eyed in silence. Had Max's words hit too close to the truth? "Besides, what do you care if I go? It'll just give you more time to shop and hang out with your snobby friends . . . who are only after your money, anyway. Or should I say *Dad's* money?"

"I . . . I can't believe you are talking to me like this," his mother whispered, her face ashen. Max had struck a nerve, and he could see a tiny sliver of a tear forming in the crease of her eyelid. "You were taught better than this, Grayson. You're just being cruel. And while I may not carry my wounds in silence, at least I keep my anger focused on the man who gave them to me: your father — the man who you're beginning to sound like more every day."

Max's mouth dropped. He had gone too far and he knew it.

"I don't have to listen to this," she said. "Go to your room. Just . . . go."

Max sprang from his seat and raced to his bedroom, slamming the door shut. He wanted to scream, but he'd probably get in even more trouble for that. Instead, he just sat on his bed fuming, contemplating the broken fragments that were left of his family.

Max awoke in the middle of the night, but didn't bother opening his eyes. He didn't have to. Max knew exactly what was going on in the shadows. He could feel them. Faeries. Several of them. They had come in through the window and were sneaking toward his bed. Some were watching Max, making sure he was still asleep. Others were intently crisscrossing in the shadows, moving closer to their quarry.

Faeries could move without being seen or heard, even by dogs. But ever since he had discovered the *Codex,* Max's senses had grown superhuman. He could, in fact, pinpoint a faerie over a mile away if he concentrated hard enough. The problem was, he rarely could focus like that for very long. He was far more interested in things like playing football, video games, and Round Table with his friends. But tonight was different.

These faeries had broken into his house before. They were Brownies, dirty little creatures that stood about a hand high. They had no wings, and their taste in fashion was questionable at best. For some reason, they seemed to have a fondness for aluminum foil hats. But clothing aside, they were expert thieves, and if one wasn't careful, they could empty a refrigerator or jewelry box faster than the blink of an eye.

The problem was that the little buggers were after the *Codex.*

That much Max knew; what they were planning on doing with it, he had no idea. In the past, whenever Max woke up, they'd simply run off, disappearing into the darkness before he could capture them.

That was about to change. As the first Brownie reached for the secret drawer where the *Codex* was hidden, the trap Max had set was sprung. A fishnet from his aquarium swung down, ensnaring one of the Brownies, as the others scattered like sparks from a wind-blown fire. Max quickly pulled off the covers and jumped down to study his catch. With wild hair springing from its head like a patch of weeds, the Brownie cursed and grumbled, shaking its little fist at Max.

That's when a cold wind swept through the open window. As Max turned his head, the Brownie pulled out a slender peapod from behind its back and blew into it like a trumpet. Suddenly, a cloud of shimmering dust filled the air. The room started to spin, and Max crashed to the floor in a daze. He couldn't move, and worse, he couldn't think straight. His trap had been turned against him.

From the edge of his blurred vision, Max saw a horrible creature slither through the gaping window into his bedroom. With sinister teeth bared, the creature Max recognized as a Púka crept closer. Spiraling horns rose from the top of a gruesome goat's head, and its skin shone deathly pale in the moonlight. Max's eyes followed the beast's long arm, bone thin with a web of stringy veins, until he caught sight of a needle, shining and ominous, clutched in the monster's bony fingers.

With gasping breaths, the Púka drove the needle into the soft flesh of Max's arm. Max tried to scream, but his mouth wouldn't work. He was paralyzed, watching in revulsion as the dark crea-ture drained his blood into a hollowed-out willow reed.

When it was finally over, the monster withdrew, disappearing from Max's feverish vision. The last Brownie was long gone, as Max lay there lost in a haze. Things slowly came back into focus, and eventually Max was able to move his toes, then his fingers, until he gained strength enough to sit up. In a panic, Max scratched at his arm, but when he looked, there was no wound. In fact, he didn't bear a single mark. Max shook his head in confusion. It must have been a crazy delusion from the faerie dust. He'd have to be more careful next time.

Frustrated, Max made his way back over to his bed and checked on the *Codex,* which had been tucked safely under his pillow. It was still there.

Max sighed and threw himself back into bed as sour thoughts raced through his head. The night had been a total disaster, start-ing with the argument he'd had with his mother. It wasn't that Max wanted to be mean. He was just hurt and confused. But as hard as the divorce had been on him and his baby sister, Hannah, Max knew it was probably even harder on his mother.

Figuring he'd apologize in the morning, Max groaned and punched his pillow. Even if he reconciled with his mom, tomorrow had its own set of problems. How was he going to tell his fellow Griffins that their trip to Scotland was cancelled?

Wednesday morning Max woke up feeling strange. He was dizzy, his skin ached, and on top of that his mouth was dry and his throat was scratchy and sore. Like a bad dream, memories of the Púka, Brownies, and peapods flooded back, and Max groaned. He didn't want to think about Logan's reaction once he heard that Max had fallen for the faeries' prank. It was a stupid mistake — luckily it hadn't been fatal.

Unfortunately, the repercussions of the faerie dust weren't the worst of his problems. Today was the day he was supposed to leave for Scotland. In fact, the rest of the Grey Griffins were already packed. But Max knew there was no way his mother was going to let him go, and if Max couldn't go, that meant Harley, Natalia, and Ernie couldn't go, either. They were almost more excited about the trip than Max was. His friends were going to be crushed, and Max didn't want to be the one who ruined Christmas for them.

Suddenly a loud knock rattled his bedroom door. It swung open to reveal Annika Sumner standing there, disheveled and red-eyed, holding a yellow telegram at her side. "Okay, Max," she said in a defeated tone. "You win. You and your little club are going to Scotland. I hope you find whatever it is that you're looking for," she said flatly, before turning and storming down the hallway to her master suite, not bothering to wait for a response.

Max's mouth dropped in amazement. What had just happened?

"Are you okay?" Harley asked.

His face pale, Max leaned against a cold flagpole in the front drive of King's Elementary School, rubbing his forearm absently. The last bell had rung, signaling the end of the school day, and the Griffins were eagerly waiting outside in the cold. Soon Logan would be there to pick them up, to whisk them away on their dream vacation to Scotland, for a winter break, as Dr. Diamonte Blackstone put it, that they would never forget.

"I'm fine," Max replied, continuing to rub at his arm. "At least, I think so. But I had this dream...."

"A dream? When?" asked Natalia, pulling out her *Book of Clues*. Dreams, in her opinion, were vitally important and needed to be reviewed each and every night. She herself had no less than fourteen dream journals filled from beginning to end.

"When the peapod dust hit me, I kinda blacked out," Max confessed. "Then I think I saw a monster leaning over me, and it poked something into my arm."

Natalia pursed her lips. "Are you sure it was a dream?"

Max nodded. "My skin doesn't have a mark on it. And it's not like it hurts. It's just that the dream felt ... well ... real."

"So why do you look sick?" asked Ernie, who was keeping his distance for fear of catching whatever Max had.

"It's just a cold," Max explained. "I woke up with it this morning. Anyway, the sooner we're out of here, the better."

Right on time, Logan's Land Rover pulled into the school's circular drive, and the Griffins cheered.

Thanks to Natalia's guidance, they had come prepared, bringing all the essentials — though she had obviously gone the extra mile. Natalia had two suitcases, a backpack, her purse, and an old steamer trunk. What was inside, no one but Natalia knew. And she wasn't telling, either — girls have to have their secrets, she pointed out.

Then Ernie got a strange look on his face as a rolling wave

undulated across his puffy ski jacket. Natalia eyed Ernie suspiciously. "You are not taking that weasel to Scotland with us," Natalia barked.

"I am, too," countered Ernie. "She'd be lost without me."

"Forget it," Natalia insisted.

"Oh, it's just a ferret," Max consented, as Winifred poked her head out from beneath Ernie's jacket. "You can bring it, Ernie. Just don't let it stink up the plane."

"Are you lot ready?" Logan interrupted, as he pulled up and opened the back hatch to the Land Rover. "We have to get a move on. The plane's fueled and ready to roll."

Natalia threw up her hands and climbed into the backseat, leaving her bags for Logan to deal with. "Just keep that stinky weasel away from me," she smoldered.

5

What Goes Up... Must Come Down

"I'VE NEVER BEEN on a plane before," Ernie commented nervously as the Land Rover sped toward the airport. It was probably the tenth time he'd mentioned that fact since he had arrived at school earlier that day. But the truth was, none of the Griffins except for Max had ever been on a plane.

A few quiet moments passed as the town of Avalon disappeared in the rearview mirror, and the countryside crept into view with its snowy hills, frozen ponds, and battered old silos. Sumner Airfield wasn't far outside the city limits, so Natalia didn't have to deal with Winifred's stench for long before the metal airplane hangar swung into view.

Logan flashed the Land Rover's headlights three times as they approached, and immediately the broad doors of the private hangar rolled open. With a quiet lurch, the vehicle pulled into the darkness, coming to rest next to a sleek jet as the doors rolled closed behind them. Logan killed the engine, and the four friends stepped out of the car to admire the plane.

Harley gaped in wonder. He loved jets. Actually, he loved anything mechanical — go-carts, motorcycles, automobiles, airplanes, rockets. If it had an engine, Harley was in heaven. But this particular piece of machinery was something more spectacular than even his imagination could have conjured.

Among many top-secret projects, Max's father ran an aerospace design center, where he had ordered his very best engineers to create a personal fleet of jets that rivaled anything the government had dreamed up. His own jets had style. Where most planes were painted a basic boring white or gray, this particular jet was constructed of polished silver panels that reflected the surroundings like a mirror. It looked like a powerful predator, ready to hunt through the skies. Harley couldn't wait to strap in and take off and see what this plane had under its hood.

"If you like this, wait 'til you get a load of the inside," Logan said, handing his bag to a man in a blue jumpsuit who was loading the cargo.

"Who's flying?" Natalia asked, looking around for the pilot.

"Yours truly," answered Logan.

"I didn't know you could fly," Ernie exclaimed.

"I can drive or fly almost anything," Logan stated plainly, scratching at his stubbled jaw. "And if the skies stay clear, I'll have you at your father's estate in no time."

"How long is *no time?*" Ernie asked hesitantly, his fear of heights intensifying.

"I've been with this ship since the design stage," Logan assured. "Trust me. It moves."

"How fast?" asked Harley. "Mach one?"

"Let's just say it's classified," Logan replied with a wink, putting his glasses back on. "And I suggest you get onboard," he called over his shoulder as he climbed the steps. "This baby is taking off in two minutes. With . . . or without you."

As promised, the interior of the airplane was even more amazing than the outside. No expense had been spared in making it the most luxurious haven for the four friends to spend a long flight across the Atlantic Ocean. The main cabin was dressed in rich mahoganies and outfitted with expansive video screens for television, movies, or video games. Even the chairs — which had each of their names embroidered on the headrests — swiveled, reclined, and massaged at the touch of a button. There was also a fully loaded refrigerator with bologna sandwiches, sodas, and other more exotic snacks like chocolate soufflés.

"Oh, my goodness," Natalia exclaimed as she walked through a nearby doorway, her eyes wide in wonder. "Have you seen my room?" Of the four Griffins, she was the only one to have her own bedroom *and* her own bathroom. The boys, if they wanted any sleep, would have to do so in the main cabin. But considering all the toys they had to play with, sleep couldn't have been further from their minds.

Winifred, on the other hand, was already passed out and, curled up in Ernie's discarded jacket.

Shortly after the plane had reached cruising altitude, Ernie found himself enjoying the view out the window. As the earth slipped away beneath them, he began to wonder what life might be like if the plane were suddenly bombarded by cosmic radiation and they were instantly transformed into superheroes. He smiled and leaned back, envisioning every possible option for a costume to accent his newfound powers: utility belts with grappling hooks, a golden cape . . . but would he wear a mask or not bother with a secret identity at all?

"Hey, what's that under your chair, Ernie?" Harley asked, pointing to an object that had caught his eye.

"Winifred," Ernie answered, not bothering to look down. He was still wary of Natalia's scorn and didn't need Harley making fun of his pet on top of it.

"Not the stupid ferret . . . the shiny thing next to her."

"Search me," Ernie said, shrugging, as he casually leaned over and discovered a small drawer beneath his seat cushion. There was a button on it with a little sticky note next to it that read, PUSH ME.

"What do I do?" he asked the others as a smile crossed his face.

"Push it, of course," Natalia prompted in curiosity. "You can't have it spelled out much clearer than that, you know." Ernie shrugged and pushed the button. The drawer slid open, exposing a single comic book enveloped in a clear plastic bag. It looked old and extremely expensive.

"Holy cow," Ernie shouted as he pulled the comic onto his lap. "It's *Fantastic Four* number forty-eight!"

"Hey, we all have drawers under our seats!" Natalia exclaimed. In a flash, she pushed her button, revealing a crystal unicorn figurine. Natalia gasped. It was so beautiful. Beneath Harley's seat was a long cylindrical device that when opened held a screwdriver, a laser pointer, a high-resolution microscope, a magnet, and countless other gadgets. Max found a picture of him and his dad laughing as they played football. On the flip side of the photograph was a little note that read, *I can't wait to see you, Maximus!* Max sat back and sighed, thinking about all the things he and his dad would do when the plane landed in Scotland.

An hour or so later, the Griffins stretched out on the floor and pulled out their Round Table cards. Ernie wanted to get his Frost Dragon card back, so he challenged Natalia to a duel. Unfortunately for Ernie, her luck was still running hot. Not only did he get destroyed by his own dragon, but he lost several more cards as well.

As night fell, Logan dimmed the lights and suddenly the main cabin transformed into a flying movie palace, complete with sodas and popcorn. But it had been a long day, and even though they tried to keep their eyes open, the Griffins were powerless against the wave of sleep that washed over them.

As the lights lowered, eyelids closed, and soon, Ernie was snoring in his chair as Winifred squeaked softly on his lap. Harley had passed out on the floor near the remote control while Max had fallen asleep with the photograph of his dad in his hand. And Natalia quietly retired to her bedroom and closed the door.

All was quiet . . .

. . . until the alarm sounded.

Max opened his eyes to see the cabin bathed in an eerie red light. He felt feverish, his forehead painted in sweat. *That stupid peapod*, he thought. Whatever that Brownie had blown all over Max wasn't going away. Then Max felt a throbbing sensation in his arm. He rolled up his sleeve, but there was still no evidence of a puncture wound from the needle that the Púka in his bedroom had stuck him with . . . if it had been there at all. But why was his arm in such pain? Max thought it was probably time to tell Logan, regardless of the repercussions. The Scotsman would know what to do.

Taking off his seat belt, Max moved toward the cockpit, but the door swung open before he could reach it. Logan stepped out, a stern look on his face.

"Get back to your seat," Logan commanded gruffly. "And buckle up. All of you."

Half-asleep, Natalia opened up her door, yawning. But it didn't take long before she was fully alert, as she surveyed the cabin, catching the serious look in Logan's eye, and rushed to her seat.

Across the aisle, Ernie tried to soothe a very nervous Winifred. "It's okay, girl. We're gonna be just fine," he murmured, hoping he wouldn't be proved wrong.

"We're in for a bumpy ride ahead," Logan said. "Don't get up for any reason. Things are about to get messy."

"Messy?" Ernie cried out fearfully, imagining an egg being smashed on the sidewalk.

"If you're in here, then who's flying the plane?" Natalia asked.

"Autopilot," answered Logan. "Just stay calm, and I'll explain more when I can," he assured the Griffins before turning back to the cockpit. "I'll let you know when it's time to worry. Right now, just remain calm, and I'll handle the rest."

Max turned to look out the window, and his visage went white as a ghost.

"What's wrong?" Harley asked from across the aisle.

Natalia shook her head. "We're not alone. . . ."

Two shadows shot out from a patch of silvery clouds on either side of the Sumner plane. They were military jets, painted stealth gray with no markings other than a strange runic symbol upon the tail. Silently, the jets flew alongside the Sumner aircraft. *What did they want?*

Max reached under his shirt and pulled out his grandfather's Templar necklace. His eyes scanned it as they had a hundred times before, wondering what was to become of him. Clearly, Logan viewed the visitors as a threat. And no wonder — these were fighter jets. If they got aggressive, how were the Griffins going to escape?

At that moment, the engines fired as the Sumner plane accelerated like a rocket, and the kids were thrown back in their seats with a rush. Like fleeting thoughts, clouds slipped by as the jet roared through the air at ever-increasing speeds.

"Holy cow," cried Harley, looking out the window as the fighters disappeared. "I bet we're moving more than two thousand miles an hour. This is unbelievable."

"Then why do I still have a bad feeling in the pit of my stomach?" Natalia complained.

"You're starting to sound like Ernie," replied Harley with a wave of his hand. "We're as good as gold. Trust me. I bet there's nothing faster than this jet."

"There's one thing faster, though," Natalia replied.

Harley smiled, up to the challenge. "And what's that?"

"Magic!"

His smile faded. Harley hadn't thought about that.

Just then, the plane groaned, lurching as it tossed the kids around in their seats with an impact that threatened to rip apart their seat belts. Out of the skies above fell a web of crackling red energy that slipped over the Sumner aircraft, swallowing it whole. Roaring, the jet engines strained like wild horses against the magical reins, but the web proved more powerful. When the first turbine burst into flames, Logan had to shut the others down. Slowly, their jet lost speed and altitude.

Max groaned as the pain in his arm grew more intense.

"Stay in your seats," Logan's voice called over the intercom. "And hang on. . . ."

"Look up there," exclaimed Harley, watching outside his window in fascination and horror. The darkness above ushered what appeared to be a battleship floating amid the clouds. All around its mighty hull a sea of lights flashed and upon its side, emblazoned in black, was the same strange rune that marked the enemy jets. Whatever it was, colossal plane or UFO, Max knew that they were in big trouble. Then, as the airship blotted out the last of the moonlight, a barrage of falling objects struck the Sumner aircraft.

"Please tell me those weren't meteors," Ernie said as he looked up to the ceiling. Then the Griffins heard what sounded like footsteps above their heads, followed by the noise of metal striking metal. The whole airplane began to shake.

"This isn't good!" Max exclaimed as he looked out to see three Kobolds standing on the wings. More intelligent than goblins and twice as deadly, Kobolds were the faerie henchmen that had served Morgan LaFey in her plot to kill Iver. And unlike other faeries,

Kobolds had two distinct advantages: They were immune to the effects of iron; and they could see through walls.

"They want the *Codex*," Natalia cried in sudden realization. "Max, you have to do something."

"I . . . I can't," Max called back, as he clutched at his arm.

"Why not?" Natalia asked. There was a wild look in her eyes, as one of the Kobolds made its way toward her window.

"It's packed down below with the rest of my luggage."

"What?" cried Ernie. "Iver told you to never let it out of your sight!"

Max shook his head in frustration. He'd made a big mistake. "I know. But I didn't think I'd need it up here. . . ."

Suddenly, the plane shuddered as a brilliant flash of light exploded outside, followed by a burst of thunder. The Griffins watched in amazement as the Kobolds tumbled off the plane, littering the sky below.

"What in the world just happened?" Harley exclaimed in stunned amazement.

"Static Shell Burst," came Logan's voice over the intercom. "Electrocuted everything touching the outside of the jet. This beauty still has some surprises left in her."

"That's amazing," Harley cheered. "I've never even read about anything like that before."

"And you probably won't," replied Logan bluntly, "but we can only use it once. The battery is depleted now. It bought us a few minutes, but not much more."

Even before Logan finished his sentence, Max heard the echo of dreadful thumps above his head, as more Kobolds landed on the plane.

"They must be jumping out of that ship above us," Harley noted, trying to get a better look out the window. "But they aren't even wearing parachutes."

Without the *Codex Spiritus,* the Griffins were helpless as more and more Kobolds began to swarm over the plane, tearing their way through its outer shell. It wouldn't be long now before they tunneled into the cabin, leaving everyone inside at their mercy. And Kobolds had no mercy. The profile on their Round Table card made that point loud and clear.

"We are so dead," whined Ernie. As he covered his eyes, the evil faeries pressed ever harder, ripping their way into the plane, sending chunks of metal rushing past the windows. Outside, the Kobolds hammered, smashed, drilled, and melted, while the plane groaned under the onslaught. *How long could it possibly hold out?*

Dust was now falling from the ceiling and the Kobolds were mere seconds from breaching the interior, when suddenly the turbine outside Max's window exploded violently. And that's all it took. Logan lost control as the nose of the Sumner plane tipped dangerously toward the ocean, launching into a fiery descent to the icy waters below. Max had only enough time to pull the photograph of his father close to his chest before their jet crashed into the water, disappearing in the murky darkness.

If it wasn't for their seat belts, the impact from the crash would have killed them all instantly. But that was hardly a consolation as the Griffins' bewildered eyes watched the dark waves outside their windows slowly swallow the plane. The children hung in the air, suspended from their seat belts as the craft listed to the left and drifted nose first down into the frigid waters.

No one thought to say a word, and for several frightful moments, they descended in silence. Then, out of nowhere, strange, haunting noises began to echo all around them. Max had heard the noises before. It was in movies, right before a submarine was crushed by the ocean's unforgiving hand. Then another strange sound echoed — like a door opening. Millions of bubbles burst outside the Griffins' windows, and to their disbelief, slowly, surely, the plane righted itself. The children were level once again.

A moment later the door to the cockpit opened, and Logan quietly walked in. "I think we've lost them . . . for now, anyway," he said in a hushed tone, peering out of one of the windows as light reflected off the water, dancing on his face. "With any luck, they'll think we're resting on the ocean floor by now."

"So we're not dead?" Ernie asked, stroking Winifred between the ears to calm her down.

Logan smiled briefly. "You're sitting in one of the finest vessels ever constructed at the Griffin Military Engineering and Applied Science division of Sumner Enterprises. What you saw . . . and what I hope the Black Witch saw . . . was a parlor trick but a good one. Controlled fuel drop and ignition, turbine-screw water fail-over conversion, followed by wing separation. Overall, it should have looked like the real thing."

"Would you mind repeating that in English?" Ernie asked, even more confused.

"He means he faked the crash," Harley explained as Natalia turned to Logan with narrowed eyes.

"You might have warned us about it, you know," she said. "I thought we were dead for sure."

"No time," the Scotsman answered, shaking his head. "If we'd waited any longer, those Kobolds would have broken through our superstructure. If that had happened, they'd have taken the *Codex* and left us for dead. As it is, I think we did pretty well."

"Except we're stuck in the middle of the ocean," Natalia pointed out.

"Unless you haven't noticed, this is more than just a plane. It's also a submarine. And submarines are right at home in the middle of the ocean," Logan reminded her.

"No way!" Harley said, jumping from his chair to get a better look out the window. "This is amazing."

His arm already feeling better, Max smiled and looked again at the photo he held tightly in his hand.

Logan patted the plane's cabin wall fondly. "But we're still not out of danger, I'm afraid." The eyes of the Griffins turned to Logan in apprehension. "The plane wasn't designed to hit the water at two hundred miles an hour," he stated. "We lost some structural integrity."

"What does that mean?" Ernie exclaimed, looking around nervously. "It sounds bad."

"It means the sooner we get to land, the better," Logan replied as he moved from Griffin to Griffin making sure no one was hurt. "Apart from a few bruises around your midsection, you should be fine in a couple days," he noted.

"Who do you think they're working for?" asked Max, though he had an idea.

"Did you see the rune symbol on the planes?" Natalia asked. "It's just like the ones on that cufflink. It can't be a coincidence."

Logan paused. "Cufflink? You didn't mention this before."

Natalia nodded, reaching into her pocket, as she placed the silver piece in Logan's hand. After only a casual glance, the body-guard's face grew pale.

"What is it, Logan?" asked Max. "Have you seen anything like it before?"

"Where did you find it?" Logan asked.

"Out by Max's house near Lethe Creek Bridge," explained Harley.

"You're certain you found this in the woods?" Logan pressed.

"Yeah," answered Ernie, clearly shaken.

"Did you see anyone?"

"Just some tire tracks and a few wolf prints," Natalia said.

"Really?" Logan said, nodding before silently disappearing into the cockpit, leaving the Griffins alone in their new underwater world.

"He knows something," Harley pointed out.

"I agree," Natalia replied. "The question is, will he let us in on his little secret?"

"As long as Ray doesn't have anything to do with it," answered Ernie.

"You can bet he does," Natalia countered. "He's like a bad penny, always turning up. Besides, those were Kobolds that attacked us. And there's only one person I know who uses Kobolds . . . the very same person who is currently in custody of Ray."

While the Sumner plane-turned-submarine had been outfitted with every conceivable super-spy gadget in the book, the crash had done some serious damage, just as Logan predicted. Soon, the air circulation systems had short-circuited, and no longer able to stay submerged, the jet was forced to surface more than fifty miles off the coast of Scotland. Thankfully, there hadn't been any sign of the Black Witch, or her aircraft, as they carved through the dark blue waters of the firth, heading toward Port Glasgow.

Eventually they found a place to moor, though it wasn't easy for them to go unnoticed. A shining silver jet that can cruise through water as easily as it can fly through the air just wasn't a common sight. Luckily, Max's father owned a marina in the vicinity, and they were able to pull into the boathouse without being seen — or so they hoped.

Logan killed the engines as the kids stepped onto a platform in the boathouse, stretching their legs. The building they were now in was cavernous, with lots of strange yellow canisters, looming cranes, glassed-in control rooms, and flights of metal stairs that led off to who knew where. But at least it felt safe. And Ernie was quite satisfied with any footing, as long as it was on dry land.

As the Griffins took their bags from Logan, they turned to find a rather tall man waiting for them. He was wearing a blue jumpsuit, with SUMNER ENTERPRISES emblazoned on the back. Without so much as a glance at the jet, the man walked past the children and pulled out a set of keys, which he handed to Logan.

"Helicopter's ready to go topside. Cleared for takeoff."

Logan nodded. "And the weather?"

"Storm's rolling in from the northwest. Ice and sleet coming with it. If you're gonna make it, you'd better leave now."

Ernie cleared his throat as the others turned to look at him. "Not that I want to be a pain, but we ran out of food hours ago. Can we stop and get something to eat before we take off?"

"Not a good idea," Logan replied. "We don't have time. Besides, the weather's gonna be choppy. If you eat, you'll wish you hadn't."

"Trust me," replied Ernie with a smile. "I just survived a plane crash. I can handle anything. Just show me the food."

"What about your diet?" Natalia looked at him skeptically. "Your parents told me to make sure you stuck to it. And you've been doing so good."

"This is an emergency," Ernie replied resolutely.

"Suit yourself." Logan rolled his eyes. "But you'll be sorry. There's a burger joint not far up the wharf. Just get it to go."

"Roger!" Ernie saluted, handing his ferret to Logan, who looked less than pleased. "And don't worry, she won't bite."

"But I do," replied Logan under his breath.

6

Home for the Holidays

THE HELICOPTER TORE through an angry winter storm, red lights flashing as winds raged over the roiling northern seas beyond. Stomach-dropping turbulence had wracked them since Glasgow, but it was finally over. Sumner Castle lay dead ahead.

No sooner had the skids touched down than Ernie shot out the door, holding his hand over his mouth, his cheeks inflated like a puffer fish's. Ernie's ashen skin was quickly turning green, as the three cheeseburgers, pile of fries, and two chocolate malts he had devoured waged war in his stomach, threatening to revolt at any moment.

Harley was next out the door, weak-kneed but making every effort to get as far away from Ernie as he could. Vomit wasn't his thing. Natalia was next as she chased after Ernie to make sure he was okay, followed by Max. Logan came out last, surveying the skies as the wind snapped through his black trench coat. The Scotsman's signature sunglasses were fixed squarely on his face.

"Oh, my," Natalia breathed, patting Ernie on the back as she admired the castle.

It was well known that the sprawling Sumner home back in Avalon, Minnesota, was an architectural masterpiece. But what towered before them now made that house look like . . . well . . . like a dollhouse.

Hewn from dark stone, now rain-slicked, Castle Sumner took the Griffins' breath away with its phalanx of towers and turrets that sat atop a jagged cliff, defying the ocean waves that crashed far below. Despite the storm, hundreds of torches flickered, lining a narrow bridge of rock that connected the Sumner Peninsula with the rest of Scotland.

Just behind the castle, lit by a flash of lightning, rose the shadow of a vast and creepy forest. Looking at it gave Max the chills. Though the woods back home were indeed old, this woodland was something altogether ancient.

"So whaddaya think, Max?" Harley asked, teeth chattering with cold. "Home sweet home?"

"I . . . I guess so," Max stammered, not quite knowing what to say. The castle was more astonishing than even he had imagined.

As they raced across the icy lawn and up the steps to the front entrance, double doors swung open in invitation, bathing the Griffins in warm light. The entry was lit by the welcoming glow of a fireplace, and before the children could even wipe their shoes on the mat, a small army of servants in pinstriped uniforms bustled in, carrying away their baggage and personal effects like worker ants streaming from a picnic basket.

The children sighed as they took in their surroundings. Opulent didn't even begin to describe the interior of the castle. Everywhere they looked, festive décor for the Christmas season shone all about, with hundreds of yards of evergreen garlands wrapped around banisters and balconies, while tall white candles glowed brightly in the windows. Yet, the most amazing of all the decorations was the Christmas tree — as tall as a skyscraper according to Ernie — with tinsel, ribbons, and thousands of white lights, glittering like stars.

"This place is amazing," Harley said, patting Max on the back. Kobolds falling from the sky could be discussed later. For now, the Grey Griffins had entered a winter wonderland, and they wanted to soak in every inch of it.

"Ahem," came a slightly agitated voice from nearby. The children turned to see a man in a uniform similar to the other servants, save for the shiny medals pinned to the front of his, as if to signify rank or prestige. He looked to have a predilection for fattening food, but despite his corpulence, this gentleman held an undeniable dignity, with perfect posture, a crisp white shirt, a spotless tie, freshly shined shoes, and a pair of diamond cufflinks. This individual was no servant. He was a master of servants.

"Welcome to Castle Sumner," he offered in a discriminating English accent as he bowed deeply. "I am Augustus, overseer of the premises."

"Hiya, Augustus," Ernie greeted cheerily, happy to be on solid ground. "Merry Christmas. My name's Ernest. But you can call me Ernie," he said, reaching out to shake hands.

Augustus looked at Ernie disapprovingly before reaching into his coat pocket and pulling out a small silver bell. Tinkling it twice, a young woman, perhaps in her early twenties, strode into the hall. Her hair was raven black, accented by a silvery white forelock, pulled back into an intricate knot. Beneath arched eyebrows were electrifying blue eyes that glowed under the warm lights of the house. Natalia marveled at the woman's impeccable taste in clothing. If she was a servant, she certainly didn't look like one.

"This is Athena," the hefty overseer introduced, as the woman bowed politely. "I apologize for her attire; however, like you, she has only just arrived. But from this moment on, it will be her responsibility to ensure your stay here is comfortable."

"Merry Christmas," Athena said with a musical voice. Her eyes skimmed the guests before coming to rest on Max. With a demure smile, she bowed slightly. "It's an honor, Master Sumner," she said, her eyes never moving from Max's. "I've heard so much about you. . . ."

Max blushed. The extra attention embarrassed him, and it didn't help that Athena was beautiful. "Um . . . thanks," he said, averting his eyes.

"Not at all," she replied. "Your father has asked that we make this the most magical holiday you've ever had, and I'm here to ensure that happens."

"Are you tellin' me we're really gonna have servants?" Harley whispered out of the corner of his mouth. He felt a bit uneasy at the prospect.

"There are many servants here," Augustus pointed out with an air of absolute authority, though the question had not been addressed to him. "All have names, but the only ones you need remember are my own, Athena's, and, of course, Magnus's."

"Magnus?" asked Ernie with a giggle as he looked around. "Is he mag-netic? Who would name their kid that?"

That's when a second figure emerged from the shadows. Standing almost seven feet tall, the man's substantial jaw was covered in a wild beard, and his brows were perched like giant caterpillars over his eyes. Enormous shoulders, arms, and a thick neck all threatened to burst the seams of his jacket. He had long blond hair pulled back in a ponytail, and a set of golden loops adorned each ear.

"This . . . ," Augustus continued with an absent wave at the hulking mass behind him, "is Magnus. And I don't recommend discussing the practicality of his name. He's not the forgiving sort."

Ernie nodded quickly and stepped behind Logan, peering out from under one of the Scotsman's arms.

"Magnus is the Lord Sumner's bodyguard. All business . . . and serious business at that," Augustus continued. "He is unable to speak, you see. Please don't bother trying any of your charming American small talk. I doubt you'll find him an appreciative audience."

"When can I see my father?" Max asked, confused. He had flown all this way for one reason and one reason only — to be reunited with his dad.

Augustus turned slowly, looking down at the Sumner boy with haughty eyes. "Yes. Your father, Ahem . . . ," the overweight overseer cleared his throat again — which sounded more like a frog croaking. "Lord Sumner is . . . well, he is indisposed at the moment; though he wanted me to extend his warmest Christmas greetings." Something in the tone of Augustus's words dripped with condescending sarcasm. In fact, it seemed to Max that he was taking some sort of perverse pleasure in disappointing the young Sumner.

"Your father's a lord?" asked Natalia. "That's so cool."

"Yes," Augustus replied, straightening himself to a more respectable height. "The Sumner blood is as blue as the sea."

"Blue blood?" Ernie's nose curled up at the thought.

"It's an expression," Natalia explained in a whisper. "It means he's related to royalty."

But Max wasn't interested. "I'm here because my father sent for me. He wants to see me."

"I'm afraid that will be quite impossible," Augustus maintained, folding his arms. "Perhaps the morning shall bring different tidings."

Max's mouth sagged in disbelief, as the Griffins gathered around him protectively. He had come so far. . . .

"Max!" called a familiar voice. Lord Sumner rushed down the polished stairs, pushing Augustus aside. He swept Max into his arms. "You made it! I've been worried sick. . . ."

Grayson Maximillian Sumner II, a distinguished man in his early forties, was wearing a formal business suit and a bold red tie. His dark hair was thick and fashionable, with light shocks of gray around the ears. Slender waist, broad shoulders, olive skin, with nails perfectly manicured and teeth as white as polished ivory — Lord Sumner was every bit as handsome as Max's mother, the former supermodel, was beautiful.

"Hi, Mr. Sumner," exclaimed Ernie with a big grin, his braces gleaming like tinsel in the firelight. He had always liked Max's dad and, like every other boy his age, wanted to grow up to be just like him. "Thanks for inviting me. This place is amazing!"

Lord Sumner smiled warmly as he turned to Ernie. "Ernest, I'm sorry about the bumpy flight over here, but you were in good hands with Logan," Max's father said, concern lining his face. "Thankfully, though, it seems like everyone's fine. That is certainly the best Christmas gift I could possibly have received. But it's great to see you. Is that a new pair of glasses?"

Ernie nodded proudly. "Mom says they make my nose look smaller."

"And who is that?" Lord Sumner asked as Ernie's ferret peeked out of his jacket. "Not Winifred, is it? She's beautiful," he commented, scratching the animal between her ears. Remarkably, the ferret didn't hiss or threaten to bite Max's dad as it did everyone else.

"How did you know her name?" Ernie asked, amazed.

"It's my job to know, Ernest. And Winifred is a welcome guest in our house," he said as Ernie shot a look of great satisfaction at Natalia.

Lord Sumner's eyes twinkled, then he turned to Harley. "And how are things with you, Harley? Have you built any go-carts lately?"

Harley folded his arms and nodded. "The fastest in Avalon, but it's no big deal."

"Not the fastest in the world, though." Lord Sumner shook his head with a grin. "But it will be. I have some ideas that my people in Sumner Labs have been working on. I think it could be just the trick to make that go-cart of yours world class."

Harley's mouth fell open. Sumner Labs? The very same labs that developed jets that converted into submarines, like the one they had rode over in?

"Just what Harley needs," exclaimed Natalia with a disapproving shake of her head. "Yet another way to put himself in the hospital."

"Natalia Romanov!" Lord Sumner bowed and offered a wink. "You look simply radiant. Always dressed for the occasion, I see ... absolutely stunning. Of course, I would expect nothing less from a young lady of your stature. And I must say your hair has taken on a golden radiance since I last saw you."

Natalia blushed, reaching back unconsciously as she ran her hand through her hair to inspect a strand or two. Girls adored Lord Sumner. And Natalia, despite her arguments to the contrary, was not immune to flattery. Especially from someone who had graduated at the top of his class in Cambridge.

"So what are we going to do first, Dad?" Max asked, beaming. He'd waited so long for this moment that Max could hardly have been blamed for forgetting that he hadn't slept in more than twenty-four hours, his plane had been shot out of the sky, and he'd narrowly managed to make his way to dry land on a super-secret submarine. But all Max could think about was playing football with his dad one more time.

Lord Sumner gave his son another hug, then rose to his feet and looked at his watch. "The first thing to do, despite my wishes, is for the secret Order of the Grey Griffins to get some sleep. It's been an exciting day, and I want to hear all about it. But not until you've had a chance to recover. And after Ernie has a full belly, of course."

"Thank you," Ernie replied with a salute, as his mouth began to water at the thought of a late-night snack.

Natalia turned and looked at him skeptically. "You just threw up!" she argued. "Don't you ever learn, Ernest?"

"But my stomach's empty now," Ernie protested. "Besides, I promise I'll eat healthy this time. Trust me."

Lord Sumner laughed. "The fridge is fully stocked, so help yourselves. I've asked the chef to keep his staff on a bit later tonight, thinking you'd be hungry from this sea air. But I must say good night, as I have a full boardroom waiting for me to return."

"At this hour?" Natalia asked in disbelief.

Lord Sumner smiled sadly. "Unfortunately, there are things in life that are bigger than ourselves, and business can be a tyrannical taskmaster. But having a son like Max and friends like the Grey Griffins makes this burden a bit easier to bear. As far as I'm concerned, there's nothing better in this whole world than a true friend. And that's an encouraging thought, don't you think?"

Max nodded, as did the rest of the Grey Griffins.

"Good. Now Augustus will see you to your rooms," Lord Sumner continued, as the Head of Staff's eyes narrowed in annoyance. Castle Sumner didn't see many guests, and Augustus was not accustomed to actual acts of service, despite the fact that service was at the core of his responsibilities. "I hope you'll find them comfortable. I don't want any of you getting homesick." He said the last line with a wink, and then turned and walked out of the room, Magnus close behind.

"As much as I would savor an opportunity to be of service, I'm afraid I have some matters of import that I must attend to myself,"

Augustus said, his voice dripping with sarcasm. "Athena and the rest of *my* staff will show you to your rooms now."

"Ah, and lest I forget . . . ," the Head of Staff said, turning his back to the Griffins as he walked down the hallway. "Lord Sumner requested that I invite you all to join him at breakfast tomorrow, which will be served promptly at six. I trust you have brought appropriate attire." With that, he disappeared, leaving an army of servants to take care of Max and his friends.

The Grey Griffins looked at one another, a bit confused. Appropriate attire? For breakfast?

Castles are, by their very nature, immense more often than not. And the rooms inside must, of course, be spacious and accommodating: dining rooms with tables as long as airplane runways, libraries with books more numerous than leaves in a forest, and kitchens with a thousand cupboards and drawers, and at least six different pantries. But the kids had no expectations for their guest rooms, apart from there being beds and perhaps an alarm clock. What they found, however, was something altogether astounding.

There were two guest rooms: one for the boys to share and one for Natalia, just down the hall, with a nameplate stating her name — THE LADY ROMANOV — placed above the entrance. Just beneath the sign were two large, gilded double doors that swung open soundlessly, revealing a treasure trove even Natalia couldn't have dreamed up in a month of Sundays.

As the four friends entered, they discovered Natalia's room

filled with light cascading from ornate Tiffany lamps. There was a table set for a tea party and a shelf full of rare novels and a stack of empty journals and calligraphy pens. It was warm, cozy, and sumptuous. But it was only the beginning.

Her room had been decorated in her favorite theme — unicorns. They were everywhere. Vast paintings hung on the walls, in which they pranced and played. High above, draping from the ceiling, was a banner made of pink and white silk with a unicorn emblazoned on it. And just below this rested the most delicious canopy bed an eleven-year-old girl could ever have dreamed.

French doors tucked behind gossamer drapery led outside to a private garden terrace, where there was a merry-go-round made especially for her. There, four unicorns rose up and down to a soft music-box melody. Natalia swayed to the music and closed her eyes, and with a rapturous smile she breathed in the magical surroundings. Quietly, Max, Harley, and Ernie left the terrace and headed back down the hallway, filled with wondrous expectation. If Natalia's room was that amazing, what would their own room be like? On the count of three, they pushed open their door together. And together, they gasped.

It wasn't a room at all. It was a playground that seemed to stretch almost a mile high. The main floor was paved in shiny black stone, and the room's outer rim was circled by an enormous aquarium of iridescent blue water where leopard sharks, eels, and even a sea turtle played among coral and anemones. There was an air-hockey table, billiards, foosball, a miniature golf course, slot-car racetracks, a giant movie screen, and even a table set up for a Round Table tournament — in fact, it was piled high with the latest Shadowlands Expansion packs, which Iver said weren't due out until after Christmas.

"Did you see this?" Max asked, walking over to a rather amazing and intricate series of tubes, tanks, and wire cages filled with everything from squeaky toys to a six-foot-high glass cage with a tree, shrubs, and dirt tunnels that looked like a giant ant farm. Ernie carefully set Winifred inside, and she tore off through the trails.

Down a set of concrete stairs, lit by flashing lights, lay Harley's ultimate dream: a go-cart garage unlike anything he could have imagined. There were at least twenty go-carts of varying colors and shapes, either on the floor or up on hydraulic lifts. Toolboxes lined the walls in military order and the garage door opened to reveal a long tunnel that gradually ramped up to the castle driveway.

Harley had no intention of leaving the garage, so Ernie and Max raced back into the main room, and up another flight of stairs where they came to a circular room brimming with row upon row of shelves stuffed with strange-looking books.

"A library?" Ernie asked, a bit surprised and more than a little disappointed.

"These aren't books," Max shouted, running over to a nearby wall. "They're comic books."

Ernie let out a whoop and ran around the room, trying to get the lay of the land. Every now and again he'd pull an issue from a shelf and let out a squeal of glee. All about them were rare comics from days long past. Some were on reading tables, while other priceless first appearances and secret origin issues aligned in alphabetical order, rank upon rank.

Models of spaceships hung from the ceiling, and there were life-sized statues of the most powerful heroes in the comic book world, not to mention a dark corner dedicated to the most sinister supervillains that ever existed.

"This *is* pretty cool," Max said, walking over to a drawing table nestled below a wall of action figures still in their packaging. On the table were sketches from famous comic artists, who had also signed the wall. But as Max walked through the aisles, his eyes alighted upon one wonder after another, until he found a second staircase. It spiraled up as if it were floating in the air, until it reached a mysterious balcony high above. "Wanna see where this goes?" he called over to Ernie.

Reluctant to leave his newfound treasure trove, Ernie pulled himself away and followed Max up the corkscrew staircase until, finally, breathlessly, they found themselves at the top. As Ernie looked back down over the balcony, his stomach grew queasy: Their beds and game tables seemed like tiny specks far below.

When Ernie turned back around, he found Max staring at a celestial observatory, complete with a towering golden telescope that poked through an opening in the roof. To the right of the hulking spyglass lay a library of books and smaller instruments. To the left was a passage to a giant orrery, which was, if possible, even more enormous than the telescope.

"What is it?" asked Ernie as he walked toward the metal beast. He thought it looked rather like a giant clock that had exploded and refashioned itself into an amusement park ride. The machine had a central sphere that was twenty feet high, with ten golden arms branching out, which attached to smaller spheres. And everything was in motion.

"It's an orrery, a map of the planets," recalled Max, thinking back to what his old Latin tutor had told him. "But it actually moves. They used to use it, I guess, to find out how all the planets moved through the solar system. See, the big globe in the middle is supposed to be the sun. And all the smaller globes are the planets."

Silently, the planets sailed over the boys' heads.

"Oh," Ernie's voice trailed as his interest faded.

"Why do you think your dad has one?" he asked, patting a circular globe that passed slowly over his head.

Max shrugged, never dropping his eyes from the marvelous structure. Why would his dad have anything?

Later that night, Max lay awake, watching the fire slowly die. His arm ached again, but it was the thought of his mother spending Christmas alone that was really eating at him. Sure, they hadn't been getting along well lately, but Max still missed her and he felt guilty for leaving. After all, she *was* his mother.

"Pssst. Max, are you awake?" a voice whispered.

"Who is it?" Max asked, sitting up and peering around the room. Ernie was snoring a few feet away, and Harley must have fallen asleep downstairs on top of a toolbox.

"It's me, of course," Natalia replied as she stepped into the light of the dying fire. She was dressed all in black, and Harley, contrary to Max's assumption, was standing behind her in similar garb.

"How'd you get in here?" Max asked, running his hand through his matted hair.

"Our balconies connect," Natalia answered quickly. "Well, they almost connect. I had to jump."

"Are you crazy?" Max exclaimed, as Ernie's snores were broken by a sleepy sneeze. "It's almost a thirty-foot drop."

"But only a couple of feet between the balconies," she answered. "I've jumped farther in hopscotch."

Max shook his head, then looked again at their clothing suspiciously. "Have you guys been sneaking around the house?"

"Not yet," Harley smiled mischievously, followed by a wink. "We thought you'd like to come along."

"We can't," Max replied. "We're supposed to be in bed. Besides, Augustus would kill us if he found us roaming around. He's just looking for a reason, you know."

"What good is flying across the world to a mysterious castle if you can't take the time to have a good snoop around?" Natalia asked.

She had a point.

"C'mon, Max. This place is awesome," Harley added. "I already checked out a few rooms. You should see everything — it'll blow your mind!"

"This castle is absolutely perfect," Natalia agreed. "One day it might even be the world headquarters for the Grey Griffins. Don't you think, Max?"

"Maybe," Max replied, as he scratched his head thoughtfully. "But I don't know. And to tell you the truth, I'm as shocked as you guys are. I've never seen anything like it. And to think it's my dad's . . ."

"Which means it's your place, too," Harley urged. "So what's the big deal if you look around a bit?"

Of Beastly Menageries and
Holiday Spirits

LINED WITH MARBLE floors and padded by thick oriental rugs, the hall outside Max's room seemed to wind its way through a virtual labyrinth of mysteries. There were fountains carved into stone walls, strange statues on crumbling pedestals, animal trophies, and priceless paintings by famous artists that Natalia was certain weren't replicas.

"Are you sure we won't get caught?" Ernie asked, looking up and down the hallway reluctantly. He hadn't brought proper sneaking-around clothes, so Ernie was left with no other option than to make the foray in pajamas and, regrettably, fluffy bunny slippers. He had tried to protest the latter, claiming he could just wear his sneakers; but as they all knew, Ernie's sneakers squeaked, and that just wouldn't do.

"Relax," Harley said. "Everything's gonna be just fine."

"Maybe we'll find a magic artifact tonight . . . like another *Codex*," Natalia wondered aloud as they crept through the quiet passageway. "Castles always have things like that."

"As long as this place isn't haunted," Ernie added, his eyes darting from the thick folds of heavy draperies to a creepy deer head looking down at him from the wall. He was starting to have second thoughts. "I swear this looks just like a movie I saw where the kids get eaten by a bunch of zombies."

"You don't make it any easier for yourself, you know," Harley pointed out. "You need to stop watching so much television. Anyway, I promise that if we run into any zombies, I'll protect you, okay?" Ernie nodded, crowding close to his big friend as they continued down the hall.

Most of the doors were locked, and the few that were open led only to empty rooms with stale air and the smell of mothballs. After almost an hour of this, the Griffins were beginning to draw the conclusion that there was nothing magical about this castle at all. As far as they were concerned, their midnight adventure had been a complete bust. But just as they were about to head back to their rooms, Harley motioned for them to stop.

"Great," he stated, pointing back down the hallway.

As one, they turned to see a lantern bouncing up and down, growing steadily closer. If there had been daylight, the children would have been spotted immediately; but the darkness was their ally. Max switched off the flashlight and pulled his friends down the hall and into a nearby alcove, signaling for everyone to stay quiet. It was a bit cramped, but at least they weren't standing out in the open.

As they looked about to get their bearings, they could see a tapestry hanging on the wall behind them depicting a howling black wolf. In the darkness, it appeared a little more lifelike than Ernie would have preferred, and he managed to let out a squeal before Harley clapped his hand over Ernie's mouth.

"Well, isn't this a fine kettle of fish we've gotten into?" whispered Natalia.

"It doesn't matter," whispered Max, trying to get another look at the approaching figure. "Whoever it was, they heard us for sure. I just hope it wasn't Augustus."

"Or Magnus . . . ," Harley added.

"Oh, great." Ernie heaved a sigh and hit his head against the back wall in exasperation. Lord Sumner's giant bodyguard frightened Ernie to the bone. And something about the fact that he wasn't able to speak made him even more threatening.

Something rattled.

"What was that?" Harley asked.

"My head," answered Ernie, rubbing his sore spot.

"No," Max said, as he pulled back the corner of the tapestry. "Something's back there."

Indeed there was — a scuffed wooden door that had no handle. Wild animals with angry eyes stared back at them from the wooden surface, and a large iron knocker in the shape of a wolf's head was affixed to the center.

"We better do something fast," Natalia said. "Either we find a way in, or we're gonna get caught for sure." They all knew she was right, as the oncoming footsteps were now only seconds away.

"We don't seem to have much of a choice," Max replied as he took a deep breath. He tried to push the door open, but it wouldn't give.

"Try the knocker," Harley suggested as Ernie shook his head to disagree. Max shrugged, wondering what good it would do as he realized they were about to get caught. With little hope, he raised the knocker and let it drop as quietly as he could — which was about as silent as a toolbox being dropped from a rooftop. Then, as if by magic, the door creaked open, and without another word the Griffins raced inside and shut the door.

What lay on the other side of the darkness, none of them could guess. It was definitely not a closet, they could not feel any walls about them. But the Griffins had no intention of staying in the secret room anyway. It was too late, and they had to get back.

Once the footsteps outside faded away, they tried to leave the way they had come. Their hearts sank. The door was locked.

"Max, shine your flashlight over here," Harley said as he searched his pockets for his lock-pick kit.

"I . . . I don't have it," Max said, embarrassed. "I must have left it in the alcove."

"Doesn't matter," Harley confessed after a moment. "I can't find my lock-pick kit anyway. Must have left it back in the room."

"Well, if Winifred was here . . ."

"What would she do, chew a hole in the door?" Natalia snapped.

"We've gotta do something," Max added. "Either that or we stand around here and wait until they come looking for us."

"How about a portal, Max?" Harley asked.

"Nope," Max sighed. Over the last few months, he had developed the ability to detect the invisible magical doorways. "I can't sense any, and I haven't since we left Avalon."

"Doesn't look like we have much of a choice other than to just keep moving then," Harley said. "Go on, Ernie. You lead the way."

The Griffins continued searching as a chill draft crept in. Eyes adjusting, Ernie could now see a soft stream of light up ahead and began to move toward it, hoping he'd discovered a way out. "Hey, I think I see something. It looks like a . . ." And that was when he walked face-first into a wall of fur. Bouncing off, Ernie landed squarely on his backside as his glasses skittered into the darkness. Practically blind, all he could make out was a hairy figure looming over him, with hungry claws outstretched. "It's a monster!" he screamed, scrambling backward like a crab.

"You nitwit," Natalia scolded, as she marched over to the beast. Though it towered over her head, Natalia wasn't the least bit frightened. She stroked the monster's thick fur as one might pet a puppy. "It's not a monster, Ernie. It's . . . well . . . it *was* a wolf."

Frozen in time, a great black wolf was stuffed in a vicious pose as it leapt over a fallen log, its paws outstretched, and a savage snarl twisted across its muzzle.

As Ernie tried to pull himself together, the other Griffins started to look around their new prison. It wasn't a very large room, but it was creepy. The moon was shining weakly through a series of small stained-glass windows high above, revealing the scattered carcasses of animals that had been stuffed and mounted in every nook and cranny. There was a bald eagle hanging from the ceiling, a roaring panther leaping from the floor, and a wall of tangled antlers covered in cobwebs.

"This place is freakin' me out," Ernie chattered, moving from one grisly beast to the next, wondering if the eyes were following him.

"It's disgusting," Natalia said, stepping away from a stuffed boar that was missing an eyeball. The scent of mold and rot was overwhelming as the Griffins continued their exploration. The longer they stayed, the more the chamber felt like a tomb.

"What do you guys think this place is?" Harley asked, walking over to a strange-looking flightless bird with an awkward beak.

"I don't know," Max answered. "I guess it's a hunter's trophy room."

"Some of these animals are on the endangered species list," Natalia commented, horrified. "You don't think your father killed them, do you?"

Max just shrugged. "He's been on safari in Africa before, and we've been duck hunting a few times, but I don't remember him ever mentioning a place like this. Maybe it was already here before he took over the castle."

"This house has been in your family for hundreds of years," Harley pointed out. "It could have been anybody — your dad may not even know this room exists."

"Well, whatever it is, somebody sure has a thing for wolves," Natalia added. "I've counted four at least. And they all look absolutely vile."

The walls were held together by moldering stone with bits of moss creeping around the mortar, and ivy roots crisscrossing the ceiling like hungry fingers. There was an old desk covered with scattered papers hidden beneath a thick layer of dust, and a crumbling skull of a monstrous wolf hung on the wall above it.

"Bet that thing could've bit you clean in half, Ernie," Harley observed as Ernie cringed at the thought.

"Look, candles," Natalia exclaimed, walking over to a tarnished candelabrum streaked with black candle wax. "Anyone got a match?"

"Did you have to ask?" commented Harley as he pulled out a matchbox.

"Why didn't you pull them out earlier?" Ernie complained.

"Because I only have two matches left." Harley walked over and set a spark to the match, but Ernie sneezed, snuffing out the flame before Harley could light even one of the candles.

Frustrated, Natalia shoved Ernie into the rotting remains of a stuffed baboon. "That's disgusting!" he shouted.

"You just stay over there until we get these candles lit . . . ," she threatened.

With Ernie out of the way, Harley lit the candelabrum without issue, picked it up, and began shining the light against the walls to investigate a way out of their predicament. He soon came upon an oil painting that was hanging askew, not far from the desk.

Remarkably, it seemed untouched by the decaying hand of time that had overcome the rest of the room. As the Griffins drew close, they could see that it depicted a knight dressed in black armor, a cloak of wolf hide snapping in the wind as he stood on the precipice of a cliff. In his outstretched hand, the knight held a mighty spear, and beneath his foot lay a broken sword.

"Look at his eyes," Ernie pointed out, walking back and forth in front of the painting. "They follow you wherever you go."

"You know," began Natalia, stepping closer to the painting as she rubbed her chin. "He looks kind of familiar."

"What do you mean?" asked Max as Natalia reached into her pocket and pulled out a small stack of Round Table cards. She fished through them, once, twice, and a third time until she pulled out the card she was looking for.

"Feast your eyes on this," she invited as the Griffins gathered close. "I got it in one of those Shadowlands Expansion packs your dad gave us, Max. This guy in the painting is Mordred, King Arthur's son . . . the one that betrayed him to Morgan LaFey. And that lance in his hand is called the Spear of Ragnarok, which is supposed to be one of the most powerful weapons in the world."

"Did I get a cool card like that?" Ernie asked, pulling out his pack of Round Table cards to look more closely.

"Now pay attention because this is important," Natalia directed as she pulled out her *Book of Clues* and took a few notes.

"I've never heard of the Spear of Ragnarok," Max admitted.

"Well," Natalia began, delighted to have an interested audience. "It has an interesting history. Thousands of years ago, they say a meteorite fell out of the sky and crashed into a mountain of ice. It sent up a cloud of dust and rain that covered the earth for forty days and forty nights. When the darkness finally cleared, a great king went up and discovered a single black rock that was still burning. Seeing it as a sign, he had the rock taken to his palace, where it was cut into two pieces. The first was made into the Spear of

Ragnarok *and* the second piece was used to forge the sword Excalibur."

"The Spear of Ragnarok?" wondered Harley. "That's a pretty cool name. How come I've never heard of it?"

"Not many people have," replied Natalia with a shrug. "Very mysterious. But if it's as powerful as people say it is, then where it is now is probably one of the best kept secrets in the history of the world."

"It's that powerful?" Harley folded his arms in skepticism.

Natalia arched her eyebrow as she looked over at him. "Big time. It's not called Ragnarok for nothing."

"What does 'Ragnarok' mean?" Ernie gulped in anticipation.

Natalia studied Ernie carefully for a moment. "It means 'Doomsday' — the end of the world. And not in a nice way."

Uncomfortable silence followed as the Griffins eyed each other nervously. They all knew firsthand that things in the Round Table cards had a disturbing habit of finding their way into the real world. And none of them wanted any part of this Spear.

"So," began Harley, hoping to change the topic, "what's the story with Excalibur?"

"Excalibur wasn't always its name," Natalia pointed out. "Actually it used to be called . . ." Natalia paused, frowned, and then her eyes opened wide with excitement as she scribbled furiously in her notepad. "Max! You're never gonna believe what Excalibur's real name is! How could I have been so blind? I must have read about it a thousand times."

"What?" asked Max, unsure if he should be excited or not.

Natalia frequently got wound up about things that few people understood.

"Caliburn!" she spouted proudly, folding her arms.

"What?" Max was confused.

"That's right," she continued. "The same name as your grandma. And your grandfather, I might add. And he was a Templar Knight. It can't be a coincidence."

Max had no idea what to think. He had already learned that he was somehow related to King Arthur, who had also been a Guardian of the *Codex* long ago. But it all had seemed like a fairy tale when Max heard it from Logan. "Wow. King Arthur's heir . . . but why would my *dad* have a painting of Mordred in his house? And why keep it locked up?" Max asked, his head spinning.

"What if he's a Templar just like you?" Natalia smiled.

"But the Templar stuff is all on my mom's side of the family," Max replied. "Why would my dad know anything about it? Besides, if he's really a Templar, you wouldn't think he'd have a painting of the guy who killed King Arthur hanging on his wall. It doesn't make any sense."

"Then explain how he knows about the Round Table. And Iver. And Logan. And how his jet was able to repel Kobolds. Max, it makes perfect sense. And now I know why your father is such a gentleman. He's a knight. A Knight Templar."

"I . . . I don't know," Max said, a bit confused as he wiped sweat from his brow. His cold symptoms were back. And, right on schedule, his arm began to ache. It was getting worse. In fact, the pain was so violent that Max nearly bit off his tongue trying to suppress a scream.

"Max, are you okay?" Natalia asked, rushing over to him. "You're pale as a ghost."

"I'm okay . . . I think," answered Max, waving her away as the pain subsided as suddenly as it appeared. "I just need to sit down for a minute. It's that stupid peapod. I . . ."

"That's it." Natalia folded her arms and looked at him sternly. "It's time we had a doctor look at you."

"Now, hold on," Max began to argue but was quickly interrupted by Natalia's stubbornness.

"You're seeing a doctor and that's that. How do you know what you have isn't catching, anyway? Do you want us all to get sick? And besides, if it's something they can fix, then it's better to do it now before it gets any worse."

Max only offered her a sour look. Natalia meant well, but whatever Max had was probably not listed in the local medical journal.

"Try some of this," offered Ernie, handing Max a bottle of Plimples he had hidden in a pocket of his bathrobe. Max took a swig, and to his surprise, he actually did start to feel better.

"Thanks, Ernie," Max replied, then turned back to Natalia. "I'm feeling better now. See? No big deal, Natalia. So can we drop it?"

"We'll see," Natalia maintained skeptically as she turned back to the portrait of Mordred. "Anyway, you have to admit that it's a pretty weird coincidence for this painting to look so much like the

Round Table card, right down to that symbol on their shields. If I only knew what it meant . . ."

"It looks like another rune," commented Harley.

"Geez," complained Ernie. "What's the deal with all the runes? First that cufflink, then the planes, and now Mordred?"

"It is a puzzle," Natalia agreed.

"I just want to find a way out of here," Harley grumbled.

"Harley, I need the light," Natalia called as she unrolled a dusty parchment on the desk where Max was sitting. All around the perimeter of the page were more runes, hundreds of them, in fact. "Check this out."

Harley walked over with the candles and the children gasped. It looked to be a map of Castle Sumner: the grounds, building, and even the dark woods that lay just outside their window. But what stood out most was a marking dead in the middle of the forest — THE WITCHING WELL.

"Cool," Ernie exclaimed. "A wishing well. Do you think wishes really come true when you throw your money in? I think so. Especially in a place like this. There was this one time . . ."

"It's not a *wishing well,*" Natalia corrected Ernie. "It's a *witching well.* You know, like Morgan LaFey? That kind of witch."

Ernie's enthusiastic smile faded immediately.

"Maybe we should take the map with us," Natalia suggested as she began to gather it up in her arms.

"What if somebody finds out we took it?" countered Ernie. "We could get in a lot of trouble."

"Do you see how much dust is piled in this room?" Natalia

replied. "No one's been in here for a bazillion years. They wouldn't notice if we took the whole desk."

"Let's just worry about getting ourselves out of here first," Max said, standing. He walked over, a bit unsteadily, and gently took the map from Natalia before placing it in his backpack next to the *Codex*. "We can look at the map later."

"Maybe there's a lever or a secret bookcase," Natalia suggested, as they moved from one mysterious item to the next in their search for a way out. But even after another hour of earnest searching, sliding of books, moving of pictures, and peering down the throats of stuffed and rotten animals, the Griffins had found nothing.

"Let's face it," Ernie said, sighing as he leaned against the dusty old desk. "There's no way out. We're going to starve to death in here."

"Don't be so cynical," Natalia reprimanded him, holding the flickering candlestick in her hands. "There's always hope."

"Hope?" Ernie asked incredulously as he peered in fascinated horror at an old bleached human skull lying on the desktop. "I have about as much hope as this guy. He probably couldn't find his way out, either."

"Wait a second," Max called out. "That's it! Ernie, you're a genius."

"I am?" Ernie asked.

"You're right, Max," Harley exclaimed as he pushed past Ernie to shed some light on their discovery.

Max smiled and reached out for the skull. Upon closer inspection, the Griffins could now see a hinge. The skull had a lid.

Harley lost no time in opening the skull. And when he did, the

Griffins, with the exception of Ernie, all moved in to get a better look. Harley whistled. Natalia gasped.

"What's in there?" Ernie asked, stepping closer, but fearful of what he might see. "Brains?"

"A button," Max replied. "A black button."

"What are you going to do?"

"Press it."

And he did.

Examinations

8

MAX YAWNED, squinting at the morning light as he pulled the pillow over his eyes. He had no idea where he was, and at the moment, he didn't care. He was so tired, he felt as if his body might fall apart into a million pieces at any moment. His eyelids felt like sandpaper.

Rolling over, Max gradually gained his wits, as the excitement of the past twenty-four hours came rushing back, sweeping away everything but the slightest shadow of fatigue. Nearby, Ernie yawned, smacking his parched lips. He looked like an emaciated bear waking up from a long winter's hibernation. Then Max whipped a pillow at Harley, who was sprawled out across his bed, still wearing his clothes from the night before. "Wake up."

Harley groaned and raised his head, blinking sourly at the other two boys. "Leave me alone," he said.

"What about breakfast?" asked Ernie. "I'm starved. And besides, aren't we supposed to meet your dad?"

"Oh, my gosh," Max gasped, scrambling out of bed. "I totally forgot. . . ."

"Breakfast was cancelled," Natalia said, pushing her way through the bedroom door as she munched on an English muffin. Unlike the boys, she was already washed, dressed, and ready for the day.

"Hey, whaddaya doin' in here?" complained Ernie, racing for a bathrobe. "Did you forget how to knock?"

"Ernie, I saw you in your pajamas last night," Natalia said, rolling her eyes.

"Oh, yeah . . ."

"Who told you about breakfast?" asked Max, hoping it wasn't because of something the Griffins had done.

"Augustus sent a servant up here a few hours ago to tell us. But you guys were still asleep."

"Did he say why my dad cancelled?"

Natalia shrugged. "No. But we're supposed to call down to the kitchen whenever we're ready to eat. I guess they are standing by."

Ernie's eyes brightened. What would it be? Pancakes sopped in butter and syrup? Or French toast made with eggnog and cinnamon? And was it all right to ask for chocolate milk in his cereal?

A short time later, several platters of sizzling food were rolled into the room by a servant who looked to be only a few years older than the Griffins. He quietly went about the task of setting the table with the finest silver cutlery and china dishes, leaving with a deep bow.

"Okay, down to business," Natalia said, clearing a spot where she unrolled the strange map they had discovered the night before. The paper was in rather poor condition, but the ink was still strong. And as it lay before them, Max's eyes flitted across the runes that were etched around the border. What was their meaning? And was it some kind of sign? Was someone trying to tell him something? More important, was that someone his father?

"So what are we looking for?" Harley asked, leaning close as he stuffed a piece of Scottish bacon through the corner of his mouth.

"No question in my mind," Natalia replied, pointing to a far corner covered by burn marks and a bit of ebony wax. "I say we check out the Witching Well."

"No, thank you," commented Ernie, who had pilfered a piece of sausage from Max's abandoned breakfast plate. "I don't want anything to do with witches. Besides, that forest looks C-R-double E-P-Y. You can count me out."

"You guys wanna go check it out?" Harley asked with a devilish grin, patting Ernie on the back. "I bet we could get out there and back before lunch. It's only a mile or so according to the map."

"Sounds good to me," replied Natalia. "And I'm willing to bet that it has something to do with Max's legacy."

"His what?" asked Ernie.

"His legacy . . . family secret. You know, the whole Mordred and Excalibur thing we discovered last night. It can't be a coincidence that both the map and the picture were hidden in a secret room. And there's nothing on this map that looks nearly as important as the Witching Well."

"I'm in," Max replied, thinking a walk in the woods would be a nice diversion from the chaos and disappointment. If they happened to unravel a few secrets at the same time, all the better.

"Good," Natalia added, pulling out her tablet. She started writing out a checklist of items they would need. "We'll have to be prepared, and that starts with the proper clothing. This is Scotland. It's not as cold as Minnesota, but it's the wet that gets you, not the frostbite."

"Maybe we should bring some iron?" Max asked as they started to gather items for the adventure. "You know, just in case we run into any faeries. Natalia, you still have those iron nails, right?"

"Naturally," she replied, reaching into her leather satchel and pulling out a fistful. She was always prepared.

At the same time, Harley twisted the iron Templar ring on his finger, which he had found at a garage sale back in Avalon. "I'm ready, too."

Just then, there was an unexpected rap at the door. Harley opened it to find Athena waiting on the other side with a smile.

"I'm sorry," she said. She was standing in the doorway, wearing a pair of blue jeans and a warm woolen sweater. Her hair hung loose, falling like a dark river down her back, while her eyes glittered in the morning sun. "Am I interrupting?"

Ernie squeaked a response that sounded like "come on in," but his voice cracked under nerves. Beautiful women always did that to him. With ice blue eyes peering out from behind delicate glasses and a warm hue to her cheeks, Athena really didn't look to be that much older than they were. Then, realizing he was still in his pajamas and bunny slippers, Ernie bolted to the bathroom, grabbing a handful of clothes on his way.

"Thank you," Athena said, laughing lightly. She curtseyed before entering, and as she walked in, the faintest scent of lilac filled the room.

"Natalia told me that you haven't been feeling well," Athena said as she sat across from Max in a high-back chair. Her eyes were concerned, yet professional. "So what seems to be the problem?"

"It's no big deal," replied Max, who was now glaring at a smug

Natalia across the room. "It's probably just a cold or the flu." How could he explain what really happened without blowing the whole secret of his magic book and connection to the Templar?

"Really?" she asked, smiling. "Well, I think I should be the judge of that. Besides," she said, lowering her voice in mock seriousness, "Lord Sumner is a persistent man. He'd never excuse me if I didn't at least give you a proper checkup," explained Athena. "And since he's the boss, there's really no way out of it. So if you don't mind, let's get down to business."

Max maintained his steady glare at Natalia, but didn't move.

"Good. Now, what seems to be the cause of your symptoms?" Athena asked as she pulled a strange metallic instrument from her handbag before peering closely in Max's eyes and ears alike.

Max shrugged. "I don't know," he said, scrambling for something to say. Athena was right; he needed to get this taken care of, but he couldn't give too much away. Besides, it wasn't likely that she'd have an antidote for faerie dust. "I just get dizzy sometimes I guess . . . and my arm starts to hurt."

"When did you first notice it?"

"Well . . . when I woke up the day we flew over here, I didn't feel that great. Maybe I have the flu or something."

"Do the symptoms pop up any time more than others?"

Max just shrugged, unwilling to explain it much further.

"Would you stop being so stubborn?" Natalia pressed, growing impatient with Max. "He had a dizzy spell on the plane, and last night, too . . ."

"Is that so?" Athena asked with an arched eyebrow as she

returned her instrument to her bag. "Roll up your sleeve, please. I want to check that arm of yours."

To Max's surprise, there was now a small green spot in the middle of his forearm with strange tentacles branching out from it. Natalia gasped. "That wasn't there last time I looked," Max confessed worriedly.

Athena pulled something out of her bag that resembled a magnifying glass, only hers was brass and had several lenses, each a different color, that swung down on a series of hinges. After aligning them, Athena took a closer look, then shook her head.

"What is it?" Max asked, growing more concerned by the minute.

"Nothing I can't handle," replied Athena, "so there's no need to worry." Her soft smile offered Max some relief. But he had the sneaking suspicion that Athena knew more about what had happened than she was letting on.

"You do know that you should have told Logan sooner," Athena continued. "With an infection like this, you're lucky you weren't hospitalized . . . not that a hospital would have been able to do much. But you already knew that, I'm sure." Athena then pulled out a small bottle, opened it, and applied a shimmering blue cream to Max's arm. Instantly, the pain was gone, and the green spot started to melt away as it foamed and sizzled with refreshing coolness. After a few more seconds, she brought out an embroidered handkerchief and wiped away the remainder of the cream and pulled down Max's sleeve.

"Where did you go to medical school?" Natalia asked, impressed with Athena's obvious talents.

"Medical school?" Athena asked. "My, but no. They don't teach this kind of thing at any medical school I know. My specialty is actually in astroarchaeology."

"What the heck is astro . . . ?" asked Ernie.

"Astroarchaeology? Well . . ." Athena smiled, sitting back down. "It's not really math, history, or literature. But I guess you could say it falls somewhere in the middle."

"Wait a second." Natalia's eyes narrowed as she tried to understand what had just happened. "If you're not really in the medical field, then what were you doing with Max?"

"Since the staff nurse is out, I'm doing what I can to help," Athena replied. "Besides, I *am* a trained emergency medical technician."

"You sure know lots of stuff," Ernie commented. "And I thought Natalia was smart. . . ."

"Well, I *am* only in fifth grade, you know," Natalia offered defensively.

"So how did you enjoy your little adventure last night?" Athena asked, changing the subject gracefully. Obviously Natalia hadn't appreciated the comparison.

"What do you mean?" Max asked, trying to keep the shock from his face.

"I can imagine how exciting it must be for you to visit a castle like this. I'd be awfully tempted to have a look around if I was in your shoes."

"Luckily that wasn't the case," Natalia replied. "We were told to go to bed, and that's exactly what we did." Athena was starting to get on her nerves. All the smiles. And the perfume! Then there was that complicated-sounding degree. How dare Ernie say Athena might be smarter than she was? Anyway, who did she think she was, spying on the Griffins?

At that moment, Augustus pushed his way into the room. A long shadow fell from his bulbous form as he glared at Athena and the Griffins in turn, looking rather like a grapefruit perched upon toothpicks. "Have you completed your medical examination, Athena?"

Athena nodded and rose from her chair. "Max seems to be in good shape. We'll want to keep an eye on him, though." She then turned to Max. "It will take a bit to heal, you know. It may feel better now, but there's going to be discomfort until it heals completely. Next time, make sure you tell Logan. . . ."

"That will be all, Athena," added Augustus, nodding slightly. "Lord Sumner will be pleased."

With a bow, Athena disappeared from the room.

"Master Sumner." Augustus looked down with an air of disapproval. "Your presence is requested by the lord of the house. He would like to speak with you immediately."

"Great!" Ernie exclaimed, thinking the trip to the woods would be cancelled in lieu of a feast of turkey and cranberry sauce. "I'll go get my shoes."

"I'm afraid that won't be necessary," Augustus sneered. "The invitation is for Master Sumner alone."

9

AUGUSTUS NEVER ONCE looked to see if Max was following, as he traveled briskly past art galleries, a billiard hall, and an indoor swimming pool, until the overseer finally led Max to a tall staircase lined with shining suits of armor. At the top, two men in dark suits waited with Magnus. The Head of Staff simply shoved his way past them, motioning for Max to do the same.

Lord Sumner was sitting at an immense desk, where a tall woman stood behind him. Her blond hair was pulled back, coiled around two narrow black chopsticks. Her eyes, green as jade, shimmered beneath slender glasses that perched upon the bridge of her nose. She was beautiful. But more than that, Max could tell by looking at her that she was intelligent, calculating, and powerful — the kind of person who should never be underestimated.

"Max!" his father called, smiling as he rose to his feet. "I can't tell you how sorry I am for cancelling breakfast this morning. I had hoped we could play catch afterward."

"It's all right," Max said, shrugging as he tried to mirror his father's smile. "You have lots to do."

"No." Lord Sumner shook his head solemnly. "It's not all right. And you should never get used to it. You are a Sumner. You will be a lord."

Max said nothing, though the idea of being a lord sounded pretty cool. But something wasn't quite right. Max felt uncomfortable, eying with uncertainty the woman standing behind his father.

Grayson II intercepted his son's gaze and gestured to the woman. "Max, this is Ursula, my executive assistant."

Ursula walked from behind the desk like a model down a runway and knelt beside Max as she lifted her glasses. Smiling, she held out her hand. *"Guten morgen.* I'm pleased to finally meet you in person . . . particularly since your father talks of you so often."

Max shook her hand in return, recoiling from Ursula's icy touch. He winced, though he tried to hide the expression. Suddenly, Max's arm started to throb, right where the creature had punctured him back in his bedroom in Avalon. Ursula simply grinned, her steady eyes holding Max's gaze intently. Physically, she reminded him a bit of his former schoolteacher, Ms. Heen. But whereas Rhiannon Heen made Max feel warm, like a favorite sweater, Ursula left a chill, like a winter's frost.

He felt a sense of relief as soon as she walked out of the room and the door clicked shut behind her. Absently, Max rubbed at his arm. It was aching slightly. Though not as badly now, thanks to Athena's medicine.

"Max." His father smiled proudly. "There's suspicion in your eye, and that's good. That kind of wariness will make you a good businessman . . . better than I am, I'm sure."

Max nodded as he looked around the office. He didn't realize his father had so many bodyguards. There were at least a half dozen guards patrolling the perimeter of a balcony just outside.

Did Castle Sumner have its own army? Max often wondered why his father needed so much protection.

"Son," the elder Grayson began, his smile succumbing to a somber tone, "I'm afraid I have more unfortunate news."

"What?" asked Max, his heart dropping.

"I received an urgent call this morning. Something terrible has happened at one of our offices in Rome. It seems there's been some sort of terrorist attack. I don't know all the details, but I do know people's lives are at stake. People that work for me, and for you, son."

Max said nothing.

"I need to go . . . to be with them and do what I can to help their families."

Max remained silent.

"I love you very much, Maximus," his father continued, his voice filled with compassion. "And I hope if you were in my place, you would do the same thing. Men of greatness must do their utmost to shoulder the responsibility that falls upon them."

"Yeah. I suppose so," Max responded sullenly.

"This isn't easy, son, but I know you'll understand when I tell you that this attack may be related to the one on your plane over the North Atlantic. If that is true, we need to move quickly . . . before this escalates any further and innocent lives are lost."

"But what about Christmas?"

"I asked myself that very same question, Max," his father replied. "And then I thought about all the people whose lives are in danger. I'm afraid they won't have a Christmas at all . . . or ever again if I don't do what I can to help."

Max fell silent, ashamed of himself for being so selfish. "I can go with you . . . if you want."

Max's father smiled, then shook his head. "I need you safe, Max. I won't put you at risk again . . . not after what's already happened. Logan and Magnus will remain behind to ensure your safety because, Max, it is vitally essential that if anything happens to me, you be here to take up the reins of our family enterprise."

Max's mouth fell open. "What do you mean if something happens to you?" he asked as his heart began to beat wildly in his chest.

"I should be back in time to open presents with you, but we always need to prepare for the worst," his father continued, pulling a briefcase from his desk before walking toward the door that Magnus held open. Then he paused and turned around, a look of uncertainty in his eyes. "Max . . ."

"Yes, Dad?"

"If something should happen . . . I want you to know that I love you. And I believe in you."

"Tell me again why it's a good idea that we're looking for a place called the Witching Well," Ernie said as Winifred rode along, peeking out of his coat pocket. The early morning air was decidedly colder than it had looked from inside.

The three of them trudged through the damp lawn that stretched toward the woods. Already, the glowing warmth of the castle lay a good distance behind them as the tree line fast approached. "So why aren't we waiting for Max?"

"Because Logan said Max couldn't come with us," replied

Natalia, her breath rising like mist through the cold air. Then she paused, looking at the forest creeping up ahead. "You know, I thought it was just a cloud before, but now it really does look like there is smoke coming up from the center of the forest."

"It's not smoke," Harley said. "At least, I don't smell anything burning. It's probably just fog caught up in the treetops."

It wasn't long after they passed through the tree line that the Grey Griffins discovered something rather strange: The air was growing warmer. So warm, in fact, that they had to remove their gloves and stocking caps. That wasn't a terribly common occurrence for a cold December day in Scotland, but it was undeniable. Not only was the forest hot now, but it was humid, too. Then Winifred started to growl.

"What's wrong with that rodent of yours?" pressed Natalia.

"I don't know," Ernie answered. "I think I heard something, though."

"That's a shock," said Harley, laughing as they moved down an old leafy pathway, which looked as if it hadn't been used in hundreds of years. "Anyway, I think it's actually warmer in here."

"Yeah. You're right," Ernie echoed, raising his ski mask and looking around.

"And the ground is softer, too," Natalia pointed out. "It actually kinda feels like carpet."

Ernie jumped up and down a few times, enjoying the sucking and squeezing sound that the ground made when he landed. "It's weird, but kind of cool. I wonder what makes it like this."

"I don't know," Harley replied with a shrug as he passed Natalia and took the lead, picking up sticks and throwing them casually as he went along. Together the Griffins made their way through the maze of trees, doing their best to follow the map they had found the night before. The trek was slow going, but Harley had come prepared with a compass, heading due north by northeast. They continued without stop, enjoying the view and their friendship until they found themselves standing, mouths agape and eyes wide at the scene before them. Engrossed in their fun, the Griffins had failed to notice that the air about them was growing even thicker and warmer as mist curled about their feet and obscured the path ahead.

Before them stood two iron gates, rusted and covered in green lichen like the trees. In fact, they had been shaped like two arched trees, their bars intertwining like meandering branches, though one now hung askew from the rusted hinges. Just beyond lay a deep pool of impenetrable murk. Everything about this place felt wrong, and immediately the hair on the back of their necks began to tingle.

"We shouldn't be here. . . ." Ernie's voice faltered as he reached in his pocket to search for his asthma inhaler.

Harley nodded slowly. "Yeah . . . I . . . uh . . . think you might be right."

But before they could turn around, Ernie's ferret jumped out of his pocket and raced through the broken gates, disappearing into the gloom.

"Winifred, wait . . . ," Ernie cried, running after her but falling to his knees before the ghostly entrance. He was torn between chasing after his beloved pet and listening to his better judgment. "I . . . I can't do it. I can't go in there. But Winifred . . ."

"That's not good," Harley observed with a shake of his head.

"We can't leave her in there," Ernie exclaimed, taking a step closer to the gates as he tried to peer around the corner. "She'll die."

"It's just a ferret," Harley replied, his voice laced with uncertainty. "I'm sure she'll be fine."

"But we have to save her," Ernie pleaded.

"Oh, good grief," Natalia exclaimed as she pointed at Ernie. "Now see what you've done? As if bringing that smelly rodent to Scotland wasn't a bad enough idea, you have to bring her along everywhere we go. She's going to be the death of me."

"So *you're* going to go in there and help me find Winifred?" Ernie asked hopefully as he rubbed his nose with his sleeve.

"No," corrected Natalia. "*We're* going in as a team. That means you, too, buster."

Harley nodded as the Griffins made their way cautiously through the gates, where they were soon standing on a soggy bank. Ernie sucked in a shot of medicine from his inhaler as he watched a blanket of fog roll over the dark body of water that stood before them. They couldn't see very far through the mist, but it was clear this was no lake or pond. The forest continued right on into the water. But if there was land somewhere on the other side, it was hidden from view. For now, all they could see were the shadows of trees and the vague ghostly shapes of something else — stones perhaps? Tree stumps? It was hard to tell, and frankly, none of them wanted to find out.

"What the heck is this place?" Ernie asked in horror. His face was washed in an eerie green light.

"A bog," Natalia replied, peering over the dead water. All around the edge, strange plant life grew: water lilies and mares' tales, black bay and creeping willow. Yet the color palette was somehow off, as though the entire clearing had been dusted in a mysterious monochromatic twilight.

Just then a ball of flame burst from the water's surface, dissipating in the rolling fog. Ernie nearly jumped into Harley's arms from fright. "What in the world?"

Suddenly, another explosion of flame flew into the air, this time closer to the shore.

"I smell gas . . . or oil," Harley commented, kneeling down at the bank of murky water. He pushed a twig into the strange liquid and pulled it back out, dripping with black goop. With a sniff, Harley curled up his nose and nodded.

"What is it?" Natalia urged.

"It's definitely oil, or something like it. I betcha anything that's what's causing those fire balls."

"So it's normal?" Ernie asked, looking none-too-sure that the fiery explosions were anything close to ordinary.

"As normal as you are," replied Harley as he moved down the shoreline where they could see a stone bridge leading to higher ground. "Follow me. If Winifred is anywhere, she probably went this way."

"Right behind you," Natalia called, pulling Ernie along.

"It's not my fault that Winifred ran off," Ernie complained as he took a cautious step. Once an artisan's masterpiece, the bridge was now just a crumbling gateway into the unknown. Luckily, crossing only took a few seconds, though by the time Ernie stepped to the other side, Harley was nowhere to be seen.

"Um . . . where'd you go?" Ernie asked nervously.

"I'm right here," answered Harley, emerging from the mist as he handed a wriggling ferret back to Ernie. "She was chasing a frog."

Ernie tucked the ferret back into his pocket, relieved Winifred was okay. "I guess this place isn't so bad after all," he admitted as he reached down to pick up a smooth stone and let it fly. The rock skittered across the murky ground before it was swallowed up by the water. As he got ready to loose a second stone, Harley caught his wrist.

"Don't touch the water," Harley ordered.

"Why?" Ernie replied with a snort. "It's just a stupid bog."

"Because I think something's in there," Harley answered. Ernie gulped.

At that moment, the fog seemed to unfold before them, revealing the ghastly landscape. Jutting up from the water like jagged teeth were the crumbling remains of old tombstones. One. Two. Ten. Dozens of them all around. The Griffins had stumbled into the remains of a forgotten graveyard, devoured by the bog and rotting in its own memory. Some of the gravestones were simple and unadorned, whereas others were massive monuments of stone, carved with shadowy figures. Yet through them all there was a common theme — crosses, though not just any kind of cross.

"This is a Templar graveyard," Natalia exclaimed.

"What's that?" Ernie asked, pointing at a stone building across the water. Sitting on a lonely island with tall statues standing guard all around, everything about the building seemed horrible.

"It's a mausoleum," Natalia whispered.

"Who do you think's buried in there?" asked Harley.

"I don't know and I don't care," Ernie said. "Besides, now that we have Winifred, can we just please go back?"

"What about the Witching Well?" Natalia turned to Harley. "Didn't that map of yours say it was supposed to be around here somewhere?"

Harley checked the parchment again. "According to the map, we should be close."

"I think we've seen enough for today," Natalia said, jotting down a few notes before closing up her notebook. "I feel like we're missing something that's obvious, and I want to review my notes and take a closer look at that map before we go any farther. We can come back tomorrow."

With that they turned to make for the old bridge. But before they could take a single step, several pairs of yellow eyes appeared on the surface of the water, lurking like ghostly crocodiles.

The Griffins were not alone.

The Black Wolf Society

MAX HAD RETURNED to his room, not knowing if he should feel proud of his father's dedication or disappointed that he'd spend Christmas without any family at all. But he was surprised to find Logan standing there with his arms crossed, waiting patiently.

"Where've you been?" Max asked.

"Staying out of trouble," replied Logan in his Scottish accent, "which is more than I can say for the four of you."

"Athena told you about last night?"

Logan ignored the question. "I'm sorry your dad has to leave. It's a rough thing . . . especially after all that's happened, but it will set itself aright."

"Thanks," Max said, looking at the floor.

"I need to pick up a package in town. Thought you could use some air to clear your head a bit. Whaddaya say to a bit of a holiday?"

Max smiled. "When can we leave?"

"The copter's waiting. . . ."

Built on a muddle of hills and valleys, Scotland's capital city of Edinburgh looked like a backdrop to a Shakespearean play, untouched by the hands of time for hundreds of years. Rivers of cobblestone streets ran into one another, connecting medieval houses that dotted the breathtaking landscape all around. The birthplace of literary giants Sir Walter Scott and Robert Louis Stevenson and home to landmarks like the Royal Mile, Edinburgh was a picturesque city, steeped in rich history.

Outside the citizens' cozy doors were the beginnings of a blustery winter storm, but despite the wind and creeping dampness, most of Edinburgh seemed festive, decked out for Christmas in finery, as hardy Scots bustled through the streets with their arms full of packages.

"What's that building over there?" Max asked as they rode in a cramped taxi that smelled of diesel. He was pointing on an enormous stone edifice to their left. Despite his dad's sad news and departure, Max tried to enjoy the excursion as best he could.

"St. Giles' Cathedral," Logan replied as sleet began to pelt down from the gray sky. "Once upon a time there was a prison right there, and more than a few witches were hung on the front steps."

"Really?"

"Unfortunately, witch burning was popular here. Thousands of people died under torture, falsely accused by superstitious mobs . . . or worse, by the educated few with dark motives."

Max shivered, sitting back in his seat, but as he looked at the moving scenery out the window, he found that holiday shoppers had been replaced with a darker sort of society that walked under the shadows.

"Pull over here, please," Logan said, directing the driver to veer off the Royal Mile and down a dreary-looking street lined with moldering shops and dingy pubs. Logan haggled with the cabby about the price before he directed Max to step back out into the cold.

"Why didn't you give him what he asked for?" Max asked in perplexity. "It wasn't that much."

"In the Mason's Close, you don't let anyone know you have money unless you want it taken from you," Logan answered.

Max grabbed the straps of his backpack, clutching them tight. With the precious *Codex* inside, he was beginning to feel he should have left it back at the castle. Max doubted many tourists came to this part of Edinburgh, and he was beginning to feel a twinge of uncertainty himself. "Are you sure my dad would approve of me coming down here?"

"No, he wouldn't," Logan replied drily. "But my job is to protect you, and I can't do that if I don't keep you close. So for now, you're stuck with me."

Max hurried to match Logan's stride as they swept down the narrow street, empty save for a tattered newspaper blowing across their path. Following the undulating rhythm of the hills, the street was lined with decrepit buildings. Home to Edinburgh's outcasts and criminals, Mason's Close, the city's underbelly, was no place to be caught alone after dark.

"Where is everybody?" Max asked, taking a step closer to Logan, just in case.

"The smart ones never come down here," was Logan's response as he pulled his jacket collar closer to his neck. "This place has always been a curse to me."

"Oh," Max replied, his teeth chattering in the cold. "Did you grow up around here?"

Logan turned to Max, the sleet running down his sunglasses.

"Look, I know you mean well, but I'm not one for talking about the good old days."

"Why?" Max asked, the innocence and sincerity of his question disarming Logan.

"Because for me, there were no 'good old days,'" Logan replied, turning back to scan the horizon. Apparently, the conversation was over.

"So why are we here again?" asked Max, changing subjects despite his curiosity. "You said you have to pick something up?"

Logan nodded as they walked along the empty street. "Got a call from an acquaintance of mine. Says he has something for me . . . something important."

"Down here?" Max asked, looking around in disbelief. "Couldn't he have mailed it or something?"

Logan laughed. "Good question. But this isn't exactly a normal sort of chap. He never leaves this place, and prefers people come to see him. Invitation only."

"Do you trust him?"

Logan smirked, wiping the sleet from his forehead. "I don't trust anybody, Grasshopper."

"Except for me," corrected Max as he and Logan rounded the corner and headed down an old alleyway.

"Fair enough . . . except for you, it is."

Together they walked along in silence for several blocks, until Logan approached a grimy building with a rotten green door hanging from makeshift hinges. Without a word, he opened it and signaled for Max to enter.

"This is it?" Max asked, looking at the entrance with reluctance. What was that bad smell that seemed to waft through the doors?

Looking suspiciously at the sky, Logan nodded as a large shadow passed overhead. At the same time, Max's arm began to throb as a fiery pain shot all the way up to his shoulder.

"Come on, Max," Logan urged. "This is no time for games."

Max nodded, grimacing as he stepped inside.

"And keep your guard up," the Scotsman directed. "Like I said, sane people don't come down to this cesspool."

The pain fading as quickly as it had come, Max loosened the zipper on his backpack — just in case. Not that the *Codex* was any help against humans. But you never knew when a faerie might be lurking in the shadows.

"What was that thing that flew over our heads outside?" Max whispered, keeping close to Logan.

"We've been ratted out," Logan answered as he moved into the darkened room ahead.

Just then, Max could hear someone laughing in the rafters overhead. It was a bone-shaking laughter — hardly human at all. The young Griffin's eyes scanned the room, looking for any sign of life, but all he saw were ropes. Hundreds of them. Perhaps thousands. They were suspended from the shadows, while others were looped around old iron pulleys on the walls. They crisscrossed here and diverted there, springing in every direction. But all led to the darkness above.

As Max looked into the vast tangle of lines, all he could think was that this must be what a fly feels like when walking into a spider's web.

"I'm so glad you could make it, Logan," came a sickly voice as a dark shape, round and bulging, lowered itself from the ceiling. As the vague traces of light hit the figure, Max recoiled in disgust. It was a man. Or rather, it had once been a man. Misshapen and ruined, all that was left of this creature was a tiny head atop an enormous belly, squeezed into what appeared to be some sort of iron bowl that was attached to his body by wires and hoses. He had no legs, and when he had to move, his long skeletal arms would reach out and grasp hold of a rope, using a series of pulleys that would lift and swing him from one area of the room to the other. He was his own puppet, a marionette, with a face as loathsome as his slime-coated body. And the smell alone was enough to make Max ill.

"Afternoon, Bishop," Logan saluted. "I seem to have picked up a tail on my way here."

Bishop, if that was his real name, laughed a condescending and truly delighted laugh. "Yes, of course I know that, Logan. I see everything."

"Who is it?"

"You know who." Bishop smiled as he swung closer to Logan. Now that Max could see the face in better light, he wished he hadn't. Bishop's skin was sallow and his eyes, set behind large round glasses, were drained of their color. But worst of all, with every word he spoke, it looked as though his teeth were rotting in his mouth.

"The Black Witch," Logan replied.

"Yes and no," Bishop replied. "They are here at her bidding."

"What are you talking about?" Max blurted out.

In a flash, Bishop turned and swung himself within inches of Max's face. "Yes, Logan. Here he is. The boy from the prophecy, and yet I wonder why you would bring him here? It wasn't a very wise decision. Very unlike you . . ." Bishop paused as he studied Max intently. Max, on the other hand, was holding his breath. The stench was making him nauseous.

"Yet," the spiderlike figure continued as he moved closer, "I can see why she wants him so badly. Yes, here it is, in his eyes. I can almost taste it. . . ."

Logan stepped between Bishop and Max, protectively. "We need information," he replied. "You said you had it."

"Oh, I do," Bishop exclaimed gleefully as he flew away in his tangle of ropes, back into the rafters. "She's getting close. Quite close indeed."

"To what?

"The Spear of Ragnarok," Bishop exclaimed, now laughing so hard that he began to cry. Max was no longer wondering if Bishop was insane. With a series of sniffs, Bishop wiped his long crooked nose on his arm and sighed. "Yes, she wants it. And this time, she'll get it. The end is near."

The Spear of Ragnarok? That was the spear that Mordred was holding in the Round Table card. Supposedly the most powerful weapon on earth. But . . .

"How close is she?" Logan asked, maintaining his controlled demeanor.

"Within days, I can only assume. Her servants are crawling all over the Continent as we speak." Bishop then lowered himself slowly until he was eye level with Logan. "When she has the Spear, she'll destroy you and your precious Templar, and then there'll be nothing left between her and the Shadowlands."

Logan nodded. "How do we stop her?"

"Stop her?" Bishop's face contorted wildly as if the idea itself was ludicrous. "You can't stop her. Not this time . . . and you know that, don't you, Logan?"

Logan took off his sunglasses and glared up at Bishop. "What makes you so sure?"

"Because her army is ready now. The army that she constructed from the bones of the Black Wolf Society so many years ago. That is why you will fail. And that is who is waiting for you outside these doors as we speak."

Logan chewed the inside of his cheek, deep in contemplation. "So what are they waiting for? Why not just rush in here and kill us all right now?"

Bishop scratched at his chest and shook his head. "I am a broker of information, and they are using me . . . for a handsome price, of course. Yet it is just as they use everyone else. Including the prophecy boy you have there behind your coattails . . . and the precious little book he carries."

Max narrowed his gaze and stepped toward the figure hanging from the network of ropes and pulleys. "If Morgan is going to destroy everything, then why are you laughing? She'll destroy you, too," he spat.

Bishop's face seemed to lighten with a glimmer of brief humanity. "Oh, my dear boy. I'm counting on it."

Logan ushered Max out the door and back into the brisk Edinburgh air. It was getting close to noon now, and the alleyway was damp, littered with rotting pamphlets and shards of broken bottles idly cast away where the sun, hidden by pollution and haze, struggled to reach them.

"What was that thing?" Max finally asked as they stepped off the sidewalk onto the slick pavement. "Can we trust him?"

Logan shook his head. "Bishop operates on his own stage of morality. Trust is irrelevant."

"I hate him," Max said, before even realizing he had formed the thought.

"He knew your grandfather," Logan replied quickly, with a brief glance in Max's direction. "And the Guardian of the *Codex* before him."

"How? I mean, he'd have to be . . ."

"He's old, Max. Older than you can imagine. You saw him in there," Logan replied coolly as they took off at a brisk pace back to where they had left the taxi waiting for them. "The story goes that Bishop wanted immortality . . . to live forever. And somehow, through forgotten paths and twisted science, he managed it. Not immortality, of course. Not in the true sense. But rather in the only way a human can . . . by taking what life he had and stretching it out across the centuries, so that while he continued to live, he also continued to die. A heavy price to pay, and now he is only a shadow of what he once was . . . more dead than alive. He cannot sleep, he cannot dream, and he cannot love. All that has been left to him, in his horrible bargain with Death, is his intellect . . . which, as you can see, has fallen and cracked.

Max shuddered. "No wonder he doesn't care if he lives or dies."

"But he should never be underestimated. Bishop is a broker of information. He knows everything and sees everything. Some even go so far as to speculate that he can see the future. . . ."

"Really?' Max asked in wonder.

"That's what makes him one of the most powerful people in the world, and one that the Templars have worked with for many long years," Logan added, as they walked a little farther. His steps were casual, but his eyes, hidden behind sunglasses, were roving and ever alert.

"Bishop also said something about Morgan . . . ," Max began, as a cold rain started to fall. "Iver told me back in Avalon that she returned, and that she had Ray with her. But he didn't mention that she had a whole army. What did Bishop mean by that?"

Just then a pair of headlights pulled into view on the far side of the alley, blocking their path. Several men in dark coats quickly exited the car and approached Max and Logan. They were well dressed, with hats, gloves, and polished boots. They didn't look like military soldiers, but each of them had an insignia on his lapel that, as they drew closer, Max could see bore the same rune and down-turned sword as the cufflink Natalia had found back in Avalon. In fact, they looked a lot like the mysterious man that Harley had seen following the Griffins back in Avalon. Who were these guys?

"Good afternoon," the lead figure greeted them with a stiff bow, his face hidden in shadow beneath a fedora. There was an accent, but it was of a kind that Max had never heard before. Suddenly, Max became acutely aware of a dull ache in his arm.

Logan remained silent as the rain continued to drizzle about them, mist rising from the cobblestones.

"I see you have brought the package," the figure continued, nodding in the direction of Max. "You will be rewarded accordingly, of course."

"I'm sorry," Logan replied. "The package is not for sale. Now I suggest you and your colleagues leave before it gets unpleasant."

The lead man laughed quietly, his wry smile flashing under the shadow of his hat as he pulled off his leather gloves, finger by finger. "Yes, of course. I was warned you might say that."

As the leader pointed in the direction of Logan, four of his black-coated companions rushed toward the Templar, crashing through the rain and muddy puddles. They were large and appeared exceedingly dangerous, and all of them looked more than up to the task of taking apart the Scotsman.

Max's bodyguard stood in silence as rain pelted down over his dark glasses. Yet even as the assailants reached their target, Logan remained motionless. It was only when the first of the brutes threw a fist that things changed dramatically. All at once Logan's coat flew wide as he spun and unleashed a flurry of kicks with such speed and precision that in less time than it took for Max to release his held breath, every one of the attackers was lying on the pavement, unconscious.

Logan crouched, waiting for a final showdown with the enigmatic leader. "Tell me who sent you and I might take it easy," Logan offered through gritted teeth.

The man said nothing as the headlights behind him cast eerie shadows in the rain.

"Last chance," Logan shouted, putting himself between Max and the stranger. "I'm not a patient man."

"Then we are two of a kind," the mysterious figure responded. Immediately, the man vanished.

"Where'd he go?" asked Max, eyes darting about nervously as he looked for any sign of the assailant.

"Oh, not far," came the strange man's accent, as he materialized directly in front of Logan, shooting his clawed fingers around the bodyguard's throat. Max could now see the stranger's eyes burning with a smoldering amber flame, like fiery jewels, and his face, grizzled and dark, was painted with strange symbols and runes. With strength unimaginable, the man raised Logan off the ground and began to squeeze. Vainly, Logan swung at his attacker, but his fists and feet flew right through him harmlessly — as if this man were a hologram. As the stranger closed his iron grip around Logan's neck, the bodyguard's strength began to fail him, and he struggled just to breathe.

In one fluid motion, Max unsheathed the *Codex*. He didn't know if the book would work against the fiery-eyed monster or not, but he had to find a way to save Logan.

Yet it wasn't the *Codex* that saved the day, as it had so many times before. Instead, before Max could even unlock his magic book, a sudden flash of light filled the alleyway — a light so bright and intense that for an instant, Max felt as if he could almost see through walls. In that same instant, the man in black dematerialized with a shriek — disappearing without a trace.

Logan hit the ground like a brick, choking and coughing as a trickle of blood fell from the corner of his mouth. Seconds later, they could hear a car door slam, and the headlights disappeared from view.

The assailant had fled.

"Looks like you scared him." Logan coughed.

"It wasn't me," Max replied with a shake of his head. "Something else scared him off."

"Quite true," came a disembodied voice. "You're a smart boy."

"Bishop?" Logan looked up and down the alleyway. But no one was there.

The voice continued, "The Mason's Close is my world . . . my kingdom. No one lives or dies here without my permission."

Bishop had saved their lives.

"But I thought you had a deal with them?" questioned Max, rubbing at his arm. "Why did you attack?"

"Aye. I did have a deal, and I abided by my oath. But there are always hidden clauses in the fine print," Bishop replied with self-reflected amusement.

"What do we owe you?" asked Logan as he raised himself back to his feet and brushed the grime off his knees.

"Consider it a gift, my lad," Bishop's voice replied. "I simply ask that you leave the remaining Black Wolves with me. You see, I . . . need things. And they will supply it. Consider it my gratuity."

Max gulped. Bishop's tone was so vicious that he almost felt bad for the assailants. But Logan nodded. It was more than fair, in his opinion. "Anything else?"

"Yes." Bishop's voice seemed to curl into a Cheshire smile. "You'll be receiving a distress call from the Sumner estate in approximately two minutes. The prognosis isn't good, from what I am hearing."

"Understood," Logan replied, his face turning to stone. Without another word, he grabbed Max and pushed him ahead into the rain. Together they raced down the deserted streets, hoping that Bishop's prophecy would prove false.

11

Bog Beasts and Bone Crunchers

WITH AN EXPLOSION of water and mud, a long gray arm of rotting flesh shot up out of the ground, wrapping its bony hand around Ernie's leg. There was a thunderous roar, and a dozen more arms rose from the mist and latched hold of Natalia and Harley as well. Then the horrible moaning began.

"Zombies!" Harley yelled. "The cemetery's haunted. Run!"

Ernie tore his leg free and raced for the bridge, avoiding the rest of the limbs that grabbed at him. Natalia and Harley were right behind him. Racing at full tilt, the Griffins had only one thought — getting across. But what awaited the children on the other side brought them to a screeching halt. Ernie nearly tumbled over the railing and into the pool, but with uncanny reflexes, Harley caught him and pulled him to safety.

A ghastly figure was rising out of the soggy earth near the far end of the bridge. First a crooked arm broke free of the mud, then the Griffins could see two bulbous eyes set in pale flesh, scaled and slimy. The creature had only nostril slits where its nose should have been, with pointed ears swept behind its head like fins.

The Griffins watched as the monster finished extracting itself from the bog floor. The beast was hunched forward, eyeing the children as its forked tongue licked its rotten teeth. It may not have been any taller than Ernie, but that didn't make the beast any less awful.

Soon, several more of the creatures were pulling themselves from the earth, and Natalia knew what they were the moment she laid eyes on them. "Bog Beasts!" Natalia exclaimed, grabbing Harley's arm. They had battled the creatures in Round Table, and though they weren't all that scary on the cards, alone in a grave-yard with no one around to hear the kids scream, the beasts looked downright terrifying.

"What? Those aren't zombies?" Ernie's teeth chattered as he edged backward.

"No. They're goblins."

"Good to know," Harley replied, pushing up his sleeves and spinning his Templar ring around on his finger. If it was a fight they wanted, then a fight they'd get. He took a moment to sur-vey their surroundings. There was a group of Bog Beasts standing between the Grey Griffins and freedom. Whatever the Griffins were going to do, they needed to do it fast or they'd be trapped there with nowhere to go except into the water — and who knew what lurked in there.

"We're gonna run for it," Harley whispered, never taking his eyes off the lead monster as it staggered ever closer.

Natalia nodded, pulling out a fistful of iron nails from the satchel slung over her shoulder. Forgetting to bring any iron him-self, Ernie looked around frantically for a weapon of some sort.

"Just follow me," Harley whispered. "And remember . . . go all the way through the gates, and whatever you do, don't look back. Now run!" he shouted as the other two followed close. In three strides he had cleared the bridge. A fullback on his junior football team, Harley used his blocking skills, driving through the Bog Beasts before they knew what hit them. And where his ring touched faerie skin, boils burned and monsters shrieked. "This way!" he yelled.

With a burst of speed, Natalia shot through, with Ernie right beside her. Together, the Grey Griffins raced through the rotten grass and creepers as more arms shot out of the earth, reaching for their legs. Everywhere, the air reverberated with the cries of the hungry monsters.

Harley reached down and began swinging a branch at the flailing arms as the Griffins kept running. But the growing mist proved confusing, as the three friends found themselves lost amid the grasping fingers.

Then, just as the mist parted and the gate to freedom loomed near, a Bog Beast managed to grab hold of Ernie's sneaker. He tumbled to the ground, disappearing under a layer of mist.

"Ernie!" exclaimed Natalia as both she and Harley reached the gate.

"Help . . . !" Ernie yelled at the top of his lungs as the twisted arms began to drag him down into the muck where he would surely be devoured.

"Stay here!" commanded Harley, gripping Natalia's shoulder. "If I'm not back in thirty seconds, run for the castle."

"I can't let you . . . ," she began, but it was too late. Harley had already plunged back into the fog, leaving her alone with nothing more than a handful of nails.

Ernie desperately clawed at the ground while more hungry hands wrapped about him, pulling him into the depths of the bog. "Harley! Anyone! Please!" he screamed.

Just then, the mist parted and Harley leapt through the air, grabbing hold of Ernie's outstretched hands. "I've got you!" he called, struggling to pull Ernie free as he simultaneously fought off more arms that burst out of the earth.

Ernie's face contorted in fear as the grip of the Bog Beasts strengthened, and though Harley pulled with all his might, he was no match for the tangle of Bog Beasts that fought for their quarry. Slowly, Harley's strength began to fail as he was dragged forward against his will. Ernie whimpered like a beaten puppy.

Harley was losing the tug-of-war and quickly decided it was time for another tactic. "Hold on!" Harley called, dropping Ernie's arms.

"What are you doing?" Ernie shouted in panic as his descent into the bog accelerated. "Pull me out of here. Are you crazy?"

"Hold on," Harley replied through clenched teeth as his hand latched ahold of one Bog Beast's wrist. A great shriek sounded as smoke rose from the creature's flesh. The iron ring had done the trick, and the creature withdrew — as did all the others. Ernie was suddenly free, but Harley didn't waste time congratulating himself. With renewed strength, he hauled Ernie's legs out of the bog. "Are you all right?" Harley asked as the angry howls intensified.

Ernie nodded dumbly, but he quickly remembered Winifred. In near panic, he opened his pocket. But there, looking a bit rumpled, sat the ferret. Ernie sighed with relief.

"Good," Harley stated, as he looked over his shoulder. "We don't have much time."

Ernie nodded as they took off at a sprint, passing out of the mist and through the towering gates. But no sooner were they through than Harley came to an abrupt stop. Natalia was nowhere to be seen. Had she taken off as Harley had told her, or did something go wrong? A pit formed in Harley's stomach as he looked down at the ground and felt something crawling beneath him.

"Natalia!" he shouted over the howling of the monsters that echoed all around.

No answer.

The pit in his stomach grew.

"Where is she?" asked Ernie, looking around in confusion. "Did she leave without us?"

"I hope so," Harley replied in uncertainty as he raced up to the gate and checked for footprints. Unfortunately, the bog had gobbled them up like snacks. There was no sign of Natalia.

Then, just as Harley was considering heading back into the mist, a shadow dropped from the trees above, landing on his back.

"Bog Beasts!" Ernie cried, stumbling back toward the gate.

Harley flipped the nasty goblin off his back, but not before the monster sunk its teeth into the boy's shoulder. Three more Bog Beasts dropped down, dragging Harley to the ground. He hammered away at the swarm, but there were too many. The monsters managed to wrestle his right arm to the earth. No longer able to wield his iron ring as a weapon, Harley was at their mercy as the monsters began to drag him down into the decaying earth.

Forgotten for the moment, Ernie shivered. He wanted to do something to save Harley, but there were simply too many of the moaning beasts. Then several Bog Beasts broke off from the pack and began making their way toward him. Ernie wanted to run, but he couldn't leave Harley behind.

Ernie picked up a nearby branch and charged straight into the monsters with a shout. "I'm coming!" Ernie yelled to Harley, who was struggling with all his might just to stay aboveground. Just at that moment, a silhouette raced into the clearing. It was Natalia. She'd come back, and she looked mad — madder than Ernie had ever seen her.

Teeth bared, Natalia drew back and let a swarm of nails fly. They sunk into the flesh of the monsters with unerring precision. And screeching in pain, the goblins rolled away from Harley, grasping at their wounds as they disappeared beneath the ooze.

In another marvelous volley, Natalia's iron missiles found the Bog Beasts that had again surrounded Ernie. With sparks of fire and smoke, they fell to the ground, joining the others in their retreat. Even those Bog Beasts unscathed by Natalia's nails or Ernie's club quickly disappeared.

"You all right?" Natalia asked, rushing over to Harley. He was bleeding from the shoulder, his jacket and sweatshirt torn.

"Yeah. I think," he answered, getting up slowly. "Those things are stronger than they look."

"Girl power." Natalia smiled.

"Griffin power," Ernie corrected as the three of them passed through the shadowy gate and back into the forest.

"You know, you did pretty well back there, Ernie. I saw you knock a couple of those monsters for a loop."

"I did, didn't I?" Ernie smiled. "I can't wait to tell Max. He'll never believe it." Just then a terrible roar shook the air, nearly knocking Ernie off his feet. "What the heck was that?" he asked, his eyes growing wide.

"I don't know, but we better not stick around to find out," Harley replied, looking back over his shoulder. "Whatever it was, it sounded big."

Though the mist was thick, the Griffins could see a towering shadow, broad and looming. It was bigger than the trees, and it was coming right for them.

Energized by fear, the three Griffins turned and sped out of the deadly bog. All they knew was that an enormous monster was after them, and the ground was trembling like an earthquake. Everywhere the Griffins looked, the world seemed to be coming apart at the seams. Even as they managed to regain the path, a tree was shattered, crashing down as they passed by it. Eyes wide with fear, they raced ahead as every second brought their doom one step closer.

Yet, with a gasp of final hope, the Griffins burst through the tree line and started a mad dash to Castle Sumner. But, if a forest couldn't hold the monster back, what good would a little wooden door do — even if a small army of Lord Sumner's guards were waiting on the other side?

"Don't look back!" Harley shouted, urging the others on. "We're almost there!"

Together they sprinted over the castle grounds, closing the distance with every footstep. When Ernie caught sight of the front entry he burst into overdrive, leaving Natalia and Harley in his wake. Like a rocket, he flew down the path as his moon boots began to come apart, leaving a trail of plastic and foam.

Ernie hit the icy stairs with his mangled boots seconds later. With a cry, he launched into the air like an ostrich shot from a cannon. He careened into the massive doors face-first, his glasses sailing in one direction, his boots another, as the rest of him slid down the door. He was out cold.

Harley and Natalia bounded up the steps seconds later. Natalia stopped to help Ernie to his feet, as Harley grabbed the doorknob. It wouldn't budge.

"Locked?" shouted Natalia as she dropped Ernie back to the ground with a thud. Desperately, Natalia wrenched at the door, but there was no use. "This can't be happening," she exclaimed, slamming her fist on the doorbell. One ring . . . two . . . five . . . twenty. Nothing. No answer.

"I think I broke my nose," Ernie groaned, staring up blankly at his friends. Harley and Natalia paid him no attention as they continued to beat on the door in a panic.

That's when a giant figure exploded out of the woods like a wrecking ball. Trees splintered and crashed; leaves spun about the emerging creature. Natalia's mouth fell agape as she took in the rampaging beast. "A Bone Cruncher . . . ," she murmured, though Harley already knew that. In all their hundreds of games of Round Table, this beast had shown up only once, and it had defeated them all — easily. If those Round Table cards really did predict the future, the Grey Griffins were in danger of extinction.

Taller than a house and almost as broad, the Bone Cruncher appeared like a jagged mountain. Its relatively tiny head sat hunched forward atop looming shoulders flecked with rocks and oozing tar. Glowing green eyes burned with hate, as two great horns erupted from either side of its head like spiraling swords, and tusks shot up from its jaw. Luckily for Ernie, he couldn't see anything without his glasses. Which was just as well.

Natalia turned back to the door, pounding her fists against it once again, screaming at the top of her lungs as a roar shattered the air all around them. The Bone Cruncher was lumbering closer and Harley could barely manage to keep his footing as the stone casement began to crumble all around them.

Then, from behind the beast descended a helicopter. Logan was manning the controls, as the blades of the airship sent a torrent of wind sweeping across the sward. A small door beneath the helicopter opened, and a riveted sphere of iron shot out, red lights blinking as it hovered in the air for a moment. Then it began to spin rapidly until its red beams fell upon the Bone Cruncher. In a flash, the contraption raced toward the charging monster, and as it flew, the sphere began to change shape. Telescoping and twisting, its shell unfolded, revealing a giant fishing net of braided iron that crackled with electricity.

Before the monster knew its peril, the netting had swallowed it whole. The Bone Cruncher bellowed and lashed out at its captor in vain; the iron webbing clung to its hide, squeezing the monster like a python. With a bewildered groan, the Bone Cruncher, caught in the weight of its own mass and speed, crashed to the earth. Like a derailed train, the unconscious Bone Cruncher skidded, carving its way across the frozen earth, tearing down trees and ripping lamp-posts aside, until it stopped just inches from Ernie's quivering nose.

"IVER!" SHOUTED NATALIA, her face lighting up as the door swung open. Ignoring the bitter cold and driving rain, Natalia pushed right past a sour-faced Augustus before throwing her arms around Iver's midsection. "We've missed you so much, and it's been . . . well . . . it's been absolutely dreadful here."

The old man chuckled, wrapping his arms around Natalia like a long-lost grandfather. "Now, now," he comforted, patting her on the back gently. "It can't be that bad, can it? It's only early afternoon yet, and after all, Christmas is right around the corner." Though everything around him was soaked, Iver was impossibly crisp and dry, as he stood beneath his gargoyle umbrella with a smile upon his face.

"Yes, it can!" Ernie said with certainty. He marched right up to Iver and crossed his arms angrily. "The whole world's gone crazy . . . just like it did back home, only worse!"

"Worse?" Iver replied, his eyebrows raised in surprise.

"Much worse," Ernie maintained.

"I see, Master Tweeny," Iver replied as Ernie stood under the blanket of the old man's shadow. "Well, then, it appears there's much to discuss, though I'm afraid now is not the time."

"Heya, Iver," Max said before getting enveloped in a giant bear hug.

"Merry Christmas, Master Sumner. And to you all," Iver proclaimed, pulling out candy canes and handing one to each of the Grey Griffins — with both hands. This of course wouldn't have seemed so strange in itself were it not that the umbrella remained hovering in the air, repelling the rain, just as it had when Iver was holding on to the handle. Now, nothing seemed to be holding it up at all. A bit dumbstruck, no one said a thing — though levitating umbrellas were certainly not something one saw every day.

"Indeed," Augustus said, clearing his voice. He looked almost serpentine, his eyes narrowing to mere slits as he watched the water pool on the floor.

"Ah . . . Augustus. So good to see you," Iver said warmly, casually reaching for his floating umbrella. "It's been far too long."

Ernie's mouth dropped. "You two know each other?" he asked, his voice breaking in disbelief.

"Know each other? Why, of course we do, Master Tweeny," Iver said cheerily. "Should that come as a surprise?"

Ernie just shrugged. "I . . . I guess not," he said, not really sure how to answer.

"If you would be so kind, I'll ask you to either come inside or allow me to close the door. I've just had the floors waxed and that rain isn't helping matters," Augustus stated, watching in unmasked disgust as rain poured in through the open doorway. Iver promptly collapsed his umbrella, tucking it under his arm, before herding the Griffins into the warm confines of Castle Sumner. Augustus hurriedly closed the door behind him, then pulled out a silver bell, tinkling it twice, and almost instantly another servant appeared.

The overseer gave the nervous servant strict instructions to bring them tea, and a mop to clean up Iver's mess.

"How many years has it been?" Iver mused, as the servant scuttled away under Augustus's careful watch.

"More than I care to remember," answered Augustus, who wasn't even attempting to be pleasant.

"Yes, it has been quite a long time," Iver mused, ignoring the snide tone as he admired an ornate crèche displayed on a mantle. "Augustus and I served together in the war," Iver mentioned as he turned to the Griffins, pulling out another candy cane and handing it to Ernie, who had already finished his first. "In fact, Augustus served under my command for several years."

"An experience I shall never have the privilege of forgetting," replied Augustus.

"Nor I," Iver agreed. "Augustus was an exemplary soldier. Scotland couldn't have asked for a finer man."

"No way!" Ernie blurted out in shock as Natalia pinched him to be quiet.

Augustus rolled his eyes and snorted before turning back to Iver. "To what, may I ask, do we owe the pleasure?" An eloquent man, Augustus's tone, or perhaps his glowering expressions, could unfortunately turn a simple "hello" into "good riddance."

"I was . . . in the neighborhood, you might say," Iver explained, smiling broadly. "So I thought I would stop by and pay my respects. 'Tis the season after all."

"Indeed," Augustus said, raising a suspicious eyebrow.

"My, what a lovely home," Iver commented, changing the

subject as he drank in the Christmas décor. He walked right past Augustus before finding his way to the crackling hearth, where he began to warm his hands.

"Wait 'til you see our room," exclaimed Ernie. "It's got comic books and go-carts and . . ."

"I'm afraid I won't be able to stay long, Master Tweeny," Iver said, cutting him off. "It's getting dark, and I'll need to find suitable accommodations for the evening."

"What?" Max asked. "Why don't you stay here?"

"I'm afraid that would be quite impossible," Augustus interrupted. "Given the recent events . . ."

Annoyed, Max spun on his heels. "Why do you have to be such a jerk all the time?" Max exclaimed. Talking disrespectfully to adults was not in his character, but Max loved Iver, and Augustus had crossed the line.

Augustus looked entirely taken aback. He couldn't remember the last time anyone had spoken to him like that, let alone a child — Lord Sumner's son or not. Flustered, the Head of Staff remained silent, looking from right to left uncomfortably.

"This is my father's house, not yours," Max continued in his admonition. "And he would never turn a friend away. Especially not now, during Christmas!"

"Is that so . . . ?" Augustus replied after a long moment. "And you would know that from personal experience, I assume? Perhaps he has told you that at a recent game of baseball, or while he pushed you on the swing. But, oh, I forgot . . . your father has spent most of his time here of late, now hasn't he? A shame. Dreadfully sorry to have opened a wound."

Max bit his lip and clenched his fists. Sadly, Augustus was right. Max *didn't* know his father that well anymore.

"Thank you for the offer of your hospitality," Iver said in a soothing voice, touching Max on the shoulder as the boy glared. "Perhaps given the circumstances I should stay . . . though only for a day or two," Iver said cautiously as he watched Augustus's rotund face contort in discomfort. The butler clearly wanted to avoid being under the same roof as Iver, but before he could object, Iver commented, "You'll hardly know I'm here."

His nostrils flaring, Augustus took a deep breath. "Very well," he said. "I shall have one of my staff show you to your quarters."

"Wonderful," Iver said cheerily. "I am deeply in your debt. Now," he said, turning to Max, "I believe you were about to apologize to Augustus for your outburst. . . ."

"But . . ."

Iver's gaze was stern, and though Max didn't at all feel like doing so, he turned back to Augustus. "I'm . . . sorry . . . ," he offered sullenly. It wasn't genuine, but at least Max managed to get the words out.

"I'm sure you are," Augustus replied with a stiff bow.

"Now is that tea I smell?" Iver asked, looking at the tray one of the servants had brought.

"It *is* teatime, you no doubt recall," Augustus noted with a roll of his eyes. "I suppose you would like a cup?"

"Absolutely," Iver replied, rubbing his hands together. "With a spot of milk and two lumps, if you please."

"Yes, I remember quite plainly how you take your tea." Livid, though controlled, Augustus realized to his dismay that his staff had retired, leaving him alone to serve the tea — something he hadn't personally done in years. Yet Augustus set about the task as quickly as he could manage, handing over the steaming cup and saucer to Iver, who had led them all to the fireplace off the entry, settling rather comfortably into an overstuffed chair. Iver's large stockinged feet, damp from the rain, were propped up near the fire, and he took the hot drink with eager delight.

"Thank you, Augustus," Iver said politely. "I think that will be all, but should we need anything, I believe the children know where to find you."

Ernie and Natalia giggled as Augustus, positively boiling at being dismissed, stormed out of the room, looking a bit like a wild hippopotamus in a tuxedo.

"Come now, my dear Griffins," Iver scolded. "It is never good to savor another's misery, whether he is a friend or foe."

"He had it coming," Harley said without remorse. "Augustus is a big jerk."

"Yeah," agreed Natalia. "No matter what we do, he's always scowling. And he follows us around like a storm cloud, spying on us incessantly. You'd think he'd at least be nicer to Max. After all, his dad does own the place."

"Don't be so quick to judge," Iver said. "Augustus has always struggled with congeniality, and he despises authority of any kind. But that is perhaps expected. His childhood was not an easy one."

"That's no excuse," argued Harley, who knew a thing or two about having it rough.

"True enough," Iver agreed. "But what if I told you that Augustus once saved my life? Would you change your mind then?"

Harley and Natalia just shrugged, hoping Iver would stop looking at them. Ernie, however, was completely lost, amused by the dancing flames in the hearth. He hadn't heard a word Iver said.

"Max . . . ," Iver prodded, awaiting a response.

"Well, I don't know," Max said, breaking his long silence. "If Augustus really did save your life, I guess I'd change my mind . . . at least a little."

"Excellent," Iver cheered with a bright smile. "That's a start. Now why don't you come over here and join us?"

Hesitantly, with his head down, Max walked over. He wasn't terribly happy with Iver at the moment. Apologizing to Augustus left a rotten taste in Max's mouth, even though Max knew it was the right thing to do. He could try and justify what he had done from a hundred different angles, but no matter what, Max knew it was wrong to talk to adults the way he had addressed Augustus. But he was finding it rather difficult to believe that Augustus would lift his finger to help someone, let alone save Iver's life.

"So why are you really here, Iver?" Natalia asked, while Max took the seat next to her, fumbling with the zipper on his backpack. She had a way of cutting to the chase. "I mean, you weren't really just in the neighborhood, were you?"

"Oh, it depends on how you look at it," answered Iver with a wink. "But I often have dealings in this part of the world, and considering the recent circumstances, I thought it best to keep an eye on you. If trouble doesn't find you, you invariably go looking for it."

"You can say that again," Ernie agreed, stirring on the sofa where he sat next to Harley. Winifred was nestled in his arms, basking in the warm glow of the fire and snoring rather loudly for a creature so small.

Iver took another sip of tea before reaching into his jacket pocket for his pipe and a pouch of fragrant tobacco that carried a hint of peppermint on its leaves. "Who's your friend, Master Tweeny?" Iver asked.

"My folks got me a ferret for Christmas," Ernie said, smiling brightly as he hefted Winifred in the air, waking her.

"A fine ferret, she is," commented Iver with a wink. "That's a wonderful little friend. Ferrets are magnificent animals."

Ernie looked at Natalia with smug satisfaction as she rolled her eyes. "I just wish your parents bought you some Ferret De-Stinker," she muttered under her breath. Ernie replied by sticking out his tongue, as Iver turned back to Max.

"Now I've heard rumors of your travels, but I'd like to hear it in your own words," he said, blowing a massive smoke ring into the air. It lofted higher and higher, until it dissipated in the top branches of the Christmas tree that sparkled with white lights.

"Well . . ."

"It's been horrible," Ernie interrupted, before Max could get a word out. "It's even creepier over here in Scotland than it is back home ... and we were really careful not to let anything out of Max's book this time, too. But there were the Kobolds on the airplane, a weird picture in a freaky secret room, Bog Beasts popping out of the earth, and a Bone Cruncher. Can you believe it? A Bone Cruncher! We can't even beat 'em in Round Table. . . . I mean, what the heck's going on?"

"Slow down there, Master Tweeny," Iver said with a chuckle, holding his hands up. "We've plenty of time, as I'm not leaving for a good while now. So please, start at the beginning."

The Grey Griffins did just that, taking turns telling Iver everything they could remember. Natalia pulled out her *Book of Clues*, which contained copious notes to account for facts the boys seemed to err on. She'd also made sketches of the Trophy Room and the Bog Beasts, too. Even Ernie had to admit they were pretty good. But when it came time to discuss the map and the Witching Well, Natalia fell silent. Max had asked the Griffins to not mention those things to anyone until after they had a chance to talk more — and Natalia had given her word.

Iver asked a few more questions, though nothing seemed to be of much surprise to him. For example, when Natalia gave him the cufflink they'd found near the bridge back in Avalon, Iver seemed to find the markings vaguely interesting, but he made no comments about them, even when pressed. "I'll have to think on it," Iver said, handing the cufflink back to Natalia.

"Well, now," the old man said, clapping his hands cheerily as he rose to his stockinged feet. "It's been an exciting holiday so far, though perhaps not in the way you would have imagined: attacked by enemy planes, nearly drowned, chased by Bone Crunchers — and of course the run-in with the mysterious and all-seeing Bishop that Logan has just told me about. But the hope of a merry Christmas is not lost yet. Not by a long shot, I should wager."

"A merry Christmas?" Ernie asked, entirely perplexed. "I wouldn't be surprised if there were vampires in the attic and were-wolves in the basement. This place is freakin' me out. You have to take me home with you. If I stay here much longer, I have a bad feeling something is going to go terribly wrong."

"Master Tweeny, things are bound to get darker, of course. It has to be that way, so that the dawn may come. You know the old saying. Yet for now you are among friends, locked in a fortress. Lord Sumner did not leave us without means, nor are we incapable of defending ourselves if pressed. Oh, we are quite safe here. Safer than almost anywhere else in the world — even Avalon, Minnesota."

"Oh, and I almost forgot. . . ." Iver paused as he pulled an enve-lope from his coat pocket and handed it to Max. "Your friend Brooke Lundgren asked me to give this to you."

"What is it?" Max asked, taking the envelope from Iver and try-ing not to blush. A letter from a girl was reason enough to get teased by his friends, but a letter that had traveled thousands of miles? This was even worse. Still, Harley looked the other way politely, providing Max some privacy while he opened it. Ernie, of course, could not have cared less and was munching on almond sugar cookies.

Carefully, Max pulled out a frosty blue Christmas card decorated with glitter. It was homemade, and as Max slowly opened
the card, butterflies flitted about in his stomach nervously. Then he
looked over at Natalia, who was still watching him.

"Well," she said impatiently with a roll of her eyes. "Are you
going to read it, or just sit there looking like a mouse who has found
his missing cheese?"

Max had no intention of reading it aloud.

Dear Max:

*Merry Christmas! I hope this card gets to you before the 25th.
And I hope you are having a good time with your dad. When you
get this, I will be skiing in Switzerland and having a blast! I
can't wait.*

Miss you,
Brooke ♥

"*Miss you?*" Natalia repeated. She had been reading over Max's
shoulder the whole time. Natalia spun away from the chair and
began walking around the room in vexation. "That's the stupidest
love note I've ever read."

"A love note?" Max echoed with a confused smile plastered
across his face. Was that what it was? He'd thought it was just a
Christmas card — but a love note?

"Way to go." Harley smiled, punching Max in the arm. "The cutest girl in school and you weren't even trying."

"Cutest girl?" Natalia stomped over to Harley. "That's a good one. I'll have you know that real beauty is more than skin deep. Besides, she's so . . . so . . . well, she's just ordinary, that's all."

Harley just smiled at her innocently. It was questionable whether he had meant his statement as a compliment to Max, or a way to get under Natalia's skin. Clearly, it had succeeded on both fronts.

Iver cleared his throat. "As charming as it would be to continue this pleasant conversation, I think I'll need a bit of a nap after my travels. I've come quite a distance, you must realize."

"Oh, sorry, Iver," Max stuttered, putting the letter in his pocket. He'd read it again later. A love letter? How was Natalia so sure? He must have been missing something.

But as Iver got up to leave and the other Griffins walked him to the staircase, Natalia still had her arms folded in disapproval. It wasn't that she didn't like Brooke. Girls like Brooke always made Natalia angry — especially with the way boys fell all over themselves for them. It was ridiculous, and she'd seen the way Brooke had been looking at Max for quite some time. It wouldn't be long before that brunette tried to get into their secret club — or worse — she'd pull Max away from his friends. Natalia wasn't about to stand for that.

"Look out for that log!" Max shouted into his headset, his silver go-cart veering out of the way just in time. Mud sprayed from the spinning tires as he tore around the corner in his number seven car. Harley and Natalia were hot on his trail, each trying to capture the lead.

Go-carting had been a great idea, and after the Bog Beasts, Bone Cruncher, and Bishop incidents, the Griffins felt as if they deserved a little bit of well-earned relaxation. This was supposed to be a vacation, after all. So as soon as the rain had stopped and Iver had disappeared to his room, the Griffins filed down to Harley's garage, fired up the go-cart engines, and raced through the tunnel and onto the frozen track without so much as alerting Logan. Yet the Griffins weren't at full strength, as Ernie had elected to stay inside to read comic books. Natalia had not-so-subtly pointed out that the only reason he wasn't out there with the rest of them was that he was too afraid to poke his head out the front door. The Bone Cruncher had scared him to death, and he was still recovering.

Max had read and re-read Brooke's Christmas card at least a half-dozen times when no one was looking. He couldn't understand why Natalia thought it was a love note. She was just his neighbor . . . and friend . . . that's it!

As their go-carts sped along, Natalia was gritting her teeth, trying to see through the splatter of muck that was now caked on her driving goggles and pink helmet. She fought furiously through the winding racetrack to overtake Harley's shining red go-cart, but to no avail.

"Nice try," Harley said into the microphone, as Natalia nearly cut him off on a sharp turn around a bird fountain.

Before the Griffins had arrived for their Christmas holiday in Scotland, Lord Sumner had commissioned a go-cart track just east of the castle grounds. It twined through a flower garden, around a small pond, and slipped into a patch of dark trees before snaking back to the house. He even had his tailor make official Grey Griffins racing jumpsuits that matched the design of each of the go-carts, complete with a communications system in their helmets, so the Griffins could talk with one another.

Round and round the Griffins raced, as Ernie glanced from the bedroom window without regret. He was in no mood to meet any more goblins. No, he and Winifred were going to have a nice, quiet afternoon while the others took unnecessary risks outside the safe walls of Castle Sumner.

"You guys give up yet?" Max asked, as he floored his gas pedal and accelerated down a straightaway, the pond on his left where flying geese reflected in the surface of the water.

"Never," growled Natalia, swerving this way and that, looking for an opening. Harley, however, wouldn't give her an inch.

"Your funeral, Sumner," Harley replied, smirking. And with that, he flipped a switch and a burst of flame shot out of his exhaust pipe. In the blink of an eye, Harley rocketed past Max, leaving a rooster tail of mud in his wake.

"What the heck was that?" Max asked through the microphone, watching in awe as Harley disappeared around a bend.

"Just a little nitro pack I rigged together," answered Harley, laughing as he tapped the brake and turned hard right. "We all got 'em."

"Really?" asked Max, looking for the controls.

"Yeah. Just to the right of your steering wheel. It's a little red switch."

"Awesome!" answered Max, but he was too slow to the trigger. Natalia found hers first, and she flew past Max. The leader of the Grey Griffins went from first to last in less time than it took for Ernie to gulp down a bottle of Plumples.

"Just make sure you only hit it on a straightaway," urged Harley. "Otherwise you're gonna end up missing a turn, and . . . wait, what the heck was that?" Harley exclaimed, his voice cracking as he passed under a bridge. "Did you guys see that thing on top of the bridge?"

"What . . . oh my . . . Max, look out!" warned Natalia as she tried to flick her nitro switch again. "It's . . ."

Max saw it too late. Standing on the bridge was a howling wolf, its black fur bristling. It stood there, readying itself to leap upon Max, its amber eyes glowing brightly even in the sunlight. There was no way to avoid the confrontation, so Max closed his eyes and flipped the red switch. The force of the explosion rocketed the go-cart forward as Max's head hit the back of his seat. Everything went into a blur as he launched ahead, disappearing under the bridge just as the wolf leapt.

"Max? Max . . . are you okay?" he heard Natalia calling in the speakers inside his helmet. "Max. Answer me."

Max remained in a daze as he maneuvered through the course, his reflexes taking over completely. "Um . . . yeah . . . I'm here," he answered, his mouth parched from fear as he ran his tongue across cracked lips. The wolf had missed. But the race wasn't over yet.

"Get in this garage right now!" she shouted.

The door leading to the garage came into sight as the howl of a lone wolf was answered by the call of others. Ernie's face was now plastered to the window. He watched in horror as at least a dozen wolves raced out of the pine trees to intercept Max.

There wasn't much time left. The lead wolf was already cutting the corner toward him. Holding his breath, Max flicked the nitro again. Nothing. It was gone. One shot. It had been designed for a single burst to the finish line, not a wolf hunt. Max leaned into the go-cart, trying to push it forward with sheer force of will, but he knew it wouldn't be enough.

Just then a shadowy figure stepped from behind a tree, a cross-bow pointed right at Max's head. It was a trap. If the wolf didn't get him, the bolt would. Max closed his eyes, awaiting the grisly end. But somehow the bolt missed, shooting past Max's ear with a hiss. Immediately he heard a yelp and a howl. The wolf was no longer following him.

"Logan . . . ," Max breathed, as he roared past his bodyguard and into the waiting garage. Once again, Max was in the Scotsman's debt. Whatever Logan was getting paid, Max was going to ask his father to double it.

"But I didn't even go out in the go-carts," Ernie complained, sitting on a couch next to the other Griffins in the boys' bedroom. "Why am I in trouble?"

Logan said nothing. His arms were folded and his eyes were fixed on Max. Logan was beyond disappointment. He was angry. Very angry.

"It's my fault, Logan. I'm sorry," Max offered, hanging his head in shame. "I should have told you where we were going."

"Wrong," Logan replied. "You shouldn't have even thought about going outside at all. It was a serious mistake. I taught you better than this."

"But . . . ," Natalia started, though her voice dissipated as Logan's smoldering eyes fell upon her. Harley just stared at his shoes. There was no excuse that was going to appease Logan.

"You might be Lord Sumner's son, but you aren't lord of this manor yet," the Scotsman admonished. "And until that day arrives, I have strict orders from your father to keep you alive. You aren't making it very easy for me. None of you are."

Max said nothing. He knew he was in big trouble, because when it came to meting out punishment, Logan was the best. Sometimes the Scotsman would sentence Max to hours of quiet contemplation, while other occasions called for physical labor. Max would be sent to wash and wax cars, paint fences, or haul wheelbarrows full of rocks up steep hills. Logan had carte blanche from Max's father to do with Max as he saw fit, and Logan wasn't afraid to exercise that authority.

"May I have a word with the prisoners?" came a deep voice from behind.

Logan spun, but seeing it was only Iver, he relaxed. "As you like," the Scotsman replied. "I'll be back shortly." After a fiery pause, he walked out of the room, shutting the door emphatically.

"Geez," Ernie complained. "Max's dad wouldn't have built that track if he didn't want us to use it. What's the big deal?"

"Come now, Master Tweeny," Iver said with a half smile. "What gave you pause to join the others in their excursion?"

"I wanted to read my comic books," he replied. "Besides, I was hungry."

"What else?" Iver pressed, peering intently into Ernie's eyes.

"Monsters," Ernie said reluctantly, looking over at the others. He sighed.

"Indeed," said Iver with a nod, rising up to his full height. He then began to walk about the room. Iver was a pacer, especially when he was thinking something through. He'd pace back and forth for hours, probably days if he needed to. "I only wish these three were as careful as you."

"What?" Natalia exclaimed in annoyance. "Ernie's just a chicken. That's the only reason he didn't go."

"Which was perhaps the only reason he alone would have survived, were it not for Logan's intervention," Iver pointed out quickly. "Logan is quite right, you know. It's his job — and mine, mind you — to keep the four of you safe. As you've seen over these last months, safety can never be assumed . . . no matter where you are. So perhaps it is best that we stick together as much as possible. What do you say?"

"I guess you're right," Harley admitted, sighing. Raised by a single mother who worked double shifts on a regular basis, Harley wasn't used to constant supervision, nor asking permission for anything. When Harley wanted to go fishing, he grabbed his rod and headed for Turtle Cove. If he was hungry, he made a bologna sandwich. When he was bored, he took his dirt bike out on the trails.

Life was pretty simple that way. Asking permission to step outside just wasn't natural for him.

"Of course, I'm right. I've lived too many years to be wrong about something like this. Now," continued Iver as he looked at each of them in turn to ensure his point was taken, "I need to discuss some matters with Master Sumner. The rest of you are excused. Logan will no doubt be waiting for you outside."

13   A Midnight Snack

"IT'S REALLY RATHER AMAZING, isn't it?" Iver pondered, ducking under the celestial planets of the orrery while they slowly glided around the glass-framed ceiling. "The complexity of this universe will never cease to astound me, nor will your father's attention to detail. This orrery is perfectly timed with the world outside. Look here, the moon is dipping into the southwest of the room, and outside the window, there is Orion rising out of the east."

"Yeah," Max agreed absently, as he ran his hand along the underside of Jupiter. He didn't think Iver invited him all the way up to the observatory just to watch the stars. In fact, his old friend had been strangely quiet since supper.

"You *do* know," Iver began, walking to the telescope, then peering into the heavens, "that Logan cares for you like you are his own son. Placing yourself in danger, as you did today, will understandably upset him."

"I know it's a tough job looking after me all the time," replied Max, shrugging.

"Job?" Iver asked, a frown clouding his wrinkled face as he pulled away from the telescope. "Is that what you think this is? Logan may be in your father's employ and bound by the oaths of the Templar, but he has never thought of your safety with so little regard as a compensatory duty. Nor have I, Master Sumner. No.

Our tutelage and protection come from something far deeper than that."

"I didn't mean . . ."

"Of course, you didn't," replied Iver, looking back into the telescope, which reached like a tower toward the sky. "But it's important to be reminded from time to time. We're a family, Max. Not a traditional family, of course. But we are a family nonetheless, and sometimes families have their disagreements. In the end, though, that bond is what means the most."

Family. The word left a hollow ring in Max's ear. It was hard to think about family with everything that had happened over the last year between his mom and dad. And finally when everything started looking as if it might be on the mend, Max found himself alone again, his father away on business and his mother and sister back home in Minnesota, thousands of miles away. That it was nearly Christmas only made things worse. He could handle Bone Crunchers and Bog Beasts, but inside, Max felt empty. Unfortunately, there wasn't a cure for that ill — at least none that he knew of. Max feared that the void of loneliness could never be filled — not by Logan, Iver, or his friends, no matter how hard they tried.

"Max," Iver said tenderly. "I wish I had an easy answer for you regarding life's recent turns, but you should know that things like love and friendship are the true treasures in this life. Those are the bonds that can never be broken."

Max turned his head, not wanting to show Iver the tears that were forming. "So why'd my parents get a divorce?"

"Now, there's a question only they could answer," Iver said, sighing. "Yet I believe there is more at work in their lives than simply falling out of love. As you are learning, there is a complex web entangling your family's history . . . on both your mother's side *and* your father's for that matter. Sometimes those knotted tangles are difficult to unravel."

Iver took a deep breath, as if to measure his coming words. "I don't know how to say this gently, so please forgive me in advance, but I believe this is an occasion that calls for plain speech."

"I'm ready," Max said as he wiped his eyes with his sleeve.

"Very well," Iver replied, pulling out his smoking pipe. "I'll start with this . . . you should know that your parents' union was arranged quite apart from their choosing. So perhaps they are not fully at fault for seeking an end to their vows."

Max sat down on a marble bench and placed the backpack at his feet. He was confused . . . an arranged marriage? No way. In America? Did that still happen?

"The courtship process that we now call dating did not exist until quite recently and even then it was stubbornly adopted. Times change, of course, but as in many things, the Templars have chosen to keep to the old ways. For our Order, marriage is sensibly based on politics and power, rather than the fleeting infatuation of young minds.

"Your parents both come from important families within the Templar ranks," continued Iver. "It only makes sense that, in order to keep the line of the Guardian of the *Codex* strong, political marriages were encouraged. You might call it a tradition. And it should not be a surprise that the High Council supported a marriage between the House of Caliburn and the House of Sumner. Both were families of enormous power — though of a different kind."

"That's crazy," Max said, not wanting to believe a single word. As far as he was concerned, if that was true — if his parents' marriage really was arranged, then Max felt he'd never really had a family to begin with. It meant his life was built on a big lie. "Besides, my dad isn't a Templar."

Iver said nothing as he lit his pipe, sitting in the viewing chair of the telescope. "No. He is not; but both his father and grandfather were."

"Then why didn't he become a Templar, too?" Max's mouth fell open.

"We may never know." Iver sighed. "It was your father's choice alone, and one that shook the Templars. We haven't had anyone turn their back on their birthright in hundreds of years. Yet your father has not wholly abandoned his legacy."

"What do you mean?"

"The Templars are, for all our power and prestige, in the end a secret society. It must be so to ensure the survival of our ways and our mission. Yet in order to perpetuate our underground existence, we must have a lifeline to the world above. Your father has provided, rather generously, I might add, tremendous resources for our operations at a time when survival was most uncertain. Without him, I wonder if the Templars would survive even into the next century."

"Then he knows all about Grandpa Caliburn and the *Codex* and . . ."

"Yes, Max." Iver nodded, placing a hand on the boy's shoulder. "He knows of your birthright and the *Codex* as well."

Involuntarily, Max grasped the straps of his backpack now resting at his feet, though he said nothing for a long while.

"Does Mom know, too?" Max asked slowly.

"She knows many things, Max. But as to the detail, I cannot say. That is *her* secret."

"But if it was so important for my parents to get married in the first place, then how come the Templars allowed them to get divorced?"

"That is an excellent question, Master Sumner," replied Iver as he chewed on the tip of his pipe. "As to the politics of their divorce, I am unaware, for I am not privy to the thoughts of the Templar High Council. But I don't want you to think your parents' marriage was merely a formality. There are many who knew them in happier times, when there was love between them."

Iver rose from his seat and crossed over to where Max was sitting, placing his hand on the Griffin's shoulder reassuringly. "I also know your parents still care deeply for you — and your sister — even when you may not always feel it. Were I you, I might take a moment to look around at all the wonderful things that surround you; and I don't just mean this castle. You have amazing friends who would go to the ends of the earth for you. That's true wealth."

Max sat in silence for a long while, then looked back up at Iver. "Natalia said she thinks I'm related to King Arthur. She also said that Excalibur, King Arthur's sword, used to be called Caliburn, just like my mom's maiden name. Is it true?"

"So some say," agreed Iver as he puffed at his pipe. "At least to the name."

"But if I'm related to King Arthur, that means I'm related to Mordred, too."

"So the logic goes," Iver replied, looking at Max intently. "Though only in a very warped sense of the term. Many generations have passed since those dark days, and Mordred's evil has since crumbled in the sands of time. I would not concern myself with such shadows. The portrait you found in the castle could be explained many ways. Remember, this has been an ancestral home in the Sumner family for generations. There is no telling who it was that brought the painting here . . . or why, for that matter.

"But enough of this dark talk." Iver smiled as he pointed out the window where a light dusting of snow was beginning to fall. "It *is* Christmas, Master Sumner, and Christmas has always been a magical time of year. Soon there'll be presents to unwrap and no doubt a feast of magnificent proportions. Your father's reputation as a host is legendary. No, Max. This is a wonderful time in your life. Let your worries fall by the wayside. Merry Christmas, Max."

"Merry Christmas, Iver." Max smiled back.

But it wasn't Christmas yet. There were still two days to go. The remainder of the evening was rather uneventful for everyone except Ernie, who had started cataloging his favorite comics, careful to leave the most precious in their protective plastic bags. Still, that didn't stop him from pressing his nose up against the corners to smell them. A single whiff could tell Ernie more things about a comic than the most seasoned veterans could fathom. Yet, the evening was stretching toward a close, and Ernie, despite being surrounded by a maze of comics, had to find his way to his bed like everyone else. Without his customary snack.

By two in the morning, hunger pangs were firing in Ernie's stomach like pistons in a race car. "You guys awake?" he whispered, peering out from under his comforter. No answer. Max and Harley were fast asleep — or at least they were pretending to be.

Though the afternoon with his comic books had been relaxing, the bout with all those monsters had fried Ernie's nerves, and when he was nervous, Ernie got hungry.

Ernie dreaded the thought of wandering the castle alone at night, but if he wanted a midnight snack, he didn't have much choice. Even Winifred was sleeping peacefully in her Habitrail, and Ernie didn't have the heart to wake her. So slipping out of the covers, he pulled on his glasses, grabbed his robe and fuzzy slippers, and snuck into the cold air of the dark hallway — alone.

Ernie could already navigate the course to the kitchen with his eyes closed. It didn't take him long to cut the distance in half, and then half again without seeing anyone, or being seen himself. For all intents, it was a quiet night in the castle, and Ernie could hear waves crashing on the rocks far below.

Something creaked nearby.

Ernie froze.

A muffled bang.

"What was that?" Ernie whispered into the dark.

Nothing.

Avalon, Minnesota, was full of older homes. In fact the Tweeny residence itself was over sixty years old. Those kinds of houses were known to have their own particular sounds, but they didn't compare with the mysterious noises produced by a place like Castle Sumner that was well over five hundred years old.

Hoping it was only the old water pipes from some distant bathroom, Ernie tiptoed on at a furious clip, closing the remaining distance to the kitchen in record time. With a sigh of relief, Ernie squeezed through the swinging double doors and took in the sweet aroma of fresh spices that wafted through the air.

Though the kitchen was dimly lit by recessed lighting, Ernie could see a slew of cookware and utensils hanging from racks mounted to the ceiling, and an array of cutlery, mixing bowls, and canisters neatly lining shelves and countertops alike. There was a special nook that looked like a greenhouse, where the chef grew his own herbs, and a walk-in refrigerator where whole cows, chickens, geese, pigs, and wild turkeys hung on oversized meat hooks, waiting to be butchered. That part was kinda creepy, actually, but Ernie tried to focus on the bright side: Food had to come from somewhere.

Glowing embers burned in a stone hearth where fresh breads and pizzas were baked, and open-fire cook tops lined an entire wall, still burning dimly.

Ernie's face lit up when he discovered just what he'd been looking for — the baker's alcove. With Christmas mere days away, this corner of confectionary delights had been a hub of activity. World-renowned pastry chefs had been busily creating rack upon rack of traditional Christmas favorites: ginger snaps, shortbread, butter cookies in holiday shapes, fresh fudge, homemade caramel, rum balls, toffee squares, krumkake. And of course, Max's father had requested a generous supply of his son's favorite: balls of peanut butter crisps dipped in chocolate. Ernie, not wanting Max to be disappointed by below-par peanut butter balls, went ahead and helped himself to one or two — just to test the quality. Besides, he'd been eating healthily for a couple months. A little cheating couldn't hurt. "Dee-licious," Ernie said with a look of delight as he wiped his mouth with his sleeve.

Of course, there was no other way to quench Ernie's thirst than milk — preferably so cold that ice crystals would form along the lip of the glass. *Bingo*. Ernie found just the trick in a nearby fridge, right next to a tub of raw cookie dough. After a heaping handful of what Ernie affectionately referred to as cookie sushi, he downed half a bottle of milk, belched rather loudly, then smiled.

Ernie's nerves now settled, and his stomach quiet once again, he realized he was, after all, a little sleepy. So, returning the milk and closing the door, he started to make his way back toward the hallway under a barrage of mouth-wrenching yawns.

Then Ernie heard voices.

He glanced at the giant wristwatch that clung loosely about his skinny wrist. "Uh-oh," Ernie moaned to himself. It was three in the morning, which meant the bakers were probably getting ready to start their shifts. Not wanting to get caught with his hand in the cookie jar, literally, Ernie scanned wildly for a place to hide as the voices, though unintelligible, drew closer.

Ernie spotted an open cupboard that was recessed into the wall above a serving table. In a mad dash, he threw himself into the hiding place, though not before grabbing a few more cookies — just in case.

Ernie squished and squirmed until he finally made himself fit. His knees were jammed up by his face, and he barely had enough room for his arms. But he was able, with difficulty, to slide the door sideways until he could see only through a small crack. That's when he realized he wasn't in a cupboard at all. It was a dumbwaiter — a kind of elevator used to carry food directly to the dining hall one floor above by a series of pulleys. Unfortunately, he couldn't work the pulleys from inside. But at least he was hidden.

Then Ernie gasped. Lying in the middle of the kitchen floor was one of his bunny slippers. Sweat beaded on his forehead as he calculated the risk of running back and grabbing it. Could he make it? Should he try? But if he had enough time for that, why not just run back to his room?

Unfortunately, it was too late for any further deliberation, as three men suddenly strode into view.

The hair stood up on the back of his neck as Ernie quickly realized these three were no bakers. They were dressed in long black leather overcoats, with well-polished boots, dark gloves, and strange masks on their faces. Ernie had seen that kind of mask before. But where? Then he knew: gas masks. Those creepy-looking black rubber masks with two round eyepieces and a protruding circular vent where the mouth might be that left a rather vacant, yet sinister expression where faces should have been.

Like ghosts, the men said nothing as they moved silently

through the room, looking neither right nor left. There was nothing specifically evil about them that Ernie could see, but he could feel it. These men were hunters, and they were looking for prey.

When one spotted the forlorn slipper, Ernie nearly wet his pants in fright.

Removing his mask, one of the men raised the slipper to his nose and sniffed at it like a hunting dog, then emitted a low growl. He turned his head one way, then another, and finally nodded toward the dumbwaiter. His lips curled into a sadistic smile as he stepped toward the cupboard and into a pale shaft of light.

Ernie stifled another gasp.

This was no man at all. His skin was as black as charcoal, with strange tattoos of runes burned across it. Thick eyebrows and long gray sideburns framed a grizzled face, and as he drew closer, Ernie could see his eyes were alight like two flaming amber jewels.

"Thank you," Natalia said, sipping gently on the tea that Athena had just poured for her. "I have to admit it's a bit embarrassing, but I just didn't know what else to do."

"There's nothing to be embarrassed about," Athena assured Natalia with a comforting smile. "When I was first transferred to Castle Sumner from the London office, I don't think I slept for a week. This place can be kinda creepy."

Though it was past two o'clock in the morning, Natalia was wide awake, sitting in Athena's room and resting in an overstuffed chair. Athena sat across from the young Griffin, perched on the end of her bed looking as fresh as she did in the middle of the day. Both girls were in nightgowns and bathrobes, as the wind howled wildly outside, rain splattering the windows.

"You know, this is really nice," commented Athena, who was nursing her own cup of tea. "I can't tell you the last time I had a sleepover. When I was your age, I didn't have many friends," she explained. "I spent most of my time studying, preparing for the university. That's all I cared about back then — which meant I didn't have much of a social life outside of the library."

"Me, too," Natalia exclaimed. "Well, I mean, I hang out with Max, Harley, and Ernie quite a bit, but there aren't many girls I talk to at school. I suppose I should work on that, but . . . well . . . I just like to read. Most girls my age only want to talk about clothes or boys." Natalia paused, thinking maybe she'd found a kindred spirit. "I don't really fit in very well."

"I find that hard to believe," Athena said. "An intelligent young lady like you? I bet you're the envy of your entire school."

Natalia blushed as she hid her face behind another sip of tea. "Thank you," she mumbled.

"Not at all," Athena said. "Are you feeling any better?"

"Thanks to you, yes," answered Natalia, setting her cup down in its saucer. "But you know, I was thinking about the things you were talking about earlier — the things you studied."

"Yes."

"Well, what do you do with those types of degrees?" Natalia asked. "I mean . . . well . . . what kind of a job does an astroarchaeologist get?"

Athena thought about the question for a moment before answering. "I suppose you could say I worked in logistics. Before I came here, I managed Lord Sumner's private collections."

"Collections of what?"

"Oh, the usual, I suppose," Athena teased with a wink. "You know: rare paintings, priceless antiquities."

"That sounds simply amazing," Natalia said, growing more enchanted with Athena by the moment.

"It can be, I suppose," agreed Athena, "though there's more paperwork involved than you'd expect. But tracking down the items Lord Sumner wants can be quite an adventure. And the auctions are always fun."

Suddenly, the sound of shattering glass filled the hall outside. Athena jumped from the bed, pressing her ear to the door. Natalia watched with growing dread as Athena's expression fell from curiosity to worry.

"What is it?" fretted Natalia.

Athena put her finger to her lip, motioning for Natalia to be quiet. "We have visitors," she whispered. With one quick motion, she pulled down on a metal sconce on the wall, and with a soft crack, a false bookshelf opened into the room, revealing a dark passage beyond.

"Take this hallway as far as it goes, and then run as fast as you can to Iver's room," Athena urged. "We don't have much time. Now go!"

Before she realized what she was doing, Natalia was racing down the passage as Athena closed the bookcase behind her.

It's Not Reindeer
on the Rooftop

"KNOCK IT OFF, Ernie," Max called from beneath his comforter. There was an annoying glow fluttering just on the other side of his eyelids. Ernie must have been sleeping with his flashlight again — a custom he'd adopted to keep the monsters in his closet at bay.

"I said knock it off!" Max repeated, rising up out of the covers, but it couldn't have been Ernie. His bed was empty. Instead, Max saw that everything was awash in a red light, though no lights were actually on. *Strange*, Max thought, and with a yawn, he pulled himself out of bed and shuffled over to the window to see what was going on. Still half-asleep, Max doubted what he saw at first. *How could it be raining red?* Then his eyes grew wide with horror as he realized . . . the castle was on fire!

Just below his window, Max could see the dark forms of strange men. They were dressed in black, their faces strapped in leather masks with eerie round goggles. As they approached the castle, a wall of ash and fire moved before them.

Why were they burning down his father's house? Max's heart skipped a beat as one of the masked men looked up at his window and pointed. They had seen him. Suddenly, a fiery explosion blasted through the window, throwing Max to the ground in a hail of glass, stone, and plaster as fumes filled the room. Everything went black.

"Max . . . Max are you okay?" he heard Harley shouting, but his friend's voice sounded distorted, as if he were underwater. What had happened? Why couldn't he see?

Then, with creaking squeals like a submarine being crushed under the ocean depths, the observatory groaned ominously above their heads. With a crack, its supports gave way and the shattered remains plummeted toward them.

"Watch out!" Harley called as he tackled Max. They both slid across the floor, coming to rest beneath the protective shell of the staircase. "The telescope! It's coming down. . . ."

With a deafening crash, the telescope smashed through the upper-level staircase before slamming into the floor, exploding into a million pieces. Then the orrery, with its planets and whirling moons, followed. It tore through walls and columns, falling with a resounding blast on top of the beds where, only moments before, Max and Harley had been sleeping.

Rain now pelted through the gaping hole above their heads as freezing winds whipped through the wreckage. "Wha . . . what happened?" Max asked slowly, regaining his senses.

"I don't know," Harley replied, watching as flames ate away at the tower.

"Have you seen Ernie?"

Harley shook his head as he handed Max his backpack with the *Codex* tucked safely inside. "I think he headed toward the kitchen an hour ago, but I haven't seen him since."

Max looked at the fire hungrily devouring the room all around them. They had to get out of there fast or the rest of the castle would come crashing down on their heads. And they had to find their friends. Suddenly the bedroom doors were blown open, revealing a dark silhouette standing against a backdrop of flame.

"Logan!" Max shouted.

"Let's go," the Scotsman urged, hurdling a fallen beam so he could help Max to his feet. "We don't have much time."

"What's happening?" Max yelled over the chaos that was raging all around, throwing sparks of fire and stinging rain against their faces.

"Black Wolves," Logan growled as he ushered Max and Harley to the doorway, stopping to survey the hall outside. "Where's Ernie?"

The boys shrugged, eliciting a frustrated growl from Logan. Above, the Griffins could see dark shapes sliding down ropes from the wreckage of the observatory, and more were crawling through the burned-out bedroom windows. Logan quickly pushed the boys into the hallway, slamming the door shut behind them before barring it with a piece of fallen timber.

"This won't hold them for long, so keep your heads down and follow my lead. We're going to find Ernie." With that, Logan ran ahead through the flaming debris, the boys following in his wake. But even as they turned the corner, Max could hear his bedroom door shatter and the sound of heavy boots racing after them.

"Who are the Black Wolves?" Harley asked, huffing as they slowed to peer around a corner that led to a split staircase and the foyer below.

"You don't wanna know," Max replied, thinking back to Bishop's alley, where he had first met the sinister figures face-to-face. Logan nodded grimly as they watched Augustus, still in his nightshirt, run through the room below. He was yelling for his chief butler, but no one was listening. In the chaos, it was every man for himself.

Just as they started toward the stairwell, two masked enemies appeared in front of them, blocking their path. Behind them, the footsteps were growing louder. The two Griffins were trapped. But as things looked hopeless, the two Black Wolves in front of them suddenly clutched at their chests and tumbled down the stairs. An instant later, Max felt a rush of wind as a black arrow flew up from the stairwell and over their heads. Three more followed, and the Black Wolves that had pursued them from the wreckage of the bedroom dropped to the floor. Logan and the boys had been saved.

"But how?" Harley exclaimed.

As they were about to set off again, Max spied a mysterious figure standing in their path. At first, Max thought it might have been another Black Wolf. But while this newcomer was certainly grim and armored, he was not wearing the black uniform of the Wolves, but rather was dressed in crimson, with high boots, studded gloves, and arm braces. Upon his chest plate was emblazoned a Templar cross and in his hand was a deadly bow with an iron-tipped arrow still notched on the string.

Walls cracking and drapes burning all around them, the Templar Knight joined Logan and the boys in their race through the burning house. The masked hero said very little, other than to shout orders at fleeing servants or warn Max to duck just in the nick of time.

"Who is this guy, anyway?" Harley asked. "He took out those Black Wolves back there like it was nothing."

"A member of Lord Sumner's Elite Force. The good guys," Logan replied. "Eyes ahead. We're almost out."

"What about Natalia and Ernie?" Max shouted over the noise of a nearby explosion.

"Iver and the girl are this way — in the Great Hall," the crimson soldier called back. So with renewed hope, Max fled through the blazing inferno, his eyes locked straight ahead. Unfortunately, between the explosions and falling wreckage, he failed to see a massive chandelier snap loose from its pulley and hurtle toward his head.

Suddenly a beefy hand reached out and scooped Max out of harm's way as the shards of crystal crashed like a wave upon the marble floor where Max had stood only seconds before. Catching his breath, Max looked up and saw Augustus's puffy eyes looking back at him.

"*You* saved me?" Max exclaimed in surprise. Where Augustus had come from was a mystery. How he could have moved so fast — or why he would even bother — had blown Max's mind.

Augustus smiled faintly, as he brushed a smudge of ash from his brow with a kerchief. "As Iver no doubt told you, I am full of surprises." He then nodded toward Logan and winked grimly. "I'll see if I can't throw them off your scent." And then, to Max's continued astonishment, Augustus disappeared back down the passageway from which they had just come.

As Max picked his way through the broken glass toward the others, he slipped. But again, he was quickly caught by the masked Templar. The soldier's grip was strong, but Max realized that whoever it was, he wasn't that big — perhaps only a head taller than Harley at best.

"Are you all right?" the soldier asked. Max nodded, as he moved alongside Harley.

"Augustus won't be able to hold them back for long," Logan noted. "We have to keep moving."

"Too late!" Harley shouted, pointing behind them.

As Max turned, he could see the shadows of the enemy quickly approaching. But these weren't fresh troops; they were the exact same ones that the masked Templar had dispatched only moments before. Max was certain of it. In fact, he could see one of them pulling an arrow out of its body and throwing it to the ground. The others were doing the same. Max stood there in shock as the enemy approached. What had happened to Augustus?

"We have to move," Logan commanded, pushing Max toward the Great Hall. "Eyes ahead. Don't look back."

"Tell me you saw what just happened," Harley breathed in astonishment.

"Why don't they stay dead?" Max shouted at Logan. "I mean . . . I saw those guys go down."

"Maybe they aren't human," Harley exclaimed as the Griffins and their Templar protectors moved quickly from one passage to the next.

"No, they aren't," Logan replied as they approached an arching doorway before stopping. Logan pulled the two Griffins behind him protectively, as the mysterious red knight moved into the light ahead. Max spied two curved swords strapped to the soldier's back.

"This isn't good," the Scotsman hissed as he peered through the doorway. And as he did, Max rushed over to get a better look. Then he gasped.

On the far side of the Great Hall, Max could see Iver and Natalia surrounded by Black Wolf soldiers, their masks reflecting the encroaching fire. Natalia had a long cut over one eye and looked terrified.

At the same moment, a figure strode into view, with at least ten more Wolves following. He crossed the Great Hall in long strides as he and his pack of soldiers cut off the path that led to Iver and Natalia. Then, turning on his heel, the strange man faced Logan. Dressed similarly to the others, the Wolf Lord's gas mask had been pulled aside, dangling from a snap near his leathered shoulder.

Max's mouth sagged in horror, for he had seen this face before. The dark runes . . . the gray sideburns . . . the amber flashing eyes . . . Before them stood the same man Max and Logan had met in Bishop's alley. It hadn't gone well for them then . . . and without Bishop's help, what chance did they have against a creature that could turn himself into a living shadow?

"So we meet again." The Wolf Lord smiled wickedly as he offered a stiff bow. His face was lined with years, and his black hair, though streaked with gray, was combed neatly back with oil. The Wolf Lord moved with a military gait, unflinching eyes, and a wave of authority that demanded respect from friend and foe alike. Was he human? Max couldn't guess; but if he was faerie, Max knew how to deal with him. . . .

"Put it away," ordered Logan as Max was ripping off his back-pack and reaching for the *Codex*. "It won't help . . . not here."

"The boy's a fighter. I like that."

"Stay clear," Logan warned as Lord Sumner's elite crimson sol-dier stood by his side. The monster would have to go through both of them to get at Max.

The Wolf Lord's eyes sparkled with amusement. "If I wanted the boy dead, he'd be dead already, Templar. But that's not why I'm here."

"So why *are* you here?" Logan asked, his eyes scanning the Wolf Lord skeptically.

"To kill *you*, of course," the Wolf Lord roared as he leapt toward Logan.

But before the dark enemy could close the distance, he fell to the ground in a heap. The mysterious red figure had let loose an arrow with blinding speed, once again saving Max and his friends from imminent doom.

"He won't stay down for long," the archer stated as the remain-ing Black Wolves closed in. Then the crimson hero slowly turned to Logan and pulled off the mask, letting it fall to the ground.

Max gasped as he caught sight of the long ponytail and silver forelock in the firelight.

"Athena!" Harley exclaimed in astonishment. Neither of the boys could believe it. A female Templar!

"We don't have much time," Athena said as her eyes met Logan's. "It's now or never."

"What are you talking about?" asked Harley.

Athena looked at the boys and smiled briefly before returning her eyes to Max's bodyguard. "You know what has to be done. We have to get the Griffins out of the house. . . . No matter what."

Logan nodded, but Max could see his jaw clenched in seething frustration. He evidently didn't like what he was hearing.

"Good," Athena replied, dropping her bow to the ground and drawing out her two curved swords. "I'll make sure Natalia and Iver are there waiting for you at the helicopter pad."

"You don't have to do this." Logan shook his head.

"You know I do . . . ," she replied softly, then turned back toward the battle scene.

The female Templar raced into the Great Hall, leaping over the fallen Wolf Lord, and the air exploded as the Black Wolves turned their deadly weapons toward their new enemy. But nothing could bring her down, no enemy could stand against her. Within seconds, she had single-handedly managed to fight her way across the Great Hall, freeing Iver and Natalia and clearing the path for their escape.

Just as Max was beginning to believe they might be able to get out alive, he caught sight of the Wolf Lord picking himself off the ground and plucking the black arrow from his body, casting it aside with a growl.

"Kill the girl and the old man," the amber-eyed Wolf Lord snarled in command to his troops. "Leave the Templar female to me."

Natalia screamed.

The Wolf Lord brushed aside his soldiers as he approached Athena with a vicious smirk. This was a man who loved battle and knew no fear, and as Athena turned to face him — her weapons shining — she knew she was up against something far beyond her.

"Get out of here," Athena called back to Iver and Natalia. "I'll hold him off as long as I can." Her faltering voice betrayed her own doubt.

Iver nodded, then took hold of Natalia and raced toward the far exit. But even as he did, more Black Wolves charged in to block their path. This time, Iver had no intention of being delayed. Reaching into his coat, he produced his umbrella with the gargoyle handle, and in the same motion he opened it, pointing the tip toward the masked villains. The Black Wolves were clearly expecting a weapon — but when they saw the umbrella, they started to laugh.

Iver, however, did not find the matter amusing. With a flick of the wrist, he let the umbrella fly, and as it tumbled through the air, it started to change shapes, until just as the carven handle came into view, a very real and very life-sized gargoyle exploded from the confines of the black silk. Before the soldiers knew what was happening, the monster was all over them, tearing and biting. It was more than a match for the assailants — Iver and Natalia bolted through the exit and disappeared with the gargoyle leading the way.

But the Wolf Lord was still in the Great Hall, and Athena had no such magic to defend herself. So as the grizzled soldier bore down on her, all Athena could rely on was her swords, her wits, and the tireless training she had fought through. It wouldn't be enough.

Never having faced this enemy before, Athena could not have foreseen her blades passing right through him, as if he were made of shadow; nor could she foresee him knocking the swords from her hands as if she were a child. With a devastating blow, Athena fell to the ground, silent and unmoving.

Throwing back his head, the amber-eyed monster howled and beat his chest before turning back toward Logan.

"You're next."

"Go!" Logan shouted as he pushed Max and Harley. "Make for the front lawn . . . as fast as you can. Don't look back!"

"What about Athena?" Max asked in horror. "She might be dead!"

"We'll all be dead if you don't move," Logan snapped. Together, they fled down a passageway, their hearts beating wildly in their chests. Flaming pictures fell from the walls, and furniture lay smashed at their feet as they rushed past; but as they drew near to the exit, Logan suddenly stopped and waited for the boys to catch up.

"What's wrong?" shouted Harley, looking around cautiously.

Logan pointed down a cramped servants' passage. "Winifred," he stated as Harley and Max both caught sight of the little ferret waddling at a fierce rate toward the kitchen door. "Follow her!"

"Why?" asked Harley in confusion.

"Because that little rodent is our only chance of saving Ernie."

Ernie exhaled slightly. He had survived everything so far from the safety of the dumbwaiter, where he decided to stay until all the explosions and shouting stopped. He didn't know what was happening outside his little haven, but Ernie knew it was better if he didn't get involved. In the dumbwaiter he was safe, or at least he could avoid being seen. To his relief it had actually worked — so far, anyway. The only thing that made it unbearable was that the tiny space was growing insufferably stuffy, and his left hand had fallen asleep.

"Maybe just a peek," Ernie whispered, cracking open the dumbwaiter door. He gasped and started choking on the smoke. The kitchen was bathed in a strange crimson light, and somewhere outside the window, a fire was burning. Across the room, a water line had broken, forming a shallow lake on one end of the kitchen. What remained of the Christmas cookies was scattered across the floor, broken and crumbled, much to Ernie's chagrin. He hated to see good food go to waste.

Then Ernie heard muffled voices and froze. Were the freaks with the masks on their way back? He slammed the door to the dumbwaiter and closed his eyes, hoping the strange men in black would go away. Now the only thing Ernie could hear was the beating of his own heart, which was, at the moment, almost deafening.

He heard the kitchen doors swing open, and taking shallow breaths, Ernie tried to calm himself down as the echo of footsteps neared. Then a scratching sound began near the bottom corner of the dumbwaiter door. He tried to ignore it. Were they looking for him? Had they brought some beast to hunt him down? Certainly from the sound of sniffing on the other side, Ernie knew his scent had been discovered. So bracing himself, he shrank back as the footsteps grew near, and the door to his hiding place was thrown open.

"Easy," Logan said. "It's just us."

Ernie blinked widely as his eyes adjusted to the scene before him, though his gaze paused at the sight of Augustus, who was busily surveying the damage, not the least bit interested in whether Ernie had been found dead or alive.

"How'd you find me?" Ernie asked as Logan handed him the missing slipper.

"You can thank Winifred," Max replied with a smile. "She led us right to you."

The ferret jumped into Ernie's arms and nuzzled against his cheek.

"You can do that later," Logan interrupted, pulling Ernie back into the passage where he could, for the first time, see the fire creeping across the walls — and how close he had come to being cooked.

Logan kicked through a burning door, and raced with the three Griffins out into the cold rainy night. Harley led the way, charging toward the light of the helipad, with Max and Ernie right on his heels. Logan was behind them, shouting into an earpiece to whomever was on the other end.

At that same moment, a picture window exploded from the first floor of the castle as a dark figure launched into the night, crashing to the ground. Next came the hulking form of Magnus, who leapt out with Natalia under his arm. Iver was right behind them, struggling to keep up.

Then, like a swarm of locusts, the Black Wolves poured out behind them, just as the fallen figure on the lawn picked himself up. The enemy was only seconds behind them now. Everyone was running toward the helicopter, but Iver's group wouldn't make it without a miracle. They had too much distance and too many enemies on their tail.

That's when Magnus set Natalia on her feet, and to the amazement of all, the Norse giant, who wasn't supposed to be able to talk, suddenly started shouting instructions for Iver to lead her the rest of the way. Magnus wasn't mute after all. In fact, his voice was so strong and deep that Max could hear it booming over the torrential storm. What they were saying was difficult to understand, but the meaning was plain enough to everyone: Magnus would hold back the foes for as long as he could.

Iver nodded grimly, took hold of Natalia's hand, and raced toward the helipad.

Magnus stood there like a gray tower in the pelting rain as the Black Wolves swarmed over him. He was almost twice their size and should have been able to tear them limb from limb, but the problem was that no matter how many times he'd send one crashing to the ground, they'd just get back up. Soon they had the giant's arms pinned behind his back, while others braced his legs. It was over. Magnus had sacrificed himself for the others, showing no regard for his own life. Max just hoped the sacrifice wasn't in vain.

A gust of wind broke over the Griffins' heads as a flash of light swiftly lit the castle grounds with the brilliance of daylight. Helicopters were flooding the skies as one landed on the lawn nearby. A stream of soldiers, dressed in red armor like Athena's, poured from the chopper. Their helmets were equipped with night vision and blinking sensors. Ernie gasped. Marines from outer space? What would he see next?

"They're with us," Logan assured the kids, pulling Natalia behind him once she and Iver arrived. The six of them were now standing on the far side of the driveway, about one hundred meters from the house. "The Sumner Elite Guard."

"What's gonna happen?" asked Max in fascination.

"They'll clean the house," Logan said grimly.

"But what about Magnus?" Natalia cried. "He's all alone."

"I don't think Magnus will have a problem now," Iver said, patting her on the shoulder reassuringly. "It looks as if the wind is changing."

As the Griffins looked on at the scene of the burning castle, they could see several of the Black Wolves fleeing as Lord Sumner's Elite Guard took to the battlefield. Too few remained to handle Magnus as the behemoth shrugged off his remaining opponents and let loose a terrifying battle cry. Magnus thumped his chest as he grabbed two masked assailants by the neck, hefting them into the air. Like a hammer to an anvil, Magnus brought his enemies crashing together and with another roar, he tossed the bodies to the ground, daring them to get back up . . . which they did. But this time, they weren't so anxious to tangle with Magnus. Instead, they turned and ran.

Suddenly, a great horn sounded, and the masked marauders fled from the castle and disappeared into the eerie light, as sleet and ash swirled down from red skies. The battle was over.

15   Ransom

Dawn . . .

The castle was a shell, smoking in the early morning rain like a fire-bombed city. Walls still stood, but they were covered in soot, the tapestries and paintings singed in the fire. Though staircases survived, they were treacherous, and the remaining staff had difficulty recognizing where they were standing — was it the ballroom or the billiard hall? Everything was black, and everything reeked of damp and smoke.

No one had slept, either. As soon as Lord Sumner's elite troops had swept the castle clean of Black Wolves, and the last of the flames were suffocated under foam, an urgent search for survivors ensued. They had found Athena, alive, under a piano. Most certainly it had saved her from the collapsing ceiling, though she had been critically wounded by the Wolf Lord. Jagged cuts and misshapen bruises covered her face; her shattered arm was in need of a splint. Natalia cried miserably as they wheeled the female Templar away, for Athena had offered her own life in place of Natalia's, and that is something the young Griffin would never forget.

Room by room, rescue parties searched, and eventually the Grey Griffins found themselves in the wreckage of the boys' once-opulent sleeping quarters, though now it looked like the remains of a war zone. Bullet holes riddled the stonework, and the twisted wreckage of the brass telescope and orrery lay hundreds of feet below the Observatory where they once rested.

Max looked hesitantly over at the aquariums, the thought of what he might find eating at his stomach, but to his amazement, they were intact. He didn't know how, or why, but Max was grateful all the same. Still, the water's surface was laced with ash, and the animals looked desperate. Max would make sure they were taken care of.

Still in his bathrobe, and nearly in tears, Ernie bent down to find melted plastic wrapped around the remains of a golden-age comic book — one of only a few of its kind in existence. Harley nudged him forward, handing Ernie some clothes he'd managed to rescue. Offering a half smile, Ernie accepted Harley's gift and rolled up the comic before poking it into the pocket of his bathrobe, though he didn't know why.

Ernie had lost his comics, Harley his go-carts, Natalia her unicorn merry-go-round, and Max almost all hopes of a happy Christmas. The fire had been relentless in its pursuit to devour the castle and everything within, including Brooke's hand-crafted Christmas card, which was now under the smoking remains of the orrery.

The motley band moved from room to room with heavy hearts, all wrapped in mismatched coats and blankets for protection from the cold. As Max and the other Griffins made their way back through the rubble leading into the main dining room, they found Magnus standing before them, his back turned and his eyes intently staring at the massive dining room table that, apart from broken glass all around, was virtually unscathed.

Suddenly Natalia gasped, pushing past the others. There upon the middle of the table lay a single yellowed envelope with a long iron dagger plunged through its heart. The blade was sinister, the pommel shaped like a snarling wolf's head.

Logan snatched up the dagger, studying the envelope in the light before handing it to Iver. The old man's eyebrows furrowed as he flipped the paper this way and that, before thrusting his finger under the flap and breaking the black seal. It opened with a hiss, and Iver muttered something under his breath before pulling forth the letter.

Max could see that it wasn't terribly long, and Iver devoured the cold words again and again. Anxiously, everyone waited until Iver was ready to speak. "It's a ransom note," Iver stated flatly as his eyes scanned the contents a final time. After a moment of silence, he turned to face Max. "I'm sorry."

"For what?"

"It's your father," Iver replied with a look of sorrow in his eyes. "The Black Wolves have taken him captive."

Max's stomach dropped.

"What are the demands?" came Magnus's gravelly voice — one which the Grey Griffins were still getting used to hearing.

"The Spear," Iver replied reluctantly, handing the note over to Magnus. "They want the Spear of Ragnarok."

It was shortly before noon on Christmas Eve day when a gray military patrol cruiser sliced through the icy waves of the Firth of Forth. Manning the helm was Logan, his black sunglasses glinting in the sun, and behind him stood four crimson-armored Elite Guards, each busily checking weapons systems, peering through binoculars, and ensuring that the cargo belowdecks was secure. Of course, the Griffins would rather not have been considered cargo, but after what had happened last night, they were just grateful to be alive.

Frustrated beyond words, all Max knew was that his father had been kidnapped by the Black Wolves and that they had demanded the Spear of Ragnarok in return for Lord Sumner's safe release. According to Bishop, it was Morgan who wanted the Spear. So the ransom note, while signed by the Wolves, might as well have been written in Morgan's hand. It was probably the Black Witch and her minions who had tricked Max's father into leaving the castle in the first place. The thought was that the Black Wolves had staged the terrorist attack in Italy to draw Lord Sumner away from the house and into their trap.

Yet, if they already had Max's dad, the attack just didn't make sense. If they wanted the Spear of Ragnarok, was it possible that they thought it was there at Castle Sumner? Or did they want to show Max that they had the power to reach him anywhere at any time. The Wolf Lord had said they hadn't come for Max. They had come to kill Logan. But why Logan? Or was it bigger than that? Too many questions . . .

The sleek boat eventually pulled alongside a stone quay that reached out into the choppy sea like the arm of a fallen giant. Iver had brought the Griffins to a rocky island off the coast of Edinburgh, though his explanation for the trip had been vague. As he stepped onto the stone pier, he conferred briefly with Logan, who would remain with the boat and ensure that they hadn't been followed.

"Come along, Griffins," Iver called as he moved down the quay toward land. "We haven't a moment to lose."

Max looked down the quay at a meandering stone staircase that carved a treacherous path up the side of the steep cliff. It wasn't an impossible climb, but it wouldn't be easy. And at the top? Max couldn't see much of anything other than a towering lighthouse that flashed every few seconds. Max couldn't imagine a human being wanting to stay on this island for more than a few minutes. It was cold, barren, and ugly.

"Where are we?" asked Ernie as he wandered along the stone pier behind Harley.

"Bass Rock," Iver replied, setting a brisk pace.

"It's so desolate," Natalia noted as she pulled her coat tightly to her neck. The wind off the water was freezing, but at least the cut over her eye wasn't hurting any longer.

"Indeed, Ms. Romanov," agreed Iver as he trotted up the stairs rather nimbly for one of his age and girth. "Volcanoes often are."

"What?" Ernie exclaimed. Had he heard right? "This is a volcano?" His eyes scanned the high cliffs to his right and a lump began to form in his throat. He had a long list of things he never wanted to encounter. Sharks, of course, were at the top of the list, followed by a Tyrannosaurus rex. Volcanoes, however, were also in the top ten. If he had known this was their destination, Ernie would have hidden himself back in the wreckage of Castle Sumner where no one, not even Winifred — which he had left in the care of Logan — could have found him.

"You'll understand soon enough," Iver maintained. "Not everything is as it appears, though I shouldn't need to tell you that any longer."

By the time Iver and the Griffins had reached the top of the staircase, their lungs were burning and legs aching, but Iver had no intention of lounging about the top. Instead, he kept right on marching across the stone courtyard and straight through to the front of the towering lighthouse.

"I'm sure glad I didn't bring Winifred. She'd be scared to death," Ernie complained through chattering teeth as he peered in the door cautiously. "Do people actually live here?"

"Oh, yes," Iver replied. "Though you likely won't see many of them. And there are far fewer as the years go by. Come along now."

"They work on a volcano?" asked Harley, blowing warm air into his cupped hands.

"The volcano has been nonoperational for quite some time," Iver answered as he breezed in the doorway, beckoning for the four children to follow him. They all expected it to be much warmer indoors, but unfortunately, they were in for a chilly disappointment.

"*Nonoperational?*" asked Natalia, her breath forming mist in front of her nose. "Do you mean dormant?"

"If I had meant *dormant,* I would have said so," Iver replied curtly. "And I always mean what I say." Iver continued briskly down the hall until reaching an old door on their left, which might have been a broom closet. He quickly reached into his pocket and pulled out a fistful of keys on a single ring, though all the keys seemed to look alike. But Iver obviously knew what he was looking for, and he quickly selected the key he wanted and inserted it into the door. A clicking sound echoed to his apparent satisfaction. "There," Iver exclaimed. "All right, Griffins. In you go."

"But it looks like a closet," complained Ernie, casting a suspicious look inside from behind Harley. "It's awfully dark in there."

Iver placed the key ring back in his pocket and smiled reassuringly. "It's only in darkness that light shines most brightly." He then nodded to the four friends and walked right in. "Come along, please. She's waiting for us."

"In a closet?" asked Natalia suspiciously. "Who lives in a closet?"

"Why, the Librarian, of course," Iver answered as though such information was common knowledge.

As the door shut behind them, a dim lightbulb flickered. The Griffins found themselves standing in exactly what they had first thought — a broom closet. A bit tight, it was complete with smelly mops and greasy gunk on the walls. Ernie was about to complain, when all of a sudden the floor shook and their stomachs turned upside down. They were falling straight down into the heart of the volcano.

Ding, came the sound of the elevator as the door fell open. Warm air and cozy yellow light rushed in to greet them. Yet just as Ernie was about to rush out, he pulled up short, nearly tripping over himself.

Sitting there blocking his path were two rather intelligent-looking cats that wouldn't stop staring at him. One was silver and white, with a pink nose. The other, which looked much like the first, was tabby-white with a brown nose. Both had ears that seemed to fold over on themselves, and unlike the Griffins, who had expected nothing short of monsters or boiling lava to greet them, these cats seemed quite relaxed, the tabby yawning broadly at Ernie.

"Griffins," began Iver. "May I introduce you to Browning and Thoreau, the official wardens of the Templar Library."

"Umm . . . do they talk?" asked Ernie, quite convinced anything was possible at that moment.

"Don't be absurd," Iver retorted with a snort. "This is a library, not a theater." Ernie immediately fell silent, but remained unconvinced. "They run this place, in a manner of speaking, and provide two unique services, one of which is to act as a security alarm."

"What's the other?" asked Ernie, peeking around Iver's coat.

"To catch mice, of course," Iver replied as he stepped out into the light. "Now be on your best behavior." He turned and waved his finger at them as a stern warning. "And, Natalia, I expect you to keep an eye on Ernie before he finds any trouble."

"Yes, sir," Natalia replied, feeling quite proud at having been picked for a position of authority. Ernie, on the other hand, didn't appreciate it at all and offered up his most scathing glare to Natalia, making sure Iver didn't see it.

Slowly, the Griffins filed out of the elevator after Iver and into the room beyond, blinking and shielding their eyes from the light.

Up, up, up their heads craned, looking skyward toward impossibly high ceilings framed by soaring stone arches that sprang from the marble floor. Everywhere they looked, more arches vaulted above them in an intricate pattern, almost like tree branches. Stacked throughout the vast chamber were millions of books. Level upon level, alcove within alcove, balcony over balcony, the floors of endless books rose above them to impossible heights.

"Holy cow," whispered Harley as his eyes grew wide in astonishment. "If the ceilings are this high, we have to be so far underground that we're under the ocean right now."

"You are in the belly of the volcano," corrected Iver as his shoes clicked across the surface of the floor. "Please keep up, Griffins. You'll have time for questions later." As the Griffins did their best to keep pace, the cats apparently found something more interesting and padded off into the shadows.

"Look," called Harley as he rushed over to a glass case that lay nearby. The Library was lined with bookcases and display boxes that held all sorts of strange and curious items, but this particular container held something of special interest: Lying upon a red velvet cloth was an ancient spearhead. It was frighteningly similar to the weapon that Mordred, the Black Knight, held in his portrait back at Castle Sumner.

"Oh, my gosh, Max," gasped Natalia, nearly giddy. "It's here! This is the . . ."

"The Spear of Ragnarok?" came an unfamiliar voice from behind them. The Griffins turned quickly to find a woman standing where none had been just moments before. "No. I'm afraid it's just a very convincing replica."

She was not much taller than Harley, with medium-length black hair and short bangs cropped across her forehead. Her dark eyes were framed in black eyeliner, and wire-rimmed glasses perched on her nose. With deep red lips and ghostly white skin, she was quite striking. From her ears and around her neck hung an assortment of jewelry that Natalia could only assume might be fashionable among vampires. Her choice in clothing was equally gothic — a long black shirt over a narrow skirt, dark hose, and thick-heeled black shoes with odd silver buckles. She might very well have been scary if it weren't for the fact that her eyes were so kind and her smile warm and mirthful. All in all, she was an attractive woman, but clearly one with her own mind about fashion.

"So you want to know about the Spear of Ragnarok," continued the woman, walking up to the case as her finger slid across the glass. "So many people do, and many more have died in pursuit of it. This replica is one of three that the Templar have traced over the years . . . each so perfect in detail that even using the marvels of modern science one cannot tell the difference. Which, of course, is the point. But until the real Spear is recovered, this, I'm afraid, is as close as any of us will ever get."

"Who are you?" asked Max suspiciously.

"Little boys should know better than to ask questions like that in someone else's house," she replied in a crisp tone, which sounded every bit as American as the Griffins' own English. "Perhaps you should try introducing yourself to me."

Max cleared his throat uncomfortably. "I'm Max," he said.

"Grayson Maximillian Sumner III," she corrected. Her eyes took in Max as if she might be cataloging him to be placed on some high shelf. "Yes, Iver had mentioned that you looked a lot like your grandfather. He's right. It's remarkable, really."

"I do?" asked Max in wonder, thinking back to the fact that Grandpa Caliburn had been the Guardian of the *Codex* before him.

"Yes, of course you do," came Iver's impatient voice as he walked up beside the woman. "And there's more than just a resemblance, but that's not the reason why we are here." He then waved in the direction of Max. "Max, this is the Librarian, and the very person we have come all this way to see. She'll be able to help us understand what we find ourselves up against."

"You're an American," Ernie pointed out.

The Librarian smiled and patted Ernie on his shoulder. "You are, too, which means you're a long way from home."

"We're from Minnesota," added Natalia. "And I bet you're from the East Coast."

"New York, to be precise," the Librarian said with a bow. "I once was a librarian in the city," she said before turning and beckoning the Griffins to follow her toward a circular desk that stood in the precise center of the room. "Now, instead of hailing taxis and fighting for elbow room on the subway, I have the honor of directing the most magnificent library in the world."

Ernie suddenly gasped and pulled at Harley's jacket sleeve anxiously, trying to get his attention.

"Knock it off," Harley growled, assuming Ernie was having another panic attack.

"Look up there," urged Ernie, and as Harley turned, he could see the object of Ernie's excitement. Across the balconies above, hundreds of books were floating in the air, the pages turning on their own accord as they shelved and unshelved themselves. Even nearby, only a few steps in either direction, Ernie could see things moving through the air. "This place is haunted. . . ."

The Librarian, who heard the comment, paused. Then, as if realizing Ernie's confusion, she suddenly laughed to herself. "No, there are no ghosts here. The books you see are being read by people all over the world . . . members of this Library."

"How can they be reading them if they aren't here?" pressed Ernie.

"It's called Remote Viewing," the Librarian replied matter-of-factly. "All Templars employ it, both in battle and in more civilized pursuits such as research. In fact, my patrons don't even need to leave the confines of their own homes. They can simply pick up a book and browse through it as if they were here. Of course, you can also check out books the old-fashioned way, if you wish."

"That's amazing!" exclaimed Natalia.

Ernie was just pleased to find out there were no ghosts lurking about. Still, it was rather unnerving to have a book float by your head, pages flipping, and not being able to see the reader. He contemplated trying to stick out his foot to see if he could trip a Remote Viewer, but then thought better of it.

"You must have a million books here!" Harley whistled.

"Oh, much more than that, I assure you. This library stores all the books, at least the ones that matter, in the world . . . even those that have been forgotten about. The great libraries of the past have been moved here for safekeeping. Alexandria . . . Pergamum . . . Caesarea . . . Atlantis. They are all here."

"Atlantis really existed?" exclaimed Natalia as she pulled out her *Book of Clues* and shook her pen to get the ink moving. "I thought Plato made it all up."

"I'm afraid we don't have time for a history lesson today," interrupted Iver, much to Natalia's disappointment. "Librarian, as I mentioned to you, we're in a bit of a hurry. I apologize for dropping in with such short notice, but we've a matter that requires your specific expertise."

"Really?" The Librarian smiled playfully. "I'm surprised you remember what my expertise is. Since you never come here anymore, I was beginning to think you had the entire Library memorized."

"I've been unavoidably detained."

"So much so you couldn't have returned Aristotle's *Lost Works of Alchemy* for the last thirteen years?"

Iver cleared his throat and looked out uncomfortably from the shadows of his long eyebrows. "Yes, well, it is in good hands, I assure you. At any rate, perhaps we can discuss my transgressions at a later time."

"Very well." The Librarian nodded with a knowing wink at the children, who didn't know if they should laugh or not. "You are here about the Spear of Ragnarok, that much I know."

"Not entirely," Iver replied. "There are threads of a very elaborate skein that we must untangle."

"Oh, I love puzzles," the Librarian exclaimed as she leaned forward on her elbows, batting her eyelashes. "Is it dark?"

"Darker than you've seen in a long age."

"Delicious," she replied. "Darkness is my specialty, you know."

"Indeed."

"What do you have?"

Iver turned and beckoned Harley to approach the desk. "Show her the cufflink."

The Connection Made

THE LIBRARIAN immediately pulled out a red velvet pillow from beneath the counter, placed the cufflink on it, and leaned in close. For several long minutes, no one said anything. In fact, Max had no idea what she was doing, or why the cufflink was suddenly so critical. Iver certainly hadn't seemed too concerned about it before now.

She looked up at Iver, then at Max, and finally back down at the strange object. "Why did you want me to look at this, Iver? You know what it is as well as I."

"Second opinion, you might say," the older Templar replied quickly. "We can't afford mistakes at this point."

"We found it in the woods behind Max's house back in Avalon," Ernie added helpfully.

"Careless of them to drop something like this, don't you think?" the Librarian said. "In fact, considering who it is, it hardly seems like an accident. They almost never make mistakes. . . . It's not in their nature."

"So why's this cufflink suddenly so important?" pressed Natalia, trying to get a better look to see if she'd been missing a clue. "And who in heaven's name does it belong to? I mean I have a guess, but . . ."

"Let me show you." The Librarian walked away from the desk, her heels clicking across the polished floor. "Luckily," her voice echoed across the hall, "this is fairly recent history. I won't have to go down into the lower levels on a wild-goose chase."

"Lower levels?" exclaimed Ernie. "You mean there are more books?"

"Books, manuscripts, mummies," she called. "We have at least one copy of everything here."

"Mummies?" Ernie's voice trailed off, his eyes wide as he watched the Librarian disappear in a flash of light and suddenly reappear several floors above them.

"Portals," Iver said, patting Ernie on the shoulder. "Volcanoes are thick with them, which makes Bass Rock an ideal place for a library with no staircases."

Ernie nodded as he looked around in wonder. He hadn't noticed the missing staircases before, but Iver was right. In Ernie's mind, with a library this size, if it wasn't for portals, the librarians would spend all their day simply going up and down stairs.

A moment later, the Librarian returned hefting a rather large book under her arm. With a thud she placed it on the desk and with startling accuracy she let it fall open to the exact page in question, turning it around for the Griffins to read.

"The Black Wolf Society," Max breathed.

"Yeah, but who are they?" asked Harley, poring over the pictures.

"They are many things," the Librarian answered with a hint of a smile. "But, at least on the surface, you could simply call them extremists and militants that rose out of the ashes of the last world war. But that hardly does them justice, does it, Iver?"

Iver said nothing.

"They attacked us last night," Natalia answered as her eyes followed the pictures on the pages before her. "But this isn't the first time something like this has happened." Natalia then went on to describe the events leading up to their plane crash into the sea, and then finished with a blow-by-blow description of the attack on Castle Sumner only hours earlier.

The Librarian listened intently. She was a fantastic audience, in Natalia's opinion — not offering a single interruption or question. It was like talking to a cool big sister. In fact, this woman charmed Natalia into telling her more than Natalia realized she actually knew. But she kept her promise to Max, and was careful not to say anything about the Witching Well or the map they'd found back in the Trophy Room.

"You certainly weave an interesting tale, Ms. Romanov," commented the Librarian.

"Thank you," Natalia replied, glowing.

"Now," Iver interrupted brusquely. "It's plain you have your suspicions, and we've not much time."

"Very well," the Librarian said with a smile as she turned to the Griffins. "This cufflink is worn only by leading members of the Black Wolf Society. The symbol upon it is their trademark . . . a downturned sword surrounded by Viking runes spelling out the words *Black Wolves.* They've had a few different symbols since 1945, but this seems to be their current favorite . . . always a flare for the dramatic, these devils."

"So who are they?" asked Max.

"The Society, as I mentioned, is not old," the Librarian continued. "They seem to have appeared a few years before the Second World War, organized by a man known only as Sigurd the Slayer . . . a darkly charming, staggeringly intelligent, yet entirely malevolent monster of a man. He was wealthy, politically connected, and led a small army of followers devoted to his cause. At that time, Europe was a highly charged environment, and a man of Sigurd's means was able to use this to his advantage. In fact, he was actually able to attract a large number of followers from almost every country . . . and the United States was no exception.

"When his political ideology first formed, it was based upon the idea that the only path toward the future was embracing the forgotten ways of magic," the Librarian continued. "This had the markings of a fairy tale to most, but for some it held a great deal of attraction . . . particularly those who wanted to pursue those old teachings to the exclusion of all else. Yet Sigurd, a brilliant man, had no intention of turning away from the advancements of the modern age. Why discard technology and all its wonder for a Luddite world of folktales and fantasy? Why not have the best of both worlds? Why not fuse them together?"

Ernie yawned. This story was losing him, so in typical fashion, he reached into his pocket and withdrew the last Christmas cookie he had managed to salvage from the kitchen back at Castle Sumner. Natalia, on the other hand, was busily trying to capture every word in her notebook. Max just wanted to know what this had to do with his father and how they were going to get the Spear.

"So what happened to him?" asked Harley. He was drawn to grim tales and conspiracies, and this one was no exception.

"No one knows for sure," replied the Librarian as one of the cats, Browning, the silver and white one with the pink nose, jumped up onto the counter next to her and began to idly knock pencils to the floor. The Librarian, with a frown, quickly picked up the cat and sent it sliding across the floor, where it disappeared into an invisible portal with a flash. Dusting off her hands, she returned to the desk.

"Sorry. It's a little game we play," the Librarian explained. "He'll return in a few minutes. Anyway, back to the topic at hand. There was some speculation that Sigurd was the one secretly behind the dark magic attributed to the Nazi SS during the war, as well as the American and British Paranormal Bureaus. But this is complete conjecture. Apparently after the war, he and his followers disappeared to a secret base from which they now operate and continue to pursue their fusion of magic and technology . . . and one other experiment . . . a far darker one."

A shadow seemed to fall over the room as the Griffins drew near for safety. "Sigurd was a genius," the Librarian continued. "There was never any doubt, and there is no denying he was successful in ways the world has yet to discover. But something seems to have occurred a few years after the war that had his fingerprints all over it, something he had been striving to create for years. . . ."

"Werewolves," came Iver's somber voice from nearby.

"Werewolves?" Ernie exclaimed, suddenly yanked back into the conversation. He didn't like the sound of that. Other kids might find werewolf stories silly, but they had never come face-to-face with one. Not like Ernie had.

"Like Morgan LaFey's driver!" Natalia recalled, thinking back to the monstrous giant that had nearly killed the Griffins only a few months back. "He was a werewolf."

"That's right!" Harley echoed.

"Oh, no." Ernie sighed with slumped shoulders. "Not again."

"Then I think another piece of the puzzle has fallen into place," the Librarian stated. "If the Black Witch was employing a werewolf and the only source for werewolves is Sigurd's Black Wolf Society, we can assume they are likely working together."

"That's what Bishop thinks," Max added. The others looked at him curiously. He hadn't shared too much of his discussion in Edinburgh with them. There just hadn't been time . . . besides, just thinking about Bishop gave him the creeps.

The Librarian paused, then looked over at Iver with confusion and concern. "Who brought this boy to see Bishop?"

"Logan," Iver replied curtly. It was obvious that Iver clearly would not have done the same in Logan's position.

"I see," said the Librarian, her eyes narrowing as she looked Max over. "Well, you seem all right. No worse for wear, but it was a huge gamble."

"Who *is* this Bishop?" asked Natalia, glaring at Max for not having shared every shred of information with her.

"Another time," interrupted Iver. "For now, I'd like to stay on the topic of werewolves."

Natalia shook her head in frustration. Bishop was important, she was sure of it. And glossing over him like yesterday's news seemed to be a bad idea.

"You said Sigurd created werewolves?" began Max, ignoring Natalia completely. "But I thought that werewolves have been around for a long time?"

"That's true," replied the Librarian. "But that older breed of werewolf was hunted to extinction by the Templars and their brothers, the Order of the Dragon. There hasn't been a werewolf, or any were-creature for that matter, on this earth for well over two hundred years. Most people would prefer to have kept it that way."

"I second that!" Ernie exclaimed as he raised his hand, earning him a reproachful look from Iver.

"I think they have more than just werewolves," added Max, thinking about the amber-eyed leader of the Black Wolves, who clearly had powers beyond just howling at the moon and surviving bullets.

"It could be that the werewolves are evolving," continued the Librarian, her eyebrows bent in concentration, as if she were chewing on some distant thought. "With Sigurd, anything is possible. Yet to have the Black Wolf Society in league with Morgan LaFey is bad enough."

"So it's Morgan who wants the Spear of Ragnarok?" asked Max.

The Librarian shook her head. "You can't know for sure, but it's a good bet and one that Bishop would no doubt take. There are things even beyond *his* ability to see . . . Morgan, for instance. While Bishop may know what she is doing at any particular moment or what her minions store in their wicked little minds, in the end he is blinded by the same thing that blinds all of us."

"What's that?" asked Max in confusion.

"Free will," replied the Librarian. "Morgan has many choices to make ahead of her, and like any chess game, her final design may not be readily apparent from the opening moves. But I can tell you this, and let you draw your own conclusions: The Spear of Ragnarok is a weapon made in the ancient world and legend claims that whoever possesses it is unstoppable. No army, no man, no faerie can withstand the Bearer of the Spear. And lest you be skeptical, I can say with certainty that so far, this prophecy has always been deadly accurate. Some of the greatest and most powerful rulers of the past can lay their success squarely at the feet of the Spear, and it was not until it fell from their hands, either in error or in old age, that they fell victim to defeat. If a weapon such as this was to fall into the hands of the immortal Black Witch, I shudder to think what would become of our world."

"But the ransom note says that if we don't give her the Spear, she'll kill my dad!" exclaimed Max, who suddenly realized the perilous nature of the required ransom. "What choice do we have?"

"I knew your father, Max," the Librarian replied coldly. "And though we didn't always see eye to eye, there is no question that he has supported us through the years . . . even in the dark times. But I can also tell you this . . . no single life is worth the horror that would result in handing over the Spear of Ragnarok to Morgan."

"What?" Max asked, confused. Was she really saying that?

The Librarian turned to Iver as the old man placed his hand on Max's shoulder. "Max, your father would tell you the same thing," Iver explained, his voice full of compassion. "We simply cannot allow Morgan to take possession of the Spear. If that happens, the results will be catastrophic . . . worse than any world war and more deadly than our darkest nightmares."

"But . . ."

"Your father was a realist," Iver continued. "And he knew when to make the necessary sacrifices."

"How do you know?" Max shook away from Iver's hand, his eyes narrowing in sudden anger. "If my dad's helped you as much as you say he has, then you owe him. How can you just leave him to die like this? Is that what the Templars are all about?"

Iver shook his head. "That's not how it works, Max. We Templars serve a higher cause, even when difficult choices must be made. There is no individual greater than the whole."

No one said a word as anger boiled within Max. He stood there defiant, fists clenched as a strange crackling energy washed over him, fueled by his rage. "Fine!" he roared. "If that's the way it's gonna be, I don't want anything to do with the Templars or this stupid book!" he screamed, whipping off his backpack and throwing the *Codex* at Iver's feet. "I trusted you," Max said. "But now I see. You and the Templars are just like everyone else . . . all you ever wanted was to use me! Was it because I'm the Guardian of the *Codex*, or were you just after my family's money?"

"Max!" gasped Natalia, who was on the verge of tears as she

watched the horrific display. Ernie could only look at his feet and pretend to be invisible.

"Grayson Maximillian Sumner!" Iver's voice turned dark and ominous, nearly shaking Max out of his shoes. All at once the kindly old man seemed to tower above him, while Max shrank back, feeling as though he'd fallen into a hole. "That is quite enough! I will not stand by and listen to you denigrate yourself and everything your family has held dear for over a thousand years. And how dare you question me or my friendship. I have been with you since the beginning, just as I was for your grandfather. You have no right to dishonor me, or your grandfather's memory. You were born into dark times, but if you see only shadows among the friends who care about you the most, you will lose yourself in your own poison."

Max remained where he was, chest heaving, but silent. Then, slowly, Harley walked over and picked up Max's backpack, holding it before his friend. Max looked at Harley, then Natalia, and finally Ernie, who turned away, frightened.

Then the guilt set in. He knew he had overstepped his bounds, but right now, all that mattered was his father. And if his father's life wasn't important to his friends, Max was going to have to carry out the mission himself. He'd worry about the consequences later.

The Librarian cleared her throat to diffuse the uncomfortable silence, as Max took his bag from Harley. "You know, this isn't the first time Morgan LaFey has sought the Spear of Ragnarok."

"What?" exclaimed Max.

The Librarian shook her head. "No, but it *is* the first time she has a serious chance at it. The last time she ran headlong into the Order of the Dragon, which was a fate LaFey had hoped to avoid. She managed to survive, as always, but her hopes of gaining the Spear were all but lost."

"So, who are the Order of the Dragon?" asked Harley. "That's a pretty cool name."

"It certainly is," the Librarian replied with a smile. "Its members were hardly what you'd call, well, social gentlemen. They were Templars, of a sort . . . rather like first cousins to our Order. They were vastly powerful, having kings and emperors in their league, yet they were also ruthless in their methods, as sometimes, I admit, we all can be when it comes down to those things that are most important. It was they alone who were able to stop Morgan from achieving her quest for the Spear, and the Dragons paid a high price for their victory." Her voice faded in somberness.

"That doesn't sound good," Natalia pointed out. "Did they die?"

"Oh, worse than that." The Librarian shook her head. "Much worse."

"I think this tale is a little too dark for these ears," voiced Iver, looking down at Natalia. "Perhaps when they are older."

"What?" complained Harley, who was just getting interested.

The Librarian slowly, almost sadly, nodded in agreement. "Still, I think it's worthwhile to know why Morgan ultimately failed and why she now needs Max to rescue the Spear of Ragnarok for her. Did you not consider why she simply could not, in all her power, reach out and take it for herself? Especially now that the Drachenorden are no longer here to stop her?"

"Who?" asked Ernie, lost.

"I'm sure it's just another way to say Order of the Dragon. Will you just pay attention?" Natalia snipped, jabbing Ernie gently in the ribs to wake him up.

Max paused in confusion. The Librarian had asked a good question. Why would the Witch need Max to do her dirty work? The thought hadn't crossed his mind, but as Max looked over at Iver, he could see that his old friend had thought very deeply about it. Why wouldn't he have mentioned it to Max? What was he hiding?

"So why *does* she need Max?" reflected Natalia, who'd slung her arm around her friend protectively.

"Because the Spear is guarded by a magic even she can't defeat. Only the boy from the Prophecy can discover the three pieces of the Spear and reassemble the weapon."

Max's mind turned back to his run-in with Bishop in Edinburgh. He had called Max the Prophecy Boy, but Max had assumed it meant something else — something about the *Codex*. Could he have been talking about the Spear of Ragnarok?

"What prophecy?" prompted Natalia.

The Librarian took off her glasses as she looked over at Max. "I actually have it here in the Templar Library . . . the original. Would you like to see it?"

Max nodded as he and the others followed the Librarian and her two cats into the darker recesses of the Library.

Soon they were standing near a stone slab, weathered and gray. It stood upright behind a giant glass case, lit from above by a shining orb of living light that hovered mysteriously in the air. Nearly as tall as Iver, the stone was wrapped in long looping ribbons tied into a series of elaborate knots. Each was decorated with runes, similar to those on the cufflink.

"This is called a rune stone," explained the Librarian, waving in the direction of the table. "It was discovered off the coast of Iceland about three hundred years ago, I believe. As you can see, the stone itself is much older than that . . . probably mid-eighth century if our guess is correct."

"What does it say?" asked Natalia impatiently as Ernie ducked. Another unattended book had shot out of a shelf, flying directly overhead.

"It is part of the Prophecy, and here"— the Librarian paused as she traced her finger along a long ribbon of runes that encircled the top of the stone —"is where it begins."

> *"Overwhelming from the Well Witching*
> *Within the blood of the Book and he that bears it*
> *Shall make it through mislaid memory and dire dragon*
> *To face the fierce flame within the ice's ire*
> *The Lightning Lance, the Shining Spear of Ragnarok."*

"The Well Witching? That sounds a lot like . . . ," Ernie started, earning another swift elbow to the ribs from Natalia. He had momentarily forgotten about the promise to keep the well a secret, which wasn't unusual. Ernie's memory was selective at best, and his ability to keep a secret was even worse.

"Clearly," continued the Librarian, who apparently hadn't

noticed Ernie's near slipup, "this Prophecy regards the Guardian of the *Codex Spiritus* and his link to the Spear of Ragnarok. There has been much debate over the translation I just recited to you. Not all Templar scholars agree with my interpretation, but despite sounding rather conceited, I'm quite correct about the whole matter. Runes are a special love of mine . . . as is the Spear."

"You don't think it's Max, do you?" questioned Natalia. "I mean, it could be referring to any of the Guardians of the *Codex*. Right?"

"Only Max would know the answer to that. Until now, unless I am quite mistaken, no Guardian has crossed paths with the Spear of Ragnarok. Therefore, in my opinion, it can only refer to Max. The only puzzle that remains is the *Well Witching*. We have no records of anything of the sort. It is in none of my books, I'm afraid, and all my searches for it have turned up empty."

Max's eyes grew wide. *The Well Witching* . . . could that be the same Witching Well that's on his father's estate? Of course it was. It couldn't be a coincidence, there was just no way. And that's exactly where Max would begin his quest to retrieve the Spear and free his father — so long as the other Griffins kept their vow of secrecy. If Iver found out, well, Max decided he'd worry about that if and when it happened.

"What about the other things in the Prophecy?" prompted Max, searching to change the topic. "They have to mean something . . . the fire and dragons and stuff."

"No one knows, but one can assume that they are tests or trials of some sort. Security devices, if you will, which protect the Spear."

Great, Max thought. *More tests.* If they were anything like the ones they faced in the Templar Catacombs, that meant big trouble — especially since he planned to go alone this time.

"At any rate," interrupted Iver, "I think we have seen enough for today. We have what we came for. Morgan is not only back, but in league with the Black Wolf Society. She seeks the Spear of Ragnarok and clearly will do anything to get it. As long as we keep her away from it, and from Max, her evil plans will never come to fruition."

"Can't we do anything for Max's father?" prompted Natalia. "I mean, if we can't give Morgan the Spear, then we still need to try some way to rescue him, right?"

Iver nodded. "I have already contacted the Templar High Council and the Grandmaster himself. I have been assured that an investigation will be pursued and a rescue attempt made, if possible."

"If possible?" exclaimed Max, his frustration rising again.

"This is not a simple task, Grayson Maximillian," Iver replied, continuing to use Max's formal name. "You can't rescue someone if you don't know where they are."

17

The Knights Before Christmas

ERNIE AND WINIFRED munched nervously on a bit of stale bread slathered with the last of the raspberry preserves, while the Grey Griffins sat around on makeshift cots. They were in the scorched remains of Castle Sumner, huddled in the warmth of the kitchen that had been left relatively intact. The brave souls who'd continued on had transformed the kitchen into sleeping quarters with an army of smoke-stained mattresses, tattered bedding, and ancient kerosene lamps. It would have to do until more suitable accommodations could be arranged.

Most of the castle's staff had already journeyed to one of Lord Sumner's country estates outside of London, and the Griffins were scheduled to be transferred there in the morning. That's where they were to celebrate Christmas – though few presents, if any, remained after the attack. Then they were set for an early return to their homes back in Avalon, Minnesota. That meant if Max was going to act, he'd have to move quickly.

"You're going after the Spear, aren't you?" Natalia asked in a hushed tone as she absentmindedly licked a handkerchief and wiped a smudge of raspberry from Ernie's cheek.

"What the heck are you doing?" Ernie asked, jumping to his feet in disgust.

"You really should work on your table manners," Natalia

remarked. She then turned back to Max, who was trying to avoid her eye. He'd been brooding since they left Bass Rock, offering little more than grunts when anyone tried to talk to him.

"But you heard what Iver said, Max," she continued, looking around to make sure no one was listening. "If Morgan gets her hands on it, there's no telling what could happen. . . ."

"What would you do if it was your father?" Harley countered in Max's defense. "Would you just sit back and let him die, or would you try to save him no matter what? We have to help Max, and it has to be tonight."

Natalia bit her lip as she thumbed through her notepad. It was one thing to know the right thing to do, and quite another to act on it. "Fine," she replied. "But if the Well Witching from the Prophecy is really the Witching Well, then that means we have to go back into the bog. You understand that, don't you?"

Ernie gulped, dropping his bread.

"It doesn't matter," Harley shrugged. "We'll figure it out when we get there."

"Thanks," Max said, breaking into a half smile as he turned to Harley. "But this time I have to go alone. This is my responsibility, not yours, and I can't ask any of you to risk your lives. . . ."

"That's noble," rumbled a rocky voice from behind them. "But extremely foolish. You'll need allies."

The Griffins spun around in surprise to see Magnus standing in the shadows. "What do you mean?" Max exclaimed, hoping the giant hadn't overheard everything.

"I work for your father," replied Magnus, in a halting voice that sounded as if each word was being forced through an iron grate. "I read the ransom note, and I know what's required. If you need to get back to the bog unseen, I can make it happen. Your father must be saved, and if you're the only one who can do it, it's my job to help you."

"How?" asked Max, doubting the word of the Norseman.

"A diversion."

"Like what?" Harley pressed.

"You'll know it when you hear it," assured Magnus smugly. "And when you do, make for the forest. Take supplies."

A loud crash shook the house as the Griffins shot up from their covers and blinked into the darkness. They didn't know what time it was, but there was one thing for certain — it was time for them to leave.

Shouts echoed through the charred hallways as footsteps rushed out of the kitchen, racing away in the direction of the blast. The Griffins quickly pulled on their coats, boots, and hats, while slipping on backpacks stuffed with everything they could think of, from food to flashlights, blankets to matches, the *Codex*, their map, and just about everything in between. Considering where they were going and the dangers that lay ahead, they needed everything they could get their hands on.

"Here, Winifred, it's time to go. Come on, girl!"

"You are not bringing that mangy rodent with us," stated Natalia plainly.

"What?" exclaimed Ernie. "I can't leave her here."

"Oh, yes, you can. We can't risk her messing anything up. When she ran into the cemetery last time, we learned our lesson. She's not coming, and that's final!"

"We have to go," urged Max as he opened the door to the back lawn. "We may not have much time. They'll be coming back to check on us."

"I can't find Winifred," argued Ernie.

"You can't go looking for her now," stated Harley as Ernie pushed toward the door. "If they spot you, we're finished."

"But I can't leave her!" he maintained. "She'll be lost without me."

"She'll be fine, Ernie," Harley assured. "It's probably safer here than where we're going."

"Oh, that makes me feel a whole lot better," Ernie muttered, his shoulders slumping.

The door swung shut quietly as four shadows fled into the wintry night, disappearing in the mist.

The path through the forest was extraordinarily clear, as the Griffins raced under the moonlight, all the while looking over their shoulders, expecting Logan to appear at any moment. It was only a question of time, and Max was constantly urging them onward, fearing his only chance to save his father was slipping through Logan's tight grip.

Soon they found themselves standing in front of the decayed iron gates as a pang of dread washed over them. Nervous eyes searched the eerie shadows for signs of Bog Beasts, Bone Crunchers, and Black Wolves. "You sure this is it?" Max asked, turning to Harley, who nodded.

"Yeah," he agreed. "The bog's just on the other side."

Max drew forth the *Codex*, and it flared with a golden light like a shining shield that cut through the foggy darkness. Their hopes were rekindled, until a dog barked behind them, followed by another. The Griffins could hear voices shouting. The search party had picked up their trail.

"Time to go," Max urged. "Are you ready?"

The other three nodded.

Together they raced through the mist, the *Codex* lighting the way like a magical torch. Without a single sign of Bog Beast or Bone Cruncher, they passed quickly over the crumbling bridge and pushed themselves along the fiery pools until they came within sight of the mausoleum.

"There," Max said, pointing as Natalia shined her flashlight into the darkness. "The Witching Well."

"You're kidding . . . right?" Ernie complained.

"No. I can feel there's a portal inside. That's where we have to go."

"Great," Ernie mumbled. "So now what?"

"We go in," Harley replied, taking a deep breath before stepping into the dark water. The other Griffins plunged in after him, thankful to find it was no more than knee-deep and really quite warm. But the sucking mud continually threatened to eat the boots right off their feet as the Griffins slowly made their way around the bursts of blue fire that leapt into the air all about them.

A few squishy minutes later, the Griffins pulled themselves onto the shores of a small island and looked up at the mausoleum in uncertainty. Perhaps several hundred years ago the mausoleum had been beautiful. But now, everything about it was downright spooky. A soggy hill, covered in dead leaves lay under the building, framed by naked trees. The structure itself was constructed of thousands of rough-hewn bricks, topped by a roof pitched upward, where gargoyles crouched. Two windows, devoid of glass, flanked a looming door of hammered iron that stared back at the Griffins hungrily.

"We really have to go in there?" asked Natalia, eyeing the structure suspiciously.

"I don't think we have a choice," Max said as he gingerly climbed the moldering step. He was holding his breath, with the *Codex* out in front of him like a shield. Nothing happened. Then he took another step. And another. Until Max stood in front of the doorway.

With a collective sigh of relief, the others joined him.

"Ready?" Max asked, before pushing open the doors.

"Right behind you," answered Natalia. "Keep the *Codex* ready. You don't know what's on the other side."

"Trust me," Max replied with a nod. The book was tightly grasped in his gloved hands.

"I'll go first," offered Harley, stepping up beside Max.

"Probably not a good idea," Max replied, moving toward the door. "If there's magic on the other side, I should be first. Just stay with me."

"I don't care which of you goes first, as long as it's not me," added

Ernie, stomping his cold feet on the ground to bring them back to life.

Taking a deep breath, Max moved forward into the shadows beyond the looming metal door, feeling as if he had just stepped into the mouth of a hungry giant. Max's eyes roved from one corner to the next apprehensively, with Harley close behind. The interior of the mausoleum was just as spooky as the exterior. It was a single room, lined with weathered stone, encircled by twelve lichen-covered statues of Templar Knights. Each one held his spear high beneath a domed ceiling etched with strange carvings and inscriptions.

In the middle of the mausoleum, surrounded by the brooding statues, stood a wide triangular pool set within three narrow walls, empty save for a pile of dead leaves.

"Is that the Witching Well?" Natalia asked, taking out her note-pad as she started to sketch.

"I . . . I don't know," Max said, running his hand along the edge of the stone. "I know the portal is here, but . . . well, I can't see it."

"Maybe it evaporated?" added Ernie, which to him sounded not only intelligent, but also pretty reasonable.

"How can a portal evaporate?" Natalia shook her head. "It's not made of water, you know."

"This one might have been," Ernie maintained.

"Look at this," Harley said, pointing to something he saw in the stones. There were three symbols, each one at a respective corner of the dry pool. Two were worn, barely perceptible. But one of them was clearly a Templar cross set within a circle.

"What do you think they mean?" asked Natalia as she moved in closer.

"A puzzle?" Max wondered.

"They kinda look like keyholes to me," Ernie mentioned casually. The other Griffins turned to look at him.

"Then where's the key?" asked Natalia.

"I don't know," Ernie said, frowning as he shrugged. "It's just a guess."

"Hey," began Harley. "You know this one kinda looks like the cross on Max's necklace."

Max's eyes lit up. "Of course," he breathed, pulling the necklace out from his coat. "Ernie, you're a genius!"

"Ernie's getting pretty sharp," Harley exclaimed. "Watch out, Natalia, or you'll have to cheat off of him in history, instead of the other way around."

"I don't cheat," Ernie complained. "Natalia made up that story."

Max slowly walked over to the side of the Witching Well with the cross and circle symbol cut deeply into it. Looking over at his friends to gather up a little extra courage, he dropped the necklace into place. Immediately, a flash of light blasted through the room, and as the Griffins' eyes adjusted, they could see that the pool had changed dramatically. Whereas before it was nothing more than a dry basin, now the pool was bursting with shimmering green light that whirled around the interior of the mausoleum like a hurricane.

The Witching Well had been activated, and the portal appeared in its depths. As the Griffins struggled to keep their feet in the storm, they heard somebody shout. Turning, they could see flashlights bouncing through the darkness just outside the door.

Logan and Iver had found them.

Max swallowed hard. It was time to make a decision — leave now or lose the chance to save his father forever. There were only seconds to choose. "It's now or never," Max yelled over the gale as he looked at his friends. "You still with me?"

With a silent nod, Harley leapt in, pulling Ernie behind him as Natalia followed. Each Griffin disappeared in a brilliant flash of light, but just as Max was about to follow, he saw Iver rush into the room. The old man's face was pale as a ghost's.

"Don't do it, Max!" he shouted in horror.

Setting his jaw in determination, Max nodded at Iver. There was no time for discussion. "I'm going to save my dad."

With that, Max turned and plunged into the Witching Well.

18

IN A BLAST OF LIGHT, Max found himself hurtling through space. Everything around him had blurred, including his own mind, so that he had no idea who he was and where he was going until he shot out of the portal, landing in a snowdrift that erupted with a powdery plop. Then everything went black.

Cautiously, Max breathed in, which meant he was still alive. That was good. All his body parts still seemed to be in the right place, which was even better. With a shake of his head, Max managed to free his face from the frozen drift, and look around. Three other figures were struggling to their feet as well.

"Where are we?" Ernie asked, wiping his thick glasses free of ice crystals.

"We're definitely not in Kansas anymore," replied Natalia, who was shaking the snow out of her braids.

As the Griffins peered over the cliff near where Harley stood, a cold breeze lashed at them, stinging noses and ears. The Griffins could clearly see that they were high up in a lofty mountain range, and farther down the slope lay a wide expanse of evergreen forest that stretched as far as the eye could see. On the edge of that forest, tiny lights from a sleepy snow-veiled village twinkled brightly up at them.

Harley was first to spot a nearby winding road that cut through the snowscape. "Check this out," he said, motioning for the others to follow him.

"No way," Natalia breathed as she read a sign that marked the icy path.

"What?" Ernie asked, ducking. He assumed some kind of terrible snow beast was rising from a drift.

"We're near Salzburg," said Natalia, blinking in wonder. "In Austria. Though I guess it could be Germany," she admitted, looking out at the mountains. "Either way, these have to be the Alps."

"Now all we have to do is find out why the Witching Well sent us here," Max said as he started to pace back and forth. The task before them was daunting — especially since the Griffins were going in completely blind. There was no outline. No map. No guide. All they had to go on was a strange prophecy with a cryptic message.

"If Iver were here, he'd know what to do," Ernie observed through chattering teeth.

"No," Max argued. "It's up to us now, and there's nothing anyone can do to help. Not this time."

"Why don't we start over there?" Harley said, pointing to something huge poking out from behind a towering drift that lay at the foot of the mountain. As he scrambled up to the snowy top, he let out a whistle. "There's a huge door back here." In fact, it was much more than a door. There was a whole archway of gleaming white stones that framed an entrance leading right into the heart of the mountain.

"KEHLSTEINHAUS," Natalia read from a sign near the entrance as the rest of the Griffins crested the top of the drift. It was a word she had never seen before, which was something of a rare phenome-non, but she quickly saw there was an English translation below it: "THE EAGLE'S NEST."

Ernie looked to the sky, searching for any giant eagles that might be hunting for their dinner, but as his eyes moved up the side of the mountain, he caught sight of what looked like a build-ing of some sort, resting at the very peak. "What's that?" he asked, pointing at the dark silhouette. Was it a castle?

"That's got to be the Eagle's Nest," Harley answered.

"But the question is," began Natalia as the Griffins started their slow descent down the other side, "whether that's where we are supposed to go."

"We're in the middle of nowhere," replied Harley. "Do you see anything else out here? If this is where the Witching Well put us, this is where we have to go."

"So why do you think Magnus helped us?" Harley asked as he assisted Natalia and Ernie down to the brick pavement that led to the door.

"Because he's loyal to my father," Max said flatly, "like all employ-ees should be. I just wish there were more people like him."

"I sure hope not," replied Ernie. "He gives me the creeps."

"Everybody gives you the creeps," Natalia pointed out.

"Hey, the door's cracked open," Max said. As he looked around, he could see some orange pylons near the entrance and a box of tools against the wall. "I think the maintenance crew is here. They're the ones that probably left the door open. I'm gonna take a peek inside."

"Whaddaya see?" asked Harley as Max peered through the opening.

"Another door up ahead, but it's open, too. And there's a long hallway beyond."

Soon all four Griffins stood beneath the arched hallway of amber stone that had been excavated right into the mountain. Electric lights flickered over their heads, causing a disorienting strobe effect as the Griffins proceeded up the steady incline.

"Do you guys think there're any bats in here?" asked Ernie, searching every crack and crevice.

"I doubt it," Harley said. "Too cold."

Quietly, they marched until the tunnel emptied into a perfectly round room lined with velvety ropes meant to guide long lines of tourists. A vast domed ceiling arched high over their heads, and electric sconces burned faintly on the walls. At the opposite end of the room stood an open doorway that led to a small parlor entirely walled in brass.

"Now what?" Max asked, frustrated. They had reached a dead end and the Spear was nowhere to be seen.

"Hey," Harley called as he entered the brass room, which was lined with green leather benches. "This isn't a room. It's an elevator!" While the others piled in, Harley smiled, motioning toward the panel of buttons on the wall. "Where to?"

Suddenly, the elevator began to rumble beneath them, whirring to life all by itself. Looking at one another, the Griffins leapt out of the elevator car and back into the waiting room. As they turned, they could see the elevator car rise and slowly disappear.

But the doors remained open, as the sounds of hammering and cutting began to echo through the parlor.

"I bet that's the maintenance crew," Max said. "They're probably just working on the elevator."

"What time is it, anyway?" Ernie asked.

"It's about a quarter after ten," replied Harley, checking his watch.

"It's actually later in Germany," Natalia reminded them.

"So I guess we can't get to the top of the mountain if the elevator's disappeared, right?" observed Ernie.

"Maybe it's not the top we're supposed to get to," Max added as the other three looked at him curiously.

"You mean you think we need to go down the shaft?" asked Harley, walking over to peer down the edge. "It's a long way down. But hey . . . what's this?"

"What?" asked Natalia, moving to take a look.

"There's a ladder here, and the lights go for a little way."

"You're not suggesting we actually climb down an elevator shaft," Natalia replied skeptically. "Do you know how dangerous that could be? What if the elevator comes down on top of our heads?"

"Yeah," agreed Ernie, thinking Natalia had finally come to her senses. "Or what if we slip and fall?"

Max closed his eyes and let his mind stretch, searching . . . looking . . . "There's a portal down there," he said plainly after a few moments. "That's where I have to go. I can't tell you why, but you have to trust me."

The shaft was lined with thick iron framing. And while the

flickering lights illuminated the way for a distance, they failed farther down where the ladder disappeared into a pool of shadows. Common sense told Max that descending into this pit was the stupidest idea in the world. The ladder was rusty and there was no telling if they could even get back up once they reached the bottom — if there was a bottom.

"You sure?" Harley asked. Max nodded.

Natalia gulped. "Umm . . . so how far down does it go?"

"Don't think about it," Harley instructed. "It'll only make you nervous. And whatever you do . . . don't look down."

"I was afraid you were going to say that," Ernie muttered as Harley handed him a length of rope that had been lying nearby.

"Tie this around your waist," he ordered as the rest of them tied themselves to the same line. "If one of us falls, they won't fall far, because we'll all be tied together."

"Or if one of us does fall, he'll drag the rest of us to our deaths," Natalia pointed out.

Harley merely shook his head and slipped over the edge, disappearing down the shaft. The others followed as Ernie took a deep breath and slowly reached his foot down to the first rung of the deteriorating ladder, which shook unsteadily under his weight.

"Nice job," Natalia assured him. "Now just keep it up."

"Eighty-three . . . eighty-four . . . eighty-five . . . ," Natalia counted aloud as they moved down the corroded ladder. Looking up, she could see that the elevator was a good distance above, and the light streaming in from the waiting room seemed almost like a remote dream. Unfortunately, the lighting below the Griffins had come to an abrupt end, though the ladder continued on into the inky blackness.

Harley pulled out his flashlight and probed the shadows with its beam. They could hear him counting under his breath for a long minute. Finally, with a whistle, he shut off the light without a word. Slowly, they resumed their descent.

"Why'd he shut off the light?" Ernie complained.

"To save batteries," Natalia pointed out.

"It's only a little bit farther," Max replied, trying to sound hopeful given the circumstances, though in truth he couldn't gauge the remaining distance.

Natalia counted seventy-three more rungs after the lights failed, when Ernie started to grow nervous. "I thought you said it was only a little farther," he complained.

"Don't worry," Harley assured him. "I'm sure it's pretty close. I . . ."

Suddenly the entire elevator shaft started to shake and rumble.

"Earthquake!" Ernie yelled as the other Griffins clung to the ladder for their lives. Above them, stones began to shake free from the walls, plummeting down around them. Soon they were caught in a maelstrom of falling rocks and debris as the force of the tremors ripped the one side of the ladder from the wall. Ernie was the first to lose his grip. With a shout, he fell from his perch, and just as Natalia predicted, she wasn't strong enough to handle the violent jerk of the rope against her waist. With a snap, she was yanked off the ladder as well. The combined weight of Ernie and Natalia hit Max like a freight train, and with a cry of dismay, he followed them into the darkness.

Harley was next in line, shouldering the oncoming avalanche of weight as best he could. Dropping the flashlight, he wrapped himself around the ladder and braced his feet. Even then, Harley knew he didn't stand a chance. The laws of momentum were stacked against him, and with a shout, he was ripped away as the screams of the Griffins echoed all around.

When Harley opened his eyes again, he found himself lying face up on something soft. All Griffins were accounted for, though none of them was particularly happy. Luckily, the fall had been brief and once Max had managed to pull out a flashlight, they could see that they had landed on a heap of overflowing garbage bags piled high and deep.

"Well, that explains the smell," Harley said as he slid down the mountain of refuse onto the rock floor below.

"Will you please get off of me?" Natalia asked furiously, pushing Ernie's smelly shoe out of her face.

"It's not my fault," Ernie retorted as he scrambled to get back to his feet. "You're the one who fell on me."

"You're the one who made us all fall in the first place," Natalia countered, brushing a dried banana peel from her shoulder as she made her way to the floor below.

"But I didn't want to come in the first place!"

"Aw, cripes," Harley complained, shaking his flashlight as it rattled dead in his hands. While the Griffins had survived the fall, his flashlight hadn't fared as well. "The bulb's busted."

"It could be worse," Natalia pointed out, handing Harley his boot, which had fallen off in their descent. "We could all be dead." She then looked back at the tower of garbage. "I never thought I'd live to see the day when litter would save my life."

"Is everyone okay?" Max asked.

"I think so," Ernie replied, straightening his glasses.

"Yeah. I'm fine," Harley assured him.

As the Griffins looked around, they found themselves standing in a wide alcove, lost somewhere in a spiderweb of rocky tunnels that branched off in a dozen directions.

"Which way is the portal?" asked Harley.

Max, who was checking to see that the *Codex* had landed safely, paused and looked around. Soon, he raised his hand and pointed down a tunnel to their right.

"That way," he stated. "No doubt about it."

"Then that's the passage we take," answered Harley as he took off at a brisk walk into the tunnel. The beam from Natalia's flashlight flitted from side to side as the Griffins filed in behind him.

The passageway they marched through was not wholly empty. Wooden crates and boxes lined its rocky walls, covered in a thick layer of dust. First, there was one, then a few others piled in stacks farther along. As the kids moved their flashlights over them, they could see flags and other symbols. Some looked distinctively American, marked with the Stars and Stripes, while others were marked by the Union Jack, German, and even Russian flags.

It didn't take the Griffins long to discover who had left the boxes. Ernie screamed as he caught sight of the first of many skeletal remains that littered the passageway. Harley was quick to wrap

his hand over Ernie's mouth to keep him quiet. There was no telling who . . . or what might still linger in these tunnels.

"I wonder what happened," Natalia said, carefully stepping over
the remains of a soldier with a German patch on his jacket shoulder.

"You don't think there's a dragon down here, do you?" fretted
Ernie, who was nearly hyperventilating. "Remember what the
Prophecy said?"

"I think it would be a little messier if these guys were killed by
a dragon," Harley pointed out.

"I guess," Ernie replied, unconvinced.

"It's weird," Harley said, kneeling by one of the skeletons. "But I
can't see any bullet holes, either."

"Maybe they got lost," offered Natalia, walking past the skeleton
of a British soldier. "Unless you know where you're going, this
place could be pretty confusing."

"That's true," Max agreed. "But we don't have time to stick
around here and find out. We have to keep moving." So Max led
them deeper into the tunnels.

"What's the deal with all this fog?" asked Harley, noticing the
path ahead was obscured by a thick mist.

"I don't think it's fog," replied Ernie, holding his sleeve up over
his nose as he started to cough. "It smells like rotten eggs."

"Eww," Natalia said with a grimace. "You're right."

Ernie's coughing continued to escalate. Natalia came to stand
next to him.

"It's your asthma," she pointed out. "Why aren't you using your
inhaler?"

Ernie shrugged and began patting down his pockets looking for his asthma inhaler. But as his coughing grew worse, Ernie realized he couldn't remember where he had put it.

"Don't panic." Natalia slapped his hand as he feverishly dumped out the contents of all his pockets. "Just breathe. Honestly, without me, you'd probably be stone dead by now." Natalia reached into her pack and pulled out a white inhaler. "I brought along an extra just in case."

Ernie grabbed it, pressing the inhaler to his lips. A moment later, his coughing fit died away. "Thanks," he said, the air returning to his lungs.

Despite the growing haze, the Griffins continued through the winding maze of tunnels with Max and his flashlight leading the way. He didn't need his eyes. All Max needed was to follow his intuition, which would lead them right to the portal, where the Spear of Ragnarok was bound to be waiting. "It's up ahead," Max called, his excitement growing. "I can feel the portal getting stronger."

"But the fog's getting thicker," Natalia complained, pulling her flashlight back out and urging the others to do the same — just in case they got separated. She pulled out an extra flashlight and flicked it on before handing it to Harley. "I always believe in bringing spares."

"Am I the only one who thinks it's getting kinda warm down here?" asked Ernie as he rolled up his ski mask and stuffed his scarf into his backpack.

"No," agreed Natalia, pulling off her gloves. "It's hot."

"Oh, I get it," exclaimed Harley as he approached the end of the tunnel where the air was thickest and pointed toward a crack in the floor. "The mist is coming up out of a hole in the ground. So's all the heat. It's got be at least a hundred degrees down here."

"Volcanic vents," Natalia stated flatly. "It makes sense. That terrible smell must be sulfur."

Slowly, the Griffins stepped near the vent and peered down. "It's not very wide," observed Harley. "Maybe we can just step over it."

Suddenly the ground trembled, sending a cloud of vapor shooting up from the fissure. The damp air smelled terrible, but even before the friends could retreat, they fell into a coughing fit. Luckily for Ernie, his inhaler cleared up the matter in no time. The others weren't so lucky, but after several moments, the rumbling stopped and so did the explosion of vapor.

"Are you sure volcanoes are supposed to stink this bad?" Ernie asked, putting his inhaler back in his pocket.

"What?" asked Natalia, who was standing there with a blank stare on her face, her long braids clinging damply to her shoulders.

"Didn't you just say that this stink is coming from volcanoes?" he asked, perplexed.

"Did I?" she replied, her brows furrowed in concentration.

"That's what I'm asking," Ernie exclaimed. "What do you think, Max?" Ernie tugged on Max's shirt, who was just standing there, doing nothing.

"Who are you?" Max asked.

Ernie shook his head and rolled his eyes. "Not funny."

Max then turned to Natalia. "Do I know you?"

Natalia shook her head. "I don't think so. I have an excellent memory, so I'd definitely remember."

"Okay, guys," interrupted Ernie, looking back and forth at them in confusion. "This isn't funny. What's the joke? I don't get it."

"Joke?" replied Harley, stumbling past the others as if in a dream. Without so much as watching where he was going, he managed to step over the volcanic vent and disappear into the mist.

"Hey! Where are you going?" Ernie called after him, but Harley didn't answer.

Max shook his head as he looked around, but everywhere his eyes landed, it just seemed to confuse him more. "I swear I've seen this place before."

"What in the world are you talking about?" Ernie's nerves began to unravel. "You guys are talking like zombies."

"I have no idea who you are," Natalia replied crisply. "But I'm sure not going to sit around with a bunch of strangers in this disgusting hole." She then turned in the opposite direction and disappeared back down the tunnel. Ernie's eyes grew wide.

"Look, Max. This isn't funny anymore. People have died down here," Ernie said, his voice quavering with panic. "Please . . . will someone tell me what's going on?"

Max just stared at him blankly, and that's when Ernie realized they weren't playing games. Something had wiped their memory, and in that instant, Ernie knew their survival rested squarely on his small shoulders.

"Okay," he said, taking a deep breath. "I want you to sit down and wait here," he instructed, gently helping Max to the tunnel's floor. "Can you do that?"

Max nodded, his eyes staring blankly as he smiled. "Oh, boy," Ernie breathed. Max's brain had gone to recess.

More comfortable with backtracking than diving into the unknown mist where Harley had disappeared to, Ernie decided to go after Natalia. His flashlight firmly in hand, Ernie took one last hit from his inhaler and headed back down the passage toward the place he last saw her.

Moments later, Ernie came to an intersection with at least a half-dozen paths, each leading to a separate tunnel. Some went up, others down, and still others wrapped around themselves like a corkscrew. "Natalia!" he shouted, hoping she would answer. Of course, she didn't.

Slowly, his bottom lip began to tremble in frustration. Just like the lost soldiers whose skeletons they had discovered, Ernie understood that the Grey Griffins were likely going to die in these tunnels. Fear grasped at his limbs, stealing what little hope he'd had. For several long moments, Ernie stared at each opening with growing desperation. Then his gaze turned down to the flashlight in his trembling hand. The batteries were fresh, but they wouldn't last forever. And when they finally did die, Ernie knew it would be all over.

That's when Ernie screamed. His voice echoed, growing to a crescendo that was a hundred times more powerful, until it sounded like the very rocks were crying out. Ernie closed his eyes and covered his ears for fear of going deaf, as the remnants of his cry filled the dark passages like the roar of thunder. When it finally passed, Ernie opened his eyes to find Natalia looking at him with irritation.

"You know, that could get very annoying," she said flatly. "You should think about opening your mouth a little less often. It might help you get along with others."

"Oh, Natalia," Ernie cried joyfully as he hugged his old friend. "You've come back."

"Come back?" she replied as she pushed Ernie away with both hands. "What are you talking about? And who's Natalia?"

"Of course, you are!" Ernie replied.

"I most certainly am not!" she answered, folding her arms in defiance.

"Yes, you are," he nodded emphatically. "You've just forgotten. You lost your memory."

"Oh, how silly is this," she replied. "I haven't forgotten my name, and my memory is very nearly perfect."

"If your memory is so perfect, then why are you wandering around this dark tunnel under the earth's surface?"

Natalia paused and looked around. "You know, that's actually a good question. I have no idea how I got here. But I certainly plan to be on my way very soon. Now if you'll excuse me . . ." She then stepped in the direction of another tunnel, but Ernie pulled her back, earning him a spiteful glare.

"How dare you touch me!" Natalia spat. "Who do you think you are?"

"I'm Ernie!" he maintained. "Ernest Tweeny. You have to

remember me. There're also Max and Harley down the tunnel back there. We're all best friends. The four of us . . . you know, the Grey Griffins."

Natalia looked at him blankly. "Then where are the others?"

"They lost their memory, too," Ernie sighed. "Same as you."

"Okay, smarty-pants. Then if three of us lost our memory, why didn't you?"

Ernie lowered his eyes to the ground. "I . . . uh . . . don't know."

"Convenient."

"It's not!" he replied with a glare. Then the tunnel rumbled to life again — though not quite as severe this time. More mist came rolling down the passage behind Ernie and poured over the two Griffins. Ernie immediately began coughing.

"Why are you coughing?" asked Natalia as she looked at him curiously.

"Asthma," he replied through tears that were forming in his eyes as he tried to catch his breath, unsuccessfully. Soon, he remembered his inhaler and pulled it out of his pocket. Taking another deep hit, he sighed. The coughing was gone.

"What is that?" Natalia asked, pointing to the inhaler.

"It's my asthma medicine," Ernie replied, wiping his tears away. "You brought the extra one here for me because I always lose things."

"Can I try it?" asked Natalia, taking it from him and looking at it curiously.

"I don't think you'd like it," he replied. "You said I have germs. . . . You won't even drink out of the same glass. . . ." Then Ernie paused as an idea unfolded in his head. The inhaler. When the vapors blasted out of the vent, all of the Griffins had been there. The only difference was that he had used his inhaler and the others hadn't.

"Natalia!" he shouted again, nearly scaring her right out of her shoes. "I have it. I know why I didn't lose my memory. The inhaler. It saved me. It somehow makes me invulnerable . . . or something like that."

"That's ridiculous," she replied, eying the inhaler skeptically.

"Okay, if you don't believe me, just try it and you'll see."

"I don't want to anymore," she replied, pushing the inhaler toward him.

"Scaredy-cat!" he replied, pushing it back at her.

"Am not!" she shouted defiantly.

"Are, too!" he replied. "You're afraid if you take it, you'll remember who I am, and then you'll know I was right about everything. Then you'll have to say you're sorry!"

Natalia weighed the possibilities in her mind before narrowing her eyes in decision. "Fine, I'll take your stupid medicine, just to show you that you're a twit!" Putting the inhaler to her mouth, Ernie helped her with the mechanism, and soon the inhalant rocketed into her lungs. Immediately, she dropped it to the floor and started coughing and hacking.

"You're trying to kill me!" she shouted at Ernie. "Are you crazy?"

"I'm sorry," Ernie cried, fearing Natalia had been hurt as he rushed to help her. "Are you okay?"

"Ernest Tweeny, can't you get anything right?"

What had just happened? Evidently, Natalia didn't know, either. Blankly, the two Griffins looked at each other for several long moments, fearing to say a single word.

"All right, point taken, Ernest," Natalia finally replied, breaking the silence as she brushed past him into the tunnel. "Let's go save Max and Harley. If they've been without me for this long, there's no telling what sort of trouble they've run into."

Ernie smiled broadly and sighed. He was a hero after all.

Max was next and didn't mind trying the inhaler one bit. He had been sitting in the dark for some time and appeared happy to see someone — even if he didn't know who they were. Moments later, he was standing next to them and pulling his backpack onto his shoulders.

"You did it, Ernie." Max smiled at his rescuer. "Using your inhaler was totally genius."

Ernie's grin stretched from ear to ear. "It's my superpower. Harley has superstrength and I have superintelligence." Natalia rolled her eyes, but her smile remained. She was proud of him, even if she didn't say so, and right there she decided to dedicate an entire page in her *Book of Clues* to Ernie's heroics.

"One more thing," began Natalia as she pulled out her notepad, leafing toward the middle. "It's part of the Prophecy, remember? Mislaid memory and dire dragon? This was the mislaid memory part. I'm sure of it."

Max looked over at Natalia and smiled. It was coming together. "One last Griffin to find," he said with determination as he looked ahead into the mist, through the volcanic vapors where Harley had disappeared. "Let's get moving. Hold your breath, everyone."

Luckily, Harley hadn't wandered too far, and his memory was swiftly brought back with a single shot from Ernie's inhaler. Soon the Griffins were once again racing down the serpentine passages with Max in the lead.

At last, the Griffins emerged from the tunnel of rolling vapors and found themselves in a wide room, perhaps the size of their school playground back at King's Elementary. But it was no cave. This room had been fashioned into a sprawling stone courtyard that lay at the foot of a Gothic cathedral carved into the rock face, dull and black. Upon its high towers was a legion of gargoyles that stared down at the Griffins. There was nothing inviting about this place.

"You don't think somebody really lives in there, do you?" Ernie asked, eying the structure nervously. In fact, only the front of the cathedral could be seen.

"No," answered Max. "It's not a real building. It's just carved into the wall to look that way."

"Whatever it is, it feels cursed," Natalia commented, stepping behind Harley instinctively.

"I agree," Max replied as something strange caught his eye. Just across the courtyard and up three wide stairs lay a grim altar that sat beneath the dark shadows of the cathedral façade. Upon it rested what Max instantly knew to be the first piece of the Spear of Ragnarok.

Slowly, the Griffins crossed the courtyard, ascended the stairs, and gathered around the mysterious altar. To their disappointment, the object that lay in front of them fell far below their expectations. It looked rather like an old piece of scrap iron with no decorations upon its black mottled skin other than a few holes and two golden X-marks carved into iron wings that sprung from the center. It wasn't beautiful. Nor did it look particularly powerful. In fact, this cold metal bit looked like something Harley might haul back from a junkyard.

"Let's grab it and get out," urged Ernie. "Before it's too late."

"Where's the rest of it? There are three pieces, right?" asked Harley, frowning as he searched the platform.

"Through that portal," Max said, pointing to a nearby doorway carved into the false cathedral.

"But that's not a real door. It's just a big stone wall — you said so yourself," Ernie said, peeking over Harley's shoulder.

"Trust me," Max implored, reaching down and taking the shard of iron in his hand. He placed the piece in his backpack next to the *Codex*. "You ready? We have another portal to catch."

"I hope it's warm on the other side," Ernie sighed as he pulled on his ski mask, preparing for the worst. "This mask smells funky."

Max smiled. First task complete. Two more and he'd have the Spear. The Prophecy was coming true.

Return of the Draconist

THE AIR SHIMMERED as they passed through the second portal. During the brief passage through time and space, the Griffins all had the sense that they were being flattened and stretched out, before getting smashed back together again like a ball of clay. It didn't actually hurt — portals never did. But it always left the traveler feeling rather disoriented, and in Ernie's case, a bit hungry.

In a brilliant flash, the Griffins jumped out of the portal, landing in the snow, in the shadow of the very same Gothic cathedral that they had left behind. However, things were different now. This time the cathedral was real, not merely a facade. And instead of a cave, they were standing under the open night sky as a heavy dusting of snowflakes fell gently on their stockinged heads.

As the Griffins turned to gauge their surroundings, they found themselves in the midst of a bright city dressed for the holidays. Everywhere they looked, garlands wrapped the lampposts, and wreathes decorated every door. Just behind them lay a narrow street lined with snow-roofed buildings huddled closely in the cold. Within their windows, the cozy warmth of flickering fireplaces and candles lit the night sky. There was no one in the streets and not a single automobile lined the curbs. The city seemed to be asleep, which suited the Griffins just fine. The less they had to explain to curious passersby, the better.

"I wonder what that is over there," Harley exclaimed, pointing into the horizon where sparkling lights flickered on and off. "An amusement park?"

Max shrugged as Natalia noticed a small slip of paper, driven by the winter wind, rush past her feet. With a quick snatch, she brought it up to the weak light of a street lamp. "It's an advertisement for the Christkindlesmarkt," she explained.

"The what?" asked Ernie, crinkling his ample nose.

"It's the most famous Christmas celebration in the whole world," she explained as though the information was common knowledge. "It takes place in Nuremberg, Germany, and I bet that's what those lights are on the horizon."

"I can smell gingerbread," Ernie sighed, his mouth salivating. "And I'm starving."

"What time is it?" Max asked.

"About two in the morning," responded Harley.

"Oh, my gosh!" Natalia exclaimed suddenly.

"What?" squealed Ernie, looking around nervously, half-expecting a monster to jump out at any moment.

"It's Christmas morning," she replied with a huge smile. "I can't believe we forgot."

The boys looked at one another blankly. In the press for time, and with all that had happened, they'd completely forgotten as well.

"Well, then," Natalia beamed, hugging each of them in turn. "Merry Christmas!"

"Um, merry Christmas," replied Max. Wishing someone merry Christmas seemed a little weird under the circumstances —

especially when their chances of surviving the night weren't very high. But still, it seemed to lighten his heart, if only a bit.

"Merry Christmas," Harley said with a smile.

"Yeah ... ah ... from me, too," Ernie offered uncomfortably, wondering if it was all right to be seen hugging a girl in public.

"Can you think of anywhere in the world you'd rather be for Christmas? It's so beautiful here," Natalia continued merrily.

"Yeah. Home in bed, under the covers, waiting for Santa to bring me some comic books to replace the ones the Black Wolves ruined," Ernie groaned.

"Don't be silly," commented Natalia. "This is absolutely glorious ... well, given the circumstances," she added, looking at Max. She knew his heart was still heavy.

"Anyway," Harley began, "Christmas or not, we should get moving. None of us speaks German, and if someone catches a group of kids wandering around the streets at night without their parents, things could get uncomfortable."

"Good point," Natalia agreed.

"So where to, Max?" Harley asked.

Max stopped and looked around, drinking in the landscape. The portal behind them had disappeared shortly after they emerged, and already another portal was calling from deep within the city.

"This way," Max said, heading in the opposite direction of Christkindlesmarkt, much to everyone's disappointment.

Natalia sighed. "What a shame. I really would have loved to have seen all the lights."

"And tasted the bratwurst," complained Ernie, who was now

drooling over an advertisement longingly. "Not to mention the gingerbread and pastries . . ."

"Maybe next time," Harley offered, catching up with Max through the falling snow as they walked side by side under the cover of darkness.

Natalia frowned. "I'll keep that in mind — if we survive long enough for there to *be* a next time."

Crossing a series of streets with tall houses on either side, the Grey Griffins became acutely aware of a change in atmosphere. Where before everything had felt festive and cozy, now the street lamps had all but disappeared as the shadows of the city fell over them oppressively. The children passed through unsavory alleyways and trekked across spooky courtyards until they found themselves walking between heavy stone buildings, pocked with blackened windows. Iron gates lay torn from their hinges with nothing to guard crumbling entrances except the baleful stares of the gargoyles above.

Ernie was about to say something regarding his uncanny nose for danger, when Harley suddenly motioned for the Griffins to freeze in their shoes. He had spotted something in the snowy mist.

"What was that?" Natalia whispered as she squinted her eyes, trying to get a better view. The snowflakes were falling so heavily now that her eyelashes were working overtime just to keep themselves clear.

Harley inched ahead a few paces and stared down a lonesome alleyway to their right. "I don't know . . . a shadow of some kind, but I don't think it was a person. Maybe a dog."

"Maybe more than one dog," added Max, looking over his shoulder nervously. "I saw them a few blocks back . . . and they weren't small."

"Why would there be . . . ," Natalia began and then reorganized her thoughts a second time. "Werewolves," she murmured as the thought struck the other Griffins at exactly the same time.

"Where are we gonna hide?" exclaimed Ernie as they set out again.

"We don't have time to hide," Max said flatly. "We just have to push on."

"Maybe they're just keeping an eye on us," Natalia reasoned as they passed under an iron lamppost and beneath a stone archway suspended atop two rather creepy-looking pillars that could have doubled as gravestones. "If they're really working for the Black Witch, I suppose they might be watching to make sure nothing happens to the Spear."

"Try not to think about it," reminded Harley. "We haven't found the other pieces yet. They still need us alive."

"You mean they need *Max* alive," Ernie promptly reminded him in turn. "Like I said, the Prophecy doesn't say anything about us. We could still end up being dog food, you know."

"Shh . . . ," Natalia hushed as she gave him a good pinch. "They can hear you, you ninny. Werewolves have dog hearing, so don't give them any ideas."

Quietly, the Griffins ushered past a particularly sinister-looking building, which had a mysterious cross-and-dragon symbol carved above its doorway. On either side of its front gate stood two terrible

dragons, fashioned from black iron. Natalia gasped. Had the dragons taken a breath as they'd passed by? No. Of course not. That
would be crazy.

Soon the Griffins found themselves standing at the entrance to
a circular courtyard bounded on all sides by gray buildings that
frowned down upon it. The only gate leading into the court lay
before them, but it had been swung open as if the kids had been
expected. Max looked around suspiciously, wondering if it might
be a trap. Once they were in the courtyard, they would have no
place to go. But he also knew this is exactly where the portal lay.
The Griffins had no choice.

Cautiously, they shuffled through the gate and looked around.
The first thing they noticed was the ominous silence that had suddenly fallen over their surroundings. They were beginning to feel
alone and very far away from the world they knew. Even the wolves
seemed to have given up the pursuit, for they were nowhere to
be seen.

The only figure to share their view was an old statue that stood
near the center of the square. Curious, the Griffins approached and
found the carven image of a man clad in heavy armor standing
upon a dais. From his shoulders cascaded a fur-lined cloak that
pooled at his feet like melted candle wax. The statue was severely
weathered, but upon his breastplate, still barely perceptible, the
Griffins could see the same strange cross-and-dragon symbol that
had decorated the sinister buildings surrounding the city square.

His long hair was swept sharply back as it fell from a widow's
peak, giving the knight the appearance of someone born to nobility.

His nose was proud and finely chiseled, as was his chin. And though his eyes were that of a conqueror, they were lined with a haunting sadness.

At this solemn figure's feet lay a stone dragon that curled about the knight's boots like a hunter's loyal pet. Its body was perhaps no bigger than a tiger, but its long tail wound about the dais several times in an elaborate series of loops. Covered in an impressive coat of armored scales and spiked protrusions, the monster had no wings, yet it appeared no less dreadful for their absence. If that wasn't frightening enough, its head was thrown back, revealing a mouthful of deadly teeth and a long, serpentine tongue.

"Um . . . can we go back now?" asked Ernie with chattering teeth. His heart pounding in his chest, Ernie's hands grew clammy beneath the woolen mittens.

"It's incredible," Natalia gasped as she drew near. "I mean, despite all the cracks, I've never seen a statue that looked so real. It's amazing." Then she had an idea. "What if this has something to do with the Prophecy?" she asked "You know, the *dire dragon* part. I mean, it can't be a coincidence." Then as she read the placard beneath the figure's snowy feet, her jaw fell, her face turning ashen.

"What now?" Harley asked.

Natalia said nothing, simply pointing to the sign beneath the figure's snowy feet. It read Vlad Dracula, and his birth year, AD 1431. Oddly, and perhaps a little eerily, there was no year marking his death.

"So what?" Ernie replied, rubbing his arms in the cold. "It's just some old dead guy. Can we please leave now?"

"You're looking at Vlad the Impaler . . . the real-life Dracula," explained Harley, who had actually done a report on the notorious vampire for school.

"A vampire?" exclaimed Ernie, suddenly forgetting his frozen toes and peering up at the dark stone figure. "This guy was a . . . a . . . a blood sucker?"

"Dracula wasn't really a vampire," Harley interjected. "People just made up those stories because they thought he was a freak. It's kind of like the kids in sixth grade who say that you eat your toenails." Ernie looked rather awkward for a moment. He hadn't realized the rumor had spread.

"I thought Dracula was a vampire, too," confessed Max, suddenly recalling the nightmare that had invaded his dreams back in Avalon — the unmistakable smile of a vampire.

"In Latin, *draco* means dragon," Natalia explained as she brushed the wet snow from her notebook in irritation. "It doesn't really have anything to do with vampires. That was just an old wives' tale."

"Yeah, Dracula was a member of the Order of the Dragon, if I remember right," Harley added casually.

"Wait. Didn't the Librarian say something about them back on Bass Rock?" asked Max. "The Order of the Dragon . . . they're kinda like the Templars, but more dangerous, right?"

"Yes, that's right," agreed Natalia, making the connection. "They were the ones who prevented Morgan LaFey from getting her hands on the Spear, but something happened to them."

"Dracula's relationship to the Templars makes sense," Harley began. "Everything I read about him said he was a pretty honorable guy. A little rough around the edges, but in those days it was kill or be killed."

"So does that mean Dracula's a good guy?" Ernie asked, growing hopeful. Though when he looked up at the statue, he had a hard time believing Vlad the Impaler had done anything virtuous in his entire life.

"That's a tricky question," Harley said, scratching his head. "Not *good* in the same way that Iver is, but he always kept his word and fought for his country to the death. He even had a family."

"That's not the Dracula we grew up hearing about," observed Natalia.

"I know," replied Harley. "He was pretty cool. And practically no one knows the truth about him."

"Look," Max began, unsure how to proceed as he felt time slipping away. "If this is the dragon from the Prophecy, where's the second piece of the Spear of Ragnarok?"

"I don't think anyone would just leave it sitting out here in plain sight," Natalia advised. "But it has to be close. Are you sure the portal is in this courtyard and not in one of the buildings around here?"

"Yeah," Max replied. "I'm positive. I just can't see it yet."

The Grey Griffins searched around the statue, but to no avail. There was no secret compartment in the base of the statue, and there were certainly no signs guiding their way. They couldn't see a single thing that resembled a rare and powerful artifact. Were they looking in the wrong place, or did they even know what they were looking for?

"Unless . . . ," Harley began as he raced around to the front of Dracula's statue. "Yes!" he called. "I found it."

"Where?" exclaimed Max, excited, though doubtful. He'd circled the statue a hundred times already and had come up empty-handed.

"Hidden in plain sight," Harley said, beaming. "Look in Dracula's belt."

Max's senses started to tingle as he approached the statue. What he'd been dismissing as a long knife was actually the missing shard of the Spear they'd been searching for all along. "Yes!" he proclaimed, eyeing the dragon warily before jumping up on the dais, but the Spear had been embedded in the statue, and it wasn't going to budge.

"Be careful," Natalia warned as Ernie stuffed his mittens in his mouth, chewing at their soggy tips.

Slowly, carefully, Max reached out for the Spear. But as he did, the cross that hung from his necklace started to burn against his skin, swallowing Max in a stream of golden light. He screamed as a single ray shot from the cross and struck Dracula's statue.

Just then, a torrent of wind rushed through the square as the iron gate slammed shut behind them, trapping the Griffins in the courtyard. They watched in horror as a stony hand wrapped around Max's wrist like a vice. Dracula's statue was coming to life!

Suddenly the courtyard was awash in a ghostly red glow that rolled off Dracula in waves, and the air was filled with a deep and violent humming. Then the statue began to hiss, as light poured forth from the fissures, nearly blinding Max in the process. More cracks formed across the statue's face and chest until there was now more light than stone. Max closed his eyes. He knew this was the end.

Then, just as suddenly as it started, everything stopped.

Slowly, Max opened his eyes and there, still holding him by the wrist, stood a very real, very menacing Vlad Dracula. He was awake.

Yet that wasn't the only thing looking at Max. Just as Dracula had come to life, so had his pet. The dragon at Max's feet slid its long tail around Max, looking at him with ravenous eyes that never blinked. Fierce-looking, yet beautiful, the dragon's shimmering scales were lacquered in a mesmerizing sheen of glacial blues and snowy whites — a perfect camouflage to the arctic backdrop of Nuremberg's winterscape.

"Please tell me this isn't happening," cried Ernie, stepping back against the iron fence.

Reflexively, Max grappled for the *Codex Spiritus* with his free hand, but it was out of reach. Would it have done any good, anyway?

Dracula looked even more frightful alive than he had frozen in stone. His skin was the color of death, and his dark green cloak was still smoking in the wet snow. Green eyes framed by dark lashes held boiling anger, as the Dark Prince seemed to peer into Max's soul. Then, apparently finding the boy was no longer a threat, he cast Max away. The leader of the Griffins landed in a heap near his friends, unhurt but very shaken.

Then Dracula turned to drink in the city around him, intrigued, yet somehow terribly sad, as the dragon stretched and yawned at his side. Vlad absently reached down to the beast, stroking its head while the dragon nuzzled against the knight's leg as though it were a mere house cat. Max could tell that the man was digesting every clue of his surroundings, from the scent of the air to the modern sounds that rang through Nuremberg. Yet, the dragon kept his gaze steadily on the Griffins.

"Please don't kill us," Ernie begged, cowering as he fell to his knees in the deep snow. "It's Christmas . . . and . . . well . . . I wouldn't taste very good anyway."

"Where am I?" The dark figure's eyes turned back to the Griffins. His accent was thick, but he evidently knew English.

"Nuremberg . . . in Germany," Natalia offered.

"Nürnberg," Dracula replied softly to himself as if someone had awakened him from a dream. "Long have I stood astride the sands of time, for the world has moved well beyond my blood and spirit."

"What's he talking about?" Ernie whispered out of the side of his mouth.

"You." The Dark Prince turned his eyes back to Max. "You are . . . familiar to me," he said, though his voice was uncertain. "What is your family?"

Max looked at the other Griffins, not sure what to say.

"Speak!" Vlad Dracula commanded, his eyes lighting up in anger. This was a man unused to waiting, and as Max eyed the dragon at his side, he thought it best to comply.

"Sumner," he replied. The man shook his head.

"No," he answered harshly, putting his hand to his sword. "Do not play games, I've no humor for it. What is your real name? Tell me, now!"

"Caliburn," Natalia exclaimed, stepping in front of Max. "He's a Caliburn and an heir to King Arthur's throne."

"Caliburn," Vlad repeated slowly as he walked over to Max, pushing Natalia aside. "Yes, this is a branch of that root. I see it now in your eyes. It has been a long time, Caliburn."

"Do you know why we're here?" ventured Max, eyeing the dragon as it clawed the frozen earth.

"Of course," Dracula answered with confidence. "You seek the Spear of Ragnarok, for the Prophecy has brought you to me."

Max nodded, wondering if admitting that very truth would get him killed.

"That's not all," Natalia added, stepping forward to point her finger in Vlad's face. "The Black Witch has kidnapped his father and is demanding the Spear as a ransom. Please . . . you have to help us."

Suddenly the dragon leapt from the dais and pinned Natalia to the ground. As the savage reptilian face closed in on hers, Natalia could feel its frigid breath, colder than the Bavarian winter, as noxious vapors plumed from its nostrils. Harley tried to rush over and help, but was met by a warning growl that could only be interpreted as "one more step and the girl gets it." Harley froze in his tracks.

Vlad turned back to Max and pulled him forward, reaching for the chain that hung around the boy's neck. With a jerk, he pulled it out of Max's shirt and studied the cross. Evidently satisfied, he let the chain fall, though he said nothing. The Griffins didn't dare utter a word — especially Natalia, who was trying not to so much as breathe.

"Who is this Black Witch?" Dracula finally asked as he called his pet back to his side, leaving Natalia to return to her feet and take several cautious steps back.

"Morgan LaFey," Harley answered, hoping Dracula was no friend of hers. If he was, Harley had just sealed their doom.

At mention of her name, Vlad Dracula's eyes narrowed and electricity seemed to ripple in the air around him. It was as though the weather itself was responding to his changing moods, and immediately a blast of cold wind howled through the courtyard, carrying stinging sleet.

The Dark Prince seethed venomously. "Morgan. The same witch that entombed me within this stone coffin to helplessly watch as lifetimes fell and crumbled before my eyes. It is because of her that my family has been cut to the vine and my lands plundered by my enemies. And for what? This Spear of Ragnarok . . ." His voice trailed off in anger as tears formed in the corners of his lordly eyes.

"Morgan LaFey did this to you?" Natalia exclaimed. "How?"

A mist closed around Vlad, the atmosphere about him seeming to emphasize his sadness. With cheerless eyes lowered, he sighed and turned to Natalia. "Because I valued an ideal over love."

"What does that mean?" asked Harley.

Dracula shook his head, lost in thought. "My name is Vlad Dracula, Prince of Walachia and the last of the Crusaders . . . the defenders of Europe. It was I who answered the call when the Black Witch marshaled her minions, and I alone stood between enlightenment and the powers of darkness. But my opposition to her evil machination's ultimately led to my demise . . . and that of my dear wife. Though I opposed the Black Witch and defeated her plans to claim the Spear again and again, my life and those of my family were destroyed one by one. In the end, she kidnapped my infant daughter to use as leverage against me."

"You turned yourself over to Morgan to save your daughter's life?" Natalia breathed in astonishment as Vlad Dracula turned from monster to hero right before her eyes.

"That was the intent, but not the result," the Dark Prince replied, taking a deeply painful breath as he stroked his dragon again. "Only after I was turned to stone did she realize that in her haste, she had mistakenly ensnared the shard of the Spear as well. It was out of her reach — protected by a magic even she could not un-make. A victory for the Order of the Dragon. But not without cost. Trapped in stone, I could do nothing to prevent the death of my daughter, who was dragged out in front of me — standing where you are now — and killed by the vengeful hand of Morgan LaFey."

The dragon roared as tears formed in Natalia's eyes. Her heart broke as she listened to the agonizing memories of the warlord. She couldn't imagine the pain that had tortured him over all those years. "I . . . I'm sorry," she said, wanting to do or perhaps even say more, though she could think of nothing. Instead, Natalia began to cry for a man she had just met.

Vlad winced, turning away from her tears. "The witch will pay," he vowed through clenched teeth. "But . . ."

The Griffins paused in expectation as the Dark Prince's eyes grew fiery once again.

"She would have known you had to come here," Vlad stated, at once taking on the air of the great military strategist that Harley had read about. "Which means she knows I would have broken free from her curse by now."

"We were followed," Harley admitted, looking over his shoulder.

Suddenly, a wolf howled, followed by the call of a dozen more as Max's arm began to flare with pain once more.

"LaFey planned this," Prince Dracula seethed, "thinking I would be weak and unaware. . . . She is wrong."

"But they're werewolves," Natalia warned. "We have to get out of here."

Vlad turned quickly to Max. "You are the One." It was said as a matter of fact, not posed as a question. "'Overwhelming from the Well Witching, within the blood of the Book and he that bears it . . .' It is you who bears the Codex now, and it is you who bears the symbol of the Templar, carrying the blood of Caliburn in your veins."

Max nodded as Dracula pulled the shard of the Spear from his belt. "The time has come for the Prophecy to be fulfilled," Vlad spoke solemnly. "I will bear it no longer, and I pray it brings you less misery than it has delivered unto me and my family."

Taking the blade in his hand, Max felt the cold metal, dark and heavy even through his glove. If he had had more time, Max might have seen a tear fall from Dracula's face. Instead, Max turned as the iron gate was blown open in a storm of shadows. Giant wolves shot through, howling and snarling, as men in black trench coats suddenly materialized from the mists nearby. At their head was a single black wolf streaked with gray, whose eyes shone fiercely like a fire. In a bone-chilling crescendo of cries and howls, the wolves circled about them.

Yet, the wolves didn't attack. What were they waiting for?

Max looked around nervously. This just didn't make sense. Why would they send him after the Spear and then kill him with one piece of the Spear remaining?

Unable to wait and eager for the kill, one of the smaller wolves leapt at Dracula, snarling. Vlad's dragon was faster. In a blur of teeth, the serpent snapped up the wolf and shook it in a horrendous motion, flinging the body of the broken creature back toward its brothers. The dragon reared up and roared, shaking the courtyard and shattering the windows of the nearby buildings.

Max quickly stuffed the shard Vlad had given him into his backpack, where the first piece of the Spear rested near the *Codex*. It was time to go. But go where? There was no portal. . . . Max still couldn't find it.

More wolves poured in. "We're in big trouble," observed Natalia.

"Get down!" Vlad commanded, pushing Natalia out of the way as a wolf pounced at her. She rolled through the snow, knocking into another wolf that turned and snapped at her. Dracula kicked the beast in its side, bones cracking under the impact of his boot. Then his sword, long frozen, came alive as it was unsheathed, arcing down upon the beast. With a cry, the wolf exploded in white light and disappeared. Had a werewolf actually just died? Max's eyes grew in wonder. After the attack back at his father's castle, Max didn't think it was possible.

That's when the rest of the wolves turned their full fury upon Vlad and his dragon, ignoring the Griffins in their onslaught. But Dracula's mighty sword did not miss. Nor did the dragon fail, sinking daggerlike teeth into its enemies, swinging its spiked tail, and lashing out with its claws. Yet, with the exception of the few that fell victim to Vlad's sword, the others soon resurrected themselves and, snapping their bones back into place, began to howl all the more. These wolves weren't stupid. They knew what they were up against, and they had a plan — Max could feel it. He just didn't want to be around when it happened.

Suddenly, the Black Wolves who maintained their human form pulled out crossbows and took aim. As one, they pulled their triggers, sending a wall of bolts toward the center of the courtyard. Max and the Griffins dove out of the way just in time — but they were not the targets. All crossbows had been aimed directly at Vlad. Yet, despite the onslaught, not a single missile reached Dracula. Acting as his shield, the dragon repelled the arrows. And just as the men in dark leather overcoats realized the futility of their efforts, the dragon shot across the courtyard with a fury and fell into their midst, ripping and shredding in a flurry of claws and body armor. Natalia tried to avert her eyes.

Vlad was now alone against the wolves, and the leader of the pack stepped forward, shaking its fur into a swirl of shadows. When the mist cleared, the Griffins could see that the dreaded amber-eyed Wolf Lord had resumed his human shape. Silently, he regarded Dracula for several long moments as the other wolves drew away.

"So this is the mighty Dracula," the Wolf Lord snarled. "I've heard of you, but I have to say, you're far less imposing than your reputation."

"Dog," Dracula spat, lowering his blade. "You have no authority here. You are but a pawn of an empty lie."

The Wolf Lord paused as if considering something, then smiled. "And *you* are nothing more than a children's fairy tale, Dracula. Your power is only a memory now. My name is Sigurd the Slayer, and I am the future. I am the evolution of everything you could have ever dreamed of!"

Suddenly, the Wolf Lord vanished into smoking vapors, only to reappear in midair as a giant wolf. So fast had it happened and so quickly had the beast moved that Max could hardly turn his head in time to see the horrific result. But Dracula was not caught unaware nor was he powerless against this dark magic. As if foreseeing every move, the Dark Prince reached out and caught the wolf by the throat. With strength unimaginable, Dracula held the immense werewolf aloft as it dangled helplessly in midair.

"Whom do you serve?" Vlad demanded, his voice growing like a rising storm.

The werewolf only snarled, saliva dripping from its fangs, but silence was not an option. Vlad Dracula applied pressure to the werewolf's throat, cutting off its oxygen. Sigurd whimpered like a beaten pup gasping for breath. "Speak, dog," pressed Vlad. "Werewolves can die, despite your reputation to the contrary. Test me if you will, but know that I have the means."

"She will have it . . . ," the wolf laughed breathlessly. "The Black Witch will soon have the Spear, and all your efforts, and the blood of your family, will have been wasted. Then, she will come for you." At that moment, acid drool dripped from Sigurd's jaws, searing the skin of the Dark Prince, burning and hissing. As the Dark Prince jerked his hand back, the Wolf Lord smiled and dematerialized into the night air.

Dracula cursed under his breath.

Then, shutting his eyes, Vlad muttered something Max could neither hear nor understand. But at that moment, the ground rumbled and the air seemed to ignite with magic. A blaze of light burst forth nearby as a doorway seemed to unfold in midair. Max's neck tingled. It was a portal.

"Go," Dracula said. "The final shard you seek awaits on the other side."

"But . . ."

"Go. There is little time," Vlad urged. "Morgan took my daughter captive, as she has your father. If you do not move quickly, his life, like that of my child's, will have been sacrificed for nothing. These dogs will not relent, I fear; and if you are the One the Prophecy spoke of, then you must fulfill your destiny. There is much I can do to aid you, but even I cannot wage war against the hands of fate."

Max nodded grimly and threw on his pack. "Let's go," he said, turning to the other Griffins.

Ernie was the first to scramble through the portal, figuring wherever they were heading was better than hanging around with the werewolves and Dracula — even if he was helping them. Next went Harley, kicking a fallen wolf as he fled the courtyard. Natalia followed, stopping to hug Dracula around his waist. "Thank you," she said quietly. The Dark Prince looked back at her as if he were looking into the eyes of his lost daughter. Then he pushed Natalia through the portal without a word.

Finally, Max passed through the magical gateway, and Nuremberg disappeared in a flash of light.

A White Christmas

"This is crazy," complained Ernie, wrapping his arms around himself as he huddled close to the other Griffins for warmth. "Did we get sent back into the Ice Age or something?"

Thanks to Dracula, the kids had narrowly escaped the wolves in Nuremberg, but now they were stranded on an endless sea of ice beneath a cheerless sun. They shivered as arctic winds tore through their clothing. Their prospects seemed even bleaker than before. To survive, the Grey Griffins needed to find shelter. Soon.

Max rubbed his hands to keep warm as he peered about the frozen surroundings. On one side lay miles of trackless ice. On the other, lay a sloping hill that ended in a precarious cliff. Max had no idea which way to go, and if there was a portal, he couldn't sense it.

"I don't think humans were meant to live here," Ernie continued through chattering teeth. Despite the ski mask and thick scarf, he was frozen clear through. As were the others.

"I don't think *anything* was meant to live here," Natalia corrected, pulling her hood up over her head, tying it tight.

"There has to be a reason we're here," Harley pointed out. "Why else would Dracula have sent us?"

Suddenly, in an explosion of wind, the sky behind them erupted, sending the four Griffins rolling to the ground for cover. Something big shot overhead, and as they looked up through squinted eyes, they could just make out the silhouette of an enormous helicopter disappearing over the cliff, its propeller sending bursts of snow swirling in all directions.

"We're down here!" Ernie shouted at the helicopter as he threw his hands in the air, waving frantically.

"We have to follow them!" Max yelled over the roar of the wind, and as one, the Griffins broke into a sprint, their frozen feet complaining with every step. Their lungs burning, they came to a hill, but luckily it wasn't very high. Harley was first to the top and signaled for them to stay where they were. The four Griffins fell to their bellies. Then, nose stinging and ears aching, Harley raced ahead, scaling a large outcropping of snow and ice.

"Whadda you see?" Max called, his voice muffled by a scarf.

"I don't know," answered Harley, waving for the others to join him. "It looks like some kind of secret base."

As the other Griffins crested the summit to join Harley, they could see they weren't standing on a cliff at all, but rather the rim of a towering escarpment of snow. Far below they could see a vast military compound set into the face of a gigantic wall of ice. No flags flew overhead to mark whose base it might be, though.

"Look . . . boats!" Harley called, pointing down to blue water that carved its way from the distant ocean through the ice before finally disappearing behind two hulking doors. The compound was a fully operational naval port.

"They look more like submarines," Ernie said, watching the torpedo-shaped vessels ply their way through the icy channel below.

"Who has a military base in the middle of nowhere?" Max wondered aloud, watching a streaming battalion of soldiers in dark uniforms march out of the doors and head down a windswept road while snowmobiles and tanks zoomed past.

"Good guys never wear black," noted Ernie as he huddled down in the snow.

The Griffins could see several roads wind their way up the icy ledges. One led to a wide compound where tanks, troop transports, and all-terrain vehicles sat, rank upon rank. Another led to an airfield farther up the slope, on top of a smooth plateau. There, the Griffins saw a towering traffic control center that brooded over a menagerie of every type of plane and helicopter imaginable. Farther up the plateau was an even more astonishing sight. Longer than three football fields, strange ships that looked like aircraft carriers hovered in the air. They were simply enormous, with landing strips lined with dozens of fighter jets and a forest of bristling cannons. Emblazoned on their hulls was the familiar rune and sword that could mean only one thing. . . .

"The Black Wolves," Natalia gasped breathlessly.

"They have a whole army?" Ernie exclaimed. He would have taken to chewing his mittens right there if they weren't already encased in a lacquering of ice.

"And I bet that's where we need to go," replied Harley.

"But," Max began, trying to reason his way out of the situation, "if this is where the third piece is kept, and the Black Wolves are already here, they must have it. So, why do they need me?"

"To hand over the other two pieces," offered Natalia.

Max nodded. It was possible.

"Either that or they're sitting on top of the third shard right now, just waiting for you to come and unlock it for them," added Harley.

"So what are we supposed to do? March down there and ring the doorbell?" Natalia asked.

"I just wonder why Morgan LaFey needs an entire army of werewolves," Ernie complained.

"To defeat the Templar," Max confessed, recalling the words he had heard only a few days before. "Bishop said that once she had the Spear, she'd hunt down and kill off the remaining members of the Knights Templar, and I don't think she has the power to do it alone."

"Maybe there's something we're missing," Natalia observed.

Just then, the ground rumbled beneath them as a blast of hot steam shot high into the air. Without hesitation, Harley ran back toward the rising steam to get a better look. "Hey!" he shouted. "It's a hot-air vent. And there's a metal grate with a hinge on it. Looks like our luck is changing."

"What do you mean?" Max called back.

"That vent's our ticket inside."

"Shh . . . ," cautioned Max, his voice echoing softly through the metal chamber. Once inside the heating duct, the Grey Griffins found themselves immersed in warm air and thawing out a bit quicker than they would have preferred. Already their noses were throbbing and their finger and toes felt like they had been hit with a mallet, but Ernie had it worst of all. With his flimsy tennis shoes, he was an easy target for the chilling bite of subarctic temperatures. Natalia had to wrap her hand around his mouth to keep him from howling during the defrosting process.

The Griffins had stumbled across a ventilation system that bore straight into the heart of the military base and were now navigating through an intricate series of gigantic heating ducts. It was slow going and very difficult as they tried not to make any noise when their boots or zippers bumped on the metal casing of the vents. Each time they nervously passed over a grate, they discovered a new room or hallway below.

"You know, I've been thinking about it," Natalia whispered a few minutes later as they crawled along through the dim light of the duct with a weakening beam showing the way. "There is only one place that can get this cold and be sunny at this time of year."

"Where?" asked Max, who had taken up a position behind Harley's lead.

"Antarctica."

Max lowered himself to his belly and peered through the register in the vent. Below him, he could see an immense room with a shiny floor that lay at least a hundred feet below where the Griffins now huddled.

"What is it?" Natalia asked impatiently.

"I'm not really sure," answered Max. "Maybe an airplane hangar . . ."

Several airships were parked inside, though they didn't look like the type of airplanes Max was used to seeing. In fact, the crafts looked more like flying saucers. Everywhere Max turned his gaze, he could see soldiers. Some of them moved to and fro, while others stood guard outside control towers and manned blinking computers. A vast army of soldiers in black uniforms stood rank upon rank across the hangar, as a senior officer inspected them. These guys meant business. Max just wondered what sort of business they were in.

"There are hundreds of soldiers," breathed Harley, who had joined Max at the vent. "And they're heavily armed, which means this isn't going to be easy."

"We'll worry about it later," Max said, cinching the straps on his backpack. "Let's keep moving . . . and remember, don't look down."

Max took the lead from Harley as they went on, twisting and turning through the vast labyrinth, past several more vents that revealed even more mysterious rooms and passageways, all filled with strange people passing through. There were lots of men in uniforms, but there were also women and children — even kids about the same age as the Griffins. This wasn't just a military installation, it was a whole city.

"That's weird," Harley noted as he peered through the vent at the passing children. "What are they doing here?"

"Even the Black Wolves were children once upon a time," replied Natalia.

"You mean those kids are werewolves, too?" Ernie asked, amazed at the prospect.

"I suppose it's possible," agreed Max. "But wait . . . who's that?"

Walking next to a uniformed officer, a striking woman had entered the hall. Her hair was blond and pulled back behind her head in an elegant twist, held in place by two black chopsticks. Her green eyes were framed by narrow glasses — a beautiful, if somewhat austere, woman. Something was familiar about her, yet Max just couldn't place her.

"Well, I don't know who she is," replied Natalia. "Never seen her before in my life."

"Me, neither," added Harley.

"Then where did I . . ." Max's voice trailed off. As the woman gave a final command to two soldiers, Max knew where he had seen her before — in his dad's study. It was his father's executive assistant.

"It's Ursula. She's in on it," Max whispered in wonder. "The Black Wolves have people working on the inside of Dad's business. This is insane."

"Okay, I'm out," Ernie exclaimed as he sat back and crossed his arms. "This is crazy. Dracula . . . a military base with an army of werewolves . . . I wanna go home."

"You're not going home," Natalia said, turning toward Ernie with a sigh. "It's too late for that now."

"Then I'll just sit here. You guys can go on without me," explained Ernie. "I'll just mess it all up anyway."

"What are you talking about?" asked Max, trying not to raise his voice too loudly. "We can't leave you here. How long do you think you'd last alone?"

Ernie looked around with eyes wide in terror, his body starting to shake. He was going into fear overload. "I'm sorry," he exclaimed a moment later through shaking lips. "But I can't take this. You know I can't. Something bad is going to happen. Besides, I'm almost out of my inhaler. What if I get an attack?"

Natalia turned back to Ernie and put her small hand on his shoulder. "Just breathe, Ernie. If you have an asthma attack, I'll help you. But we've got to get through this together, no matter what. We need one another. We need you."

"What did you say?" Ernie asked in sudden interest.

"I said we need you," Natalia repeated with a roll of her eyes. He sat there in the heating duct as the hint of a smile slowly crept over his face. Did Natalia really mean what she'd just said?

"That's right," Harley added with a reassuring smile. "If it wasn't for you, we'd never have gotten this far. You saved us back at the Eagle's Nest."

"Seriously," Max added. "You're the one with the nose for danger. You're our radar. Besides, without you, we're not really the Grey Griffins."

"Well, I'm only coming if you really mean it," Ernie maintained, looking around at his friends.

"I wasn't going to say this before," Natalia said, "but I'm going to dedicate an entire page in my *Book of Clues* to how you saved us from getting lost."

"Besides," added Harley, "it's Christmas. So what could happen?"

"That's right. Nothing bad ever happens on Christmas," Max said, nodding with a smile.

He hoped that was true. It sure sounded good, anyway. In fact, it even made him feel a little better just to say it. Maybe there was something magical about Christmas that would allow the Griffins to claim the Spear of Ragnarok and rescue his dad — all the while defeating Morgan's attempt at world domination. It could happen. They were the Grey Griffins. After all, look what they had come through so far.

It was at that moment that the ventilation shaft started to shake all around them. At first, it sounded like small shufflings in the distance; but as the noise grew, the Griffins looked at one another nervously.

"Footsteps!" Harley whispered, pointing in the direction from which they had come. Something was in the shaft with them — lots of somethings — by the sound of it. The beam of Harley's probing flashlight stretched across the dark distance behind them, picking up the flickering of several yellow eyes that peered angrily back.

Ernie shrieked.

"Kobolds!" Harley exclaimed, recognizing the evil faeries in an instant. The first time he had seen them, they had been torturing Iver. The last time, they were pulling the Sumner airplane apart as it flew over the Atlantic Ocean. The Griffins were in trouble.

"Move!" Max shouted as the children scrambled down the heating passage as fast as they could, narrowly avoiding a fan blade that took the tassel right off of Natalia's ski cap.

The Kobolds flew through the vents faster than their short legs should have allowed. The noise from their heavy boots grew ever closer as the Griffins swung into a dark passage that sloped downward, challenging their footing with the slick metal. A second later, the floor fell out from under them, sending the Griffins blindly down a long stretch of ductwork that twisted and turned like a corkscrew roller coaster. Spinning and yelling, rolling and screaming, the Griffins slid out of control through the darkness. Desperately, their fingers stretched out, grasping for something, anything to slow their meteoric descent, but by now they were moving so fast that they didn't know if they were upside down or right side up.

Then the heating duct abruptly ended, and the four children found themselves tumbling into the darkness with no ground in sight.

As he fell through a gray mist, Max's eyes barely had time to recognize that it was no longer dark before he plunged into the warm waters of a shallow underground lake. The fall hadn't hurt, which was a good thing, but he was soaked to the bone. And lost. Not to mention, the Kobolds were on their way.

Harley was already up and headed toward shore, which wasn't far off, when Natalia and Ernie splashed down unceremoniously. Max waded over and helped them to their feet, as the four friends found themselves standing in an underground cave, surrounded by high walls, steep and craggy. The ceiling was capped by rolling clouds of mist. The air shaft they burst through must have been somewhere high above that.

"We've got to get out of here," Harley shouted as he pointed to a double door only a short distance away. "Those Kobolds will be on top of us in no time."

"I can't," Max called back, wading around in the water with a frantic look on his face. "My backpack . . . I lost it. It must have sunk in the water."

"We'll have to come back for it," Harley said. "There are too many . . ."

"We can't," shouted Max as he pushed passed Natalia. "I have to find those shards . . . my dad's life depends on it."

"Look out!" shrieked Natalia.

Suddenly, the Kobolds could be seen breaking through the low-lying clouds, plummeting into the water. Any hope of the little monsters being stunned by the fall evaporated as they rose quickly to their feet. The Griffins were surrounded by the ugly creatures with yellow eyes, long snouts, wiry whiskers, and foul tempers. Kobolds were described in the game of Round Table as the smarter cousin to the common goblin — though hardly more attractive for all their intelligence. Apart from being expert diggers, they had two very special traits that made them ideal for Morgan's services: They could see through walls and were immune to the only weapon known to affect other faeries — iron. That immunity rendered Harley's ring and Natalia's nails useless. Without Max's book to provide its powerful backup, the Griffins were in deep trouble.

Grunting and snarling, the grotesque creatures moved in on them. They weren't much taller than Ernie, though they were twice as broad and strapped in leather armor. Max eyed their swords nervously, as the Kobolds drew blades slowly from their belts. Then one of the Kobolds, presumably their leader, stopped suddenly. Curiously, he kicked his foot underwater, as if he had stumbled upon something. Its eyes looked into the water, then back up at Max, as it smiled knowingly.

"Oh, no," Max gasped as his heart fell.

Sinking its arm into the shallow water, the Kobold clutched at something, then raised Max's backpack from the lake and dangled it in the air before him.

Natalia gasped. Ernie trembled. Max shook his head in disbelief. Everything they had fought for was now lost, all because Max had been too careless. But thoughts of regret quickly vanished when Max saw the lead Kobold pulling out a long crooked knife, preparing to cut the backpack open.

Natalia and Ernie stared on in horror, but Max had moved past anguish and shifted right into hatred. In fact, the more he looked at the Kobolds, who had taken possession of the only thing that could save his father's life, the more his anger mounted. It wasn't fair . . . the Prophecy . . . everything. It couldn't end like this, not after he had betrayed Iver and Logan, sacrificing everything to save his father. His devotion had to count for something.

Something within Max snapped. A well of raw power broke like flood as Max's body ignited in a sheath of blue flame. It shot out from his fingertips, racing up his arms, and within seconds, he was completely enveloped in a spectral fire.

"Max!" Natalia's eyes grew wide as she shouted over at her friend. "You're glowing!"

"Oh, my gosh!" Ernie shouted.

The Kobolds didn't know what to make of it, either; so, nervously looking at one another, they continued their approach, rusty blades extended.

His vision was blurred, and the only thing Max could hear was the beating of his own heart. All he knew was that he hated the Kobolds with every fiber of his being and that they had come between him and his father. All at once, the fire shot out from Max, and though it somehow passed harmlessly through the Griffins, the Kobolds weren't so lucky. The tentacles of flame reached for the monsters as they froze in the water, unable to cry out or run away. The Kobolds shook violently, their skin smoldering and hissing under the power of the fire.

"Oh, my gosh," Natalia screamed in realization. "Max, you're killing them!"

But Max didn't respond. He was aware of his surroundings, but only in a vague sense, as if in a dream. Instead, the single thing that reached out from his subconscious was his hatred of the Kobolds.

"Max!" Natalia screamed in desperation.

Suddenly, Harley threw himself at Max, tackling him and knocking him into the water. In a flash, the blue fire was extinguished. The Kobolds staggered for a moment before they fell back into the water. They were alive, but barely, and their clothing sizzled as they floated on the water's surface.

With a gasp, Harley surfaced with Max's backpack in hand and pulled the Griffin leader to shore, shouting at Natalia and Ernie to join them.

"Wha . . . what happened?" Max sputtered as he tried to get his bearings.

"You went nuclear," Ernie exclaimed in amazed admiration. "How'd you do that?"

"I went what?" Max asked.

"You totally lit up," Harley replied, handing Max his backpack. "Like fireworks."

Max tried to gather his wits. It had been several months since his last episode, but this burst was even stronger than before. Max could feel it in his bones — his body was drained and depleted of energy as if he had swum across the waters of Lake Avalon. Each time the flames appeared, he seemed to black out, leaving him with the uncomfortable feeling that he'd lost all control.

"Um . . . did I . . . ," he began, unable to speak his worst fear. He hadn't intended to kill the Kobolds, but as Max looked over at their floating bodies, his stomach began to churn. Was he responsible?

"No," replied Natalia, wringing out her braids thoroughly. "They're alive. . . ."

"But they'll think twice before tangling with you again," added Harley, though the words fell on deaf ears. Max still couldn't think clearly.

"Yeah," Ernie said, excited as he cleaned his glasses in the warm water. They kept fogging up in the cave, making it difficult to see. "That was awesome."

"But I don't remember anything."

"I'll give you the recap later," Harley said, looking over his shoulder at the door.

Max nodded as he slowly pulled the *Codex* out of his backpack, checking to ensure the shards of the Spear were still there. To his amazement, the book wasn't even wet.

"What are you doing?" asked Ernie.

"He's making sure that when these Kobolds wake up, they won't be able to follow us," Harley replied as he helped steady Max, who was still a little weak from the experience. Soon, Max called forth the magic that he had come to know so well. Fifteen balls of crackling blue flew from the pages, ensnaring the unconscious Kobolds. With a flash, the orbs pulled the monsters back into the pages where they should have been all along — in the confines of the *Codex Spiritus.*

If only it worked on werewolves, their job would be a whole lot easier.

"It's geothermal heat." Natalia nodded in appreciation of her surroundings, turning around in circles, looking at the cloud above them.

"What are you talking about?" asked Harley as they made their way over to the door.

"This whole base," Natalia continued, turning her pockets inside out to let them dry. "It's heated by lakes like this — warm springs deep underground. Which means there has to be a volcano around here somewhere. It's ingenious. Free heat. These guys think of everything."

"I wish they didn't," replied Max with a shake of his head. Thoughts of wandering around inside a volcano were unsettling.

"Let's just get out of here before more Kobolds show up," Harley urged. "Anyway, once we get through here, things will get better."

"I sure hope so," Max returned, rubbing his arms to get some feeling back in them. "Just don't count on me doing that again. I feel drained . . . kinda like a dead battery."

"Don't worry," Natalia said as she pushed a button. The door in front of them began to open. "Together, we can handle anything. . . ."

A blast of heat shot through the door to greet them as the Griffins looked up to see two Black Wolves. In an awkward silence, the Griffins gasped when the soldiers raised their weapons and took aim. It was all over.

Then, from out of nowhere, a shadow rose up behind the Wolves, and two meaty hands wrapped around their heads, driving them together with a tooth-jarring crash. As the soldiers fell to the earth in a heap, Max spotted the hulking form of Magnus, his father's bodyguard. And he had a smile on his face.

24 Roasting on an Open Fire

"MAGNUS!" Max exclaimed in shock. "What are you doing here?"

The giant replied with a slight bow. "I serve your father, and like you, I'll do anything to ensure his safety."

"You've come to rescue Lord Sumner, too?" Natalia asked.

Magnus nodded, then his stern eyes fell upon Max. "You have the other two pieces?"

"He sure does," replied Ernie. "And you should have been there. There were skeletons, and werewolves . . . oh, I guess you already know that part. But then we met Dracula."

"Good," Magnus replied after pausing for a moment on hearing Dracula's name. "Please, come with me. And you can leave your wet jackets; you won't need them any longer. I've located the final piece."

Max looked over at Harley in amazement. Just as things couldn't look any worse, the Griffins now had the muscle and leadership they so desperately needed — not to mention a clear path to the final piece of the Spear of Ragnarok.

"How's Athena?" Natalia asked in a worried tone. She hadn't been able to stop thinking about her since the attack. "Will she . . . be all right?"

"She's in bad shape," reported Magnus. "But the female is in good hands."

As they followed the giant into the sterile hallway, the Griffins looked around inquisitively. Apart from the two guards at the entrance, they could see no one else. Max couldn't help but think that the most powerful weapon on earth should have warranted a little more security around it than a maze of empty hallways.

"Did you know that Ursula is a Black Wolf?" Natalia asked the giant, who had saved her life twice in as many days.

Magnus nodded slowly, but his eyes remained locked ahead. "She may not be the only one."

Was it true? Had his father actually been surrounded by Morgan's agents the whole time? "But how could my dad not have known?" asked Max.

Magnus shook his head. However, Max could see anger boiling in the man's eyes. Max shuddered at the thought of Magnus getting his hands on Ursula. She would be sorry that she'd betrayed Lord Sumner. Max would see to it one way or another.

As they neared an open door, Magnus signaled for the Griffins to halt. "Ahead is a river of lava, marked by an archway with runes," he explained, pointing down the passageway. "You should find what you're looking for there."

"Let's go," Harley exclaimed, pushing up his sleeves.

Magnus put out his hand in front of Harley. "The runes say Max must go alone."

"Are you saying you know how to read runes?" Natalia asked in astonishment.

"Never judge a book by its cover," the Norseman replied curtly. "It could be a very dangerous mistake.

"No way," Harley argued, unfazed by Magnus. "We go together."

"Yeah. We Griffins don't abandon our own," supported Natalia.

"If you go, you die . . . all of you," Magnus growled in reply. "According to the runes, there is only one who can pass safely through the fiery gates that lay ahead. Disobeying the runes puts not only yourselves at risk, but Max's father as well."

Max nodded. That's all he needed to hear. With a heartfelt good-bye, Max waved to his fellow Griffins, promising he'd return soon. Then he disappeared down the hall, leaving his friends behind.

Max moved quickly down a long flight of stairs, not bothering to look back. Every moment counted, as his father's life hung in the balance. Together, the Griffins had succeeded in rescuing the first two shards of the Spear. Max was confident that he would pass the third and final trial as well. There was no other option.

As Max descended through the dark passage, he was greeted by an overpowering wall of heat. The river of fire was close, he knew. He had already shed his winter gear, leaving it at the top of the stairs. If everything worked out, Max would be able to reclaim his clothes on the way back. If not . . . well, he didn't want to think about it.

When he reached the bottom of the steps, Max found himself at the edge of a vast and terrible cavern of fire, its ceiling shrouded in swirling mist. All about, the haunting glow of molten rock flickered, and his lungs began to sting with each breath. Then Max recalled that perilous line from the Prophecy . . . *"to face the fierce flame within the ice's ire."*

A narrow stone pathway snaked out across the molten lava. It was smoothly polished and ascended high above the surface of the fiery lake toward a flight of stairs that connected to a narrow bridge. What lay beyond, Max could only guess.

Taking a deep breath, he stepped out onto the path. Then he took another step. And another. Progress was slow as Max tried to keep to the middle of the narrow walkway, ever mindful of what a misstep might mean. That's when Max began to understand the value of all those hours spent balancing on posts that Logan put him through during his martial arts training. It paid off.

Out of breath and his nerves on the edge of breaking, Max finally completed the ascent and found himself at the next stage of his journey: the dizzying staircase. Each step was steep and dangerously narrow, forcing Max to use his hands to pull himself up. Looking over the edge, he could see the lava exploding hundreds of feet below. And though it took every ounce of strength he had to make the ascent, Max did it.

He rested at the top, trying to catch his breath. Now Max could see what lay beyond: a long arching bridge supported by three massive columns of white stone that rose up out of the sea of fire. The bridge disappeared into a mighty cascade of lava that flowed down from the ceiling above. But between him and the wall of fire awaited three gateways: giant rings that hovered in the air, encircling the bridge. Whether magic, illusion, or other, whatever kept these rings from crashing down and tearing the bridge apart was anyone's guess.

As Max approached the first ring, his gaze moved over the

intricately carved surface. Like the rune stone in the Templar Library, this gateway was similarly designed with a never-ending ribbon that twisted itself into impossible knots — but it was the runes that lay within the knots that were the most interesting. Max couldn't read them, of course, but they spoke to him in a way he could never explain — as though he had been present so many hundreds or thousands of years ago when they were originally inscribed, and that their meaning was just a memory away.

On the side of the gateway, Max spied a round slot that looked exactly like the one in the Witching Well. Was Max supposed to use his Templar necklace as a key once again? Looking around, he couldn't see anything else he could do, other than to simply walk right through. But he had a feeling doing so would be the end of him. If it were that easy, anyone could have done it.

Quickly, Max pulled his necklace out and placed the cross in the slot at the top of the pillar. Immediately, the center of the gateway flashed and a portal opened in front of him. He had done it. One gateway down. Two to go. Taking another big breath, Max walked through.

Max now found himself standing on the other side of the gateway. It didn't seem to transport him anywhere. The bridge was still under his feet and the fiery lake was still hissing below. So with little choice, Max approached the second gateway. More runes awaited, as well as a keyhole, though this one was different. Its shape was narrow and jagged. What could possibly fit in there?

Max scratched his head. The Prophecy had been clear. He was

the only one who could do this, but how was he supposed to get past this? What sort of key would only the One in the Prophecy have?

"Think," Max ordered himself. "You've got to have something."

Could the magic book get him through? Max narrowed his eyes and shook his head in frustration. He didn't know how that would work. This gateway needed a key, not some sort of cosmic faerie prison.

Then he realized: the shards of the Spear of Ragnarok!

Max carefully swung his backpack around and unsnapped the cover. Without pulling them out — for fear of accidentally losing them over the edge — he studied the shards carefully. And to his relief and excitement, the piece they had found under the Eagle's Nest looked to be a perfect fit.

Drawing it out slowly, he took a deep breath and placed it in the keyhole — where, to Max's dismay, the shard was somehow pulled inside, then disappeared. Max's mouth hung open in disbelief as the second gateway crackled to life. There was no turning back.

Max's heart fell. He knew he needed to keep moving, but what would happen when he didn't have the second piece of the Spear? Max sullenly passed through the second gateway, and when he emerged on the other side, he could see the wall of fire dead ahead — as well as the last remaining gateway. Max swallowed hard. The heat seemed unbearable, but he marched on, though his body was burning as sweat poured from his brow, soaking his shirt. It felt as if he were being cooked alive.

As Max approached the last gateway, he hesitated before

placing the remaining piece of the Spear in the keyhole, wondering if there was some other way he could get through without losing the second piece — not that it probably mattered. When Morgan realized Max's quest was now incomplete, there was no way she was going to release his father. He sighed in defeat, sliding his last shard into the hole.

The third gateway roared to life, but no portal appeared. Instead, a giant mirror hung suspended, reflecting Max's own image back at him.

For a long moment, he looked into the mirror as images appeared, slowly swirling about before assembling in ghostly visions of his best friends, the Grey Griffins. Max turned around to see if the others were really there, but they weren't, of course. They all looked so happy in the reflection. Then the green hills of Avalon rolled in the distance beyond. He could see the bright flags of King's Elementary snapping in the wind, and Max caught sight of the tree house his father had built for the Grey Griffins' headquarters. Relief filled Max, and the worries of the moment melted away.

Max saw Logan and Iver wave to him as they smiled. Then his mother appeared, but unlike the others, she was angry. Annika Sumner hadn't wanted Max to come to Scotland in the first place. She told Max he'd be sorry, and from the looks of things, she had been right.

The reflection in the gateway shifted again, and Max could see a dark sky under which the smoking remains of a large fortress appeared. Everyone else had disappeared, save Max, who now looked a bit older. But then something strange happened in the mirror — blue flames burst forth, enveloping his image.

Max's stomach began to tighten as a grisly scene that had played in his subconscious was cast in the mirror. It was a path of destruction and terror. Everywhere he looked, Max saw dead goblins and trolls lying broken on the field of some great battle. Everything was on fire — blue fire — and somewhere in the distance, a great portal, like Oberon's Gate, was hanging in the air, dead and smoking.

In front of all this, Max's likeness stood with deep shadows under his eyes, the azure flame burning about him, coursing over his body. Sadly, Max realized it was him — his older self — that was responsible for the destruction. As his eyes met his own reflection, Max knew that he had brought about this great calamity for sport — not out of necessity — and a pit grew in his stomach, filled with revulsion and bile. Would this be what he was to become?

Then a shadowy figure emerged from the smoking ruin and placed its hand upon Max's shoulder, heedless of the powerful flame. Max knew who it was. Even with his eyes closed, he would have known. It was his father.

Then, without warning, the image shifted a third time, and now Max saw Brooke standing there, smiling with affection. Both of them were older now, perhaps teenagers, but he knew it was Brooke. All around her was a shining golden aura that intertwined Max's blue flame. His mouth fell open. As her eyes locked onto his own, refusing to let go, Max blushed. Then he watched his reflection look away, unsure what to do next.

Then something unexpected happened. Max saw his reflected

image step toward him, to the very edge of the gateway, and raise its hand. There, to Max's amazement, was the Spear of Ragnarok, the three shards now assembled to form the whole, all of them bound together upon a long shaft for the first time in a thousand years. All Max had to do now was take it.

His eye grew wide, but he couldn't resist the gift. Carefully, Max reached out, the flesh of his hand passing across time and space, as he took hold of the completed Spear, drawing it back through the mirror. His hand tingled, and he never felt more alive as he finally grasped the cold metal of the treasure that would free his father.

Then the image in the gateway faded into oblivion as Max hefted the heavy spear, breathing a sigh of relief. He'd done it. . . .

Suddenly everything exploded around him as the three giant rings broke free from their invisible supports, smashing through the bridge with a horrendous crash. Max barely managed to keep the Spear from tumbling over the edge as he scrambled to save himself from falling. But the damage done to the bridge was far too great. First, one of its columns began to shake, then another began to crumble. The bridge was coming down. Max had only seconds before he'd be plunged into the fire below.

Yet, looking on either side of him, there was no place to go. He certainly couldn't go back the way he had come. The gateways had torn massive gaps between where he stood and the staircase leading down. Even on his best day, he couldn't have made that jump.

Then Max remembered Iver's words concerning volcanoes. They were *"thick with portals."* Max's senses tuned and readjusted themselves instantly. Soon, he located a portal not far off, though it was suspended in the air high above the fiery lake. He squinted to gauge the distance, catching the subtle shimmer of the portal as it hung in midair. If he dared, the jump wasn't going to be easy — especially with the Spear. But as the path began to crumble beneath his feet, Max realized there wasn't much of a choice — jump or fall. So, gathering himself and all his energy, Max took a deep breath and launched himself out over the fiery waves.

A flash of light.

Max crashed down upon a cold stone floor and the Spear of Ragnarok fell from his hands, skittering away. He had made it. And though the lava had nearly taken his life, somehow, miraculously, he had survived with only a few bruises to show for it. Max slowly raised his eyes into the bright lights and rose to unsteady feet.

Standing in a colossal hall that stretched for what seemed like a mile, Max was in awe. Its walls and ceiling were crafted from ice, held in place by a framework of stone and steel. The roof was supported by lofty pillars that stood in solemn procession down the length of the hall, draped with red banners that bore the dreaded sword of the Black Wolves, encircled by those strange runes. But that was only the beginning. . . .

Beneath its towering ceilings, filling the entire hall, endless ranks of Black Wolf soldiers stood at attention. Max had never seen so many people in one place. There were tens of thousands of them in formation, standing shoulder to shoulder under the waving banners, as a crimson carpet broke the sea of black uniforms, stretching the remote distance until it finally rose up a flight of wide stairs to the platform where Max was now standing.

"Welcome, young knight," came a darkly familiar voice.

"Oh, no . . . ," Max breathed, turning slowly to face her. There, standing upon a dais before a throne, was Morgan LaFey in all her glory. She was tall, with long raven hair and cruel eyes that seemed to bite with every glance. Her coat was lined with sable fur, and upon her head she wore a mighty crown of onyx.

The relief at having survived the lake of fire evaporated as Max met the gaze of the Black Witch. He was helplessly alone, trapped between a vast army of Black Wolves and the sinister sorceress. Max chanced a look to gauge his distance, but the Spear of Ragnarok was now out of reach, and the *Codex* strapped to his back would do no good.

Morgan was not alone on the dais. Behind her throne stood two figures that left Max unnerved. The first was an albino man with flickering red eyes and black tattoos upon his face. He looked much like the Wolf Lord, and that was an ill tiding. Next to him was none other than Ursula, Lord Sumner's so-called assistant. If Max thought she had looked evil in a business suit, he realized the black leather uniform of the Black Wolves only enhanced this impression. Coldly, the woman who had betrayed his father regarded Max with a self-assured smile.

"I can't tell you how pleased I am that you could join us," the Black Witch continued, her voice dripping with sarcastic delight, as if she had planned every step of Max's journey herself. All eyes in the hall were upon Max as Morgan gloated before him. "I must say that I admire your punctuality. Right on time."

"I brought the Spear," Max stated in a low but firm voice.

"Yes, that was the deal, wasn't it? Well, I am a woman of my word," she replied. Her eyes seemed to bore into Max's soul as he frowned in confusion. "Dear boy, that may surprise someone like you, but there are things in this world that bind even the powerful . . . though perhaps I should strike you down for your impertinent meddling back in Avalon. But no," she said mockingly. "I will honor our bargain. You have brought me the Spear of Ragnarok, so I will return your father. . . ." She paused. "But first, there are some guests I'd like you to meet. . . ."

Morgan motioned to a soldier nearby, who in turn saluted and pushed aside a heavy curtain to reveal an open door. Magnus strode through wearing the leather of the Black Wolves, and behind him marched the three Griffins, shackled together at the ankles with their heads hung low.

It was all a setup — and Magnus was in on it.

"What are you going to do to them?" Max cried, pulling his venomous stare from Magnus as he turned to Morgan. "I brought you the Spear. What else do you want?"

"Think of them as an insurance policy," Morgan replied coldly.

An insurance policy? That didn't make any sense. She already had the Spear; what else was she after? Then, to his surprise . . .

"Hello, Max," came the familiar voice that he had been longing to hear.

"Dad!" Max called as Lord Sumner walked into view, though his heart dropped a bit as he saw his father flanked by two Black Wolf soldiers. But when Max saw that he hadn't been hurt, relief washed over him.

"Max, you did it," Lord Sumner praised his son as he approached the Spear of Ragnarok that lay nearby. "You brought the Spear."

"I did it for you," Max exclaimed.

"I know you did, son." His father smiled proudly as he bent down to take a closer look at the weapon. "I knew you could do it . . . you were the only one who could. The Prophecy was right all along."

Max's smile faded. Wait. How had his father known about the Prophecy?

Lord Sumner then rose to his feet with the Spear of Ragnarok held tightly in his hands.

Max's jaw dropped. Was his father supposed to do that? But the Black Wolves didn't move, and neither did Morgan.

"Dad . . ."

"You did well, son," Lord Sumner assured Max as he studied the Spear. "Exquisite, isn't it?"

"I . . . I don't understand," Max whispered, his mind going a million different directions all at once. "What's going on?"

"You see, Max," his father began. "As I've always told you, there are times when life is not as clear as comic books . . . when strange alliances become necessary." Lord Sumner took a deep breath. "Max, I know you will understand. You're my son . . . my blood. I can't tell you how long I've wanted to tell you about the plans I've made for you and me."

An alliance? With the Black Witch? Surely Max had misunderstood. "But . . . she tried to kill me," Max said in frustration, pointing at Morgan LaFey as tears formed in his eyes.

Lord Sumner shook his head. "It was an illusion, Max. You were never really in danger. I would never allow it, though the façade was necessary to allow you to discover the Prophecy . . . to show you your destiny. Max, there are things in motion you don't understand . . . things greater than both of us."

"But . . ."

"Max, we needed you. I need you; and together, working with Morgan, our family can change the world."

Max was dumbstruck.

"Not with charity balls and fundraisers to save the rain forest," his father continued. "No, Max. We can change the world in ways you've never dreamed possible. So now, you must decide."

"Decide what?" Max asked, taking an uneasy step back in apprehension.

"To join me." Lord Sumner's words seemed to hang in the air like smoke. Here, at his fingertips, was the offer Max wanted . . . a relationship with the father he had yearned for. But where was the man who had tossed around the football in the backyard and taken Max to countless baseball games? What had happened to the loving father who'd stood by his bedside when Max was in the hospital with a broken arm? Had that person ever existed, or was it all just a sad nightmare?

Morgan took a step closer. "Enlightening, isn't it, young Grayson Maximillian," she began. "I know this might be difficult for you to comprehend . . . you must be feeling so fearful . . . and yes, cautious. But in your hesitation, you dishonor your father."

"Leave me alone," Max replied with a glare. "You don't know anything about me."

Morgan replied coolly, "It is you who appears to have known nothing of your father. You who claim to love him most neither knows him nor supports him when he offers the world to you."

"What about my friends?" Max shouted, looking over at the other three Griffins across the room. "What are you going to do with them?"

"Their lives are in your hands." Morgan's voice penetrated. "I suggest you consider our offer carefully."

"And if I say no?" Max had to ask.

Morgan laughed. "Then everyone dies, of course. Including you."

Max's heart fell, but not at Morgan's words. It was the fact that his father hadn't even flinched when she threatened his life. He knew now there would be no happy ending — and worse, Max had been betrayed by his own father. "You can't kill me," he replied slowly, his mind reeling, "You need me to fulfill the Prophecy. You said so yourself."

"That, I think, will no longer be a problem," Morgan replied crisply. Suddenly a gong sounded as the beat of drums filled the air. As one, the Black Wolves, countless in number, let out a great howl. At the same time, two massive snow beasts, big as trolls, with shaggy white fur and giant tusks, lumbered in from opposite sides of the hall. The monsters bellowed savagely and took hold of thick chains that rose up out of the floor before disappearing into the roof far overhead. With a groan they heaved, and Max watched as a section of the wall high above Morgan's throne lifted away, revealing a ghostly figure that was suspended in a chamber of cloudy water. It was a boy about Max's age — or at least he had once been, and his arms and legs were strapped to his sides. His eyes were closed, as tubes of glowing liquid ran in and out of his body.

"Ray . . ." Max moved his lips, but no sound came out. The nemesis of the Grey Griffins, Ray Fisher was back. A ghastly reflection of his old self, Ray's skin was now covered in blue scales, and black horns spiraled from his head.

Then Max caught sight of a strange scar on Ray's arm, and his own arm began to throb in turn. It was a twin to the wound Max now carried, and he gasped as the puzzle pieces started to fall together.

"I'm surprised you understood so quickly," Morgan continued, her voice taut with venom. She walked up to Max's father and placed her hand upon his shoulder. "Yes, we needed *the blood of the Book and he that bears it.* However, we also knew that obtaining your complicity could not be certain . . . despite your father's hopes to the contrary. Contingencies were planned, and now your blood courses through Ray Fisher. He will be our Guardian if you refuse, and unlike you, Ray will not shrink like a coward when he is called upon. The future has arrived, and you must choose your destiny; though realize that you are but a luxury, Grayson Maximillian Sumner, *not* a necessity. But choose quickly, for Ragnarok has come."

"That is all I need to know," came a dark disembodied voice. And upon hearing it, Morgan's expression froze in astonishment.

It was at that moment that a brilliant flash of light broke through the room, sending a shock wave rippling across the floor nearly knocking Max off his feet. A portal had been torn from the fabric of the air, and it now hung, smoking and flickering. It wasn't the sort of portal Max had encountered before. Instead, it felt as if it had been forced against its will — split open from the inside.

As all faces turned to view the spectacle, a dark figure emerged from the portal's fiery pit. The intruder was cast in shadows, and from his gloved hand hung the lifeless corpse of an enormous wolf, its amber eyes no longer flickering. With a thud, the man let the carcass fall to the ground. The Wolf Lord was dead. Vlad Dracula had arrived.

A roar echoed throughout the chamber, shaking the floors as Max turned to see Magnus transform right before his very eyes. Buttons flew and leather cracked as the giant's body twisted, growing to massive proportions. Gray hair emerged from bulky arms, shining claws ripped out of his fingertips, and fangs filled his mouth. Magnus, too, was a werewolf.

Standing well over nine feet in height now, Magnus towered over the Griffins like a nightmare as he ripped out a massive chunk of the wall, launching it toward Vlad Dracula. The missile struck the Dark Prince, then shattered in a hail of deadly ice shards. With a howl, many of the Black Wolf soldiers fell to the floor.

"You clumsy fool!" the witch roared at Magnus as she raised her hand, and immediately a wall of black light shot around her and Lord Sumner, shielding them from the deadly debris. When the smoke finally settled, Max could see that Vlad Dracula was unmoved and untouched.

Max pulled himself back up to his feet, just as he heard Natalia scream. Turning, he could see her kneeling over Ernie's form lying motionless on the floor. His glasses were shattered, and blood ran down the sides of his face.

Like a wraith, Dracula moved across the flagstones, bearing down upon Magnus. The werewolf howled in battle fury, but not even the might of Magnus could stand up against the rage of Vlad Dracula. In one sweeping motion, the Dark Prince unsheathed his sword and drove the blade deep into the heart of the werewolf. In a howl of pain and anguish, the werewolf blazed with fire, then erupted in a ball of light, vanishing as Vlad withdrew the blade and turned toward Morgan LaFey.

Though the room was filled with thousands of her deadly soldiers, not a single Black Wolf dared to move or say a word. This was a fight between two giants of magic, and there was nothing anyone could do to stand in its way.

"I will end your evil reign this night," the Dark Prince growled, approaching the dais. "For five hundred years you have held me in your curse, witch. You have defamed my legacy with lies and propaganda, and worse, you have destroyed my family. No longer, for now you shall face me in all my power!"

Morgan's eyes narrowed. "Dear Vlad . . . I have not been idle while you slept in your stony grave. Nor am I diminished in my strength. Do you think I have come all this way to be bested by a forgotten hero?"

"So be it," Vlad replied, casting aside his cloak like a matador.

Max watched as the Dark Prince strode across the floor, his eyes locked on Morgan LaFey. He had come for his revenge.

"Max!" Harley shouted across the room. Max turned to see Harley holding Ernie's bleeding body as he and Natalia moved toward Dracula's portal. "We have to get out. Ernie doesn't have much time!"

Max turned to look for his father, but Lord Sumner had fled with the remaining Black Wolves. The Spear of Ragnarok was gone. And so was Ray.

Vlad and Morgan were now locked in a battle of wills, but this was only the beginning, Max was certain. At any moment the whole place might explode and come falling down on their heads. Yet neither Morgan nor Dracula seemed terribly concerned that the Grey Griffins — or the Black Wolves for that matter — would be caught in the crossfire.

"Max!" Harley yelled again. "Let's go!"

Max nodded. He had no choice. Ernie's life was in jeopardy. His friends needed him, even if his father did not. So Max rushed toward the portal, tears streaking down his face.

The other three had already passed through, and Max was preparing to follow when he heard a familiar voice.

"Don't go, Maximus."

Max turned to see his father standing in the doorway, and tears welled in his eyes, though he tried to be brave. "But I have to help Ernie. . . ."

"Max," his father's voice deepened as it grew somber. "If you leave now, I can never offer this to you again. You have to under-stand that those are the rules. If you turn your back on me, you turn your back on your destiny . . . and your family."

"I'm sorry," Max whispered as he bowed his head in sorrow. Unable to meet his father's disappointed gaze, Max stepped into the portal and disappeared just as the throne room exploded.

22 Revenge

THE SKY HUNG like a mourner's veil over a shadowy city. It was late. Or perhaps it was early. Max didn't know anymore as he stood with Natalia and Harley, looking out a high window. The hospital room smelled of rubbing alcohol and medicine. The Griffins had been there for days, sleeping only when they could no longer force their eyes to stay open. Taking turns, they set a round-the-clock vigil at Ernie's bedside, praying that he would come out of his coma. The prognosis wasn't good. Ernie lay broken with a life support system forcing oxygen into his lungs.

"It wasn't your fault," Harley said, turning to Max. "We all knew what we were getting into. Heck, Ernie probably knew more than any of us. But we stuck together, and even now I bet Ernie wouldn't have changed that."

Natalia wiped away a tear from her bloodshot eyes. It had been nearly two days since she'd slept, and she refused to eat or drink anything except a drop of water. She sniffed miserably. "Why did it have to be Ernie?"

Max sighed in frustration. "Next time it could be any one of us."

"Maybe there doesn't have to be a next time," Natalia said, blowing her nose.

Harley cleared his throat, glancing back at the hospital bed where their friend lay. "No, it's too late for that. We can't give up. Not now."

"So are you sure you guys are still in?"

Harley nodded. "It's not like we have a choice anymore. People are depending on us."

Natalia nodded with her back to the others, staring out the window toward the stars.

"Okay, then," Max replied, drawing in a deep breath. "As soon as we get back to Avalon, things are going to have to change. Iver and Logan are already rallying the Templar. They think there'll be a war."

Natalia rubbed her arms against the cold and pulled on a sweater. "The werewolves . . . that's what really bothers me. How could they get so close? They were working side by side with Templars, like Logan and Athena, without anyone realizing it. If they can fool people like that, they can fool anyone. Who knows, they could even be in our schools, our governments. . . ."

"Or even our families," Max growled, wincing at the thought of his father's betrayal.

"Morgan's gonna pay," Harley said, glancing over at Ernie, who was tied to the respirator, fighting for his life. Natalia broke into renewed sobs.

"Then we've got a lot to do between now and then," Max said with grim determination before walking over to Ernie. "You're in good hands here," he said, a lump of sadness forming in his throat. "So hurry up and get better."

Natalia and Harley nodded. They had known this was to be

their last night with Ernie. It was now time to begin planning, and every second counted. Quickly, they gathered their things and filed toward the door.

"We love you, Ernie," Natalia said with a quivering lip as a tear dropped from her cheek. "And we'll pray for you every night. I promise. Just come home soon. . . ."

As the Griffins disappeared from view, a flash of light shimmered in Ernie's hospital room and a shadowy figure stepped into view. It scanned the room, the flickering lights from the life support system reflecting off its luminous eyes. The creature was hardly bigger than a house cat, with spiky fur and a long scaly tail.

Hesitantly, it limped across the floor until it reached Ernie's bed, where it paused for a long while, watching the Griffin struggle for breath. Shaking its head, a tear spilled from the creature's eye, and it shivered.

"Sprig is back," a dark voice ushered from the creature's lips. "And now Max Sumner will have his revenge."

A Round Table Glossary

Black Wolf Society ⊨ A mysterious and powerful underground secret society first appearing around the time of the Second World War. Mingling technology with magic, the Black Wolves are rumored to have perfected their darkest experiment yet.

Bog Beast ⊨ Burrowing in the depths of swamps and bogs, the Bog Beast is a loathsome faerie closely related to the common goblin. Due to its rotting flesh and the noxious odor it produces, a Bog Beast is often confused for a zombie. That would be a mistake. Unlike the undead, Bog Beasts are quick, and much more cunning. Living in groups of no less than a dozen, the Bog Beast is the size of an average eleven-year-old human child and hunts in packs. It has frog-like eyes, allowing it to see in all directions, as well as clawed hands and webbed feet.

Bone Cruncher ⊨ A fearsome beast from the Shadowlands, the Bone Cruncher is a towering nightmare that lurks just beneath the fetid waters of slimy bogs. The monster is so large, in fact, that its shoulders and back, which often can be seen above the water line, are mistaken for hills where trees and bushes have taken root. With a thick hide covered in rough spikes, the Bone Cruncher is rumored to be impervious to dragon fire. While they may be juggernauts of strength, they are relatively dim-witted beasts. The undersized skulls that hold their pea-sized brains are adorned with giant tusks.

Brownie ⊨ Nocturnal, Brownies are scruffy little faeries that stand little more than hand-high. Though Brownies have traditionally lived peacefully among humans, aiding in household chores in exchange for bits of food, dishes of milk, sewing needles and old clothes, they can be a troublesome lot when riled. They are expert thieves capable of causing havoc to homeowners through alarming and mischievous acts. Most humans find a Brownie's taste in fashion peculiar, as these faeries tend to have a fondness for wearing discarded socks with holes cut away for their arms, and hats made of tinfoil.

Codex Spiritus ⊢ The *Codex Spiritus* is a mysterious book that was found by Grayson Maximillian Sumner III and holds within it perhaps one of the greatest secrets the world has ever known.

Crimson Guard ⊢ An elite group of super soldiers operated by Sumner Enterprises to handle extremely hazardous situations.

Dragon ⊢ The dragon is indisputably one of the most terrifying monsters on earth. While most are capable of flight, all of them are armor plated with rows of sharp teeth, long claws, piercing eyes and alarming intelligence. They prefer to eat sheep and other livestock, but will snap up almost anything if they are hungry enough. Dragons are rumored to be immortal and continue to grow throughout their lives based upon their breed: frost dragons, fire dragons, sea serpents, etc. Therefore, they can range dramatically in size (from arm length to the size of a battleship). While not belonging directly to the dragon family, the following creatures are closely related and share some of the dragon's traits: basilisks, drakes, cockatrices, and wyverns. As far as the faeirie food chain goes, dragons are on top. Only Griffins are the dragon's natural enemies. But to take down one of these large serpents, the Griffins must hunt in packs.

Faerie Hill ⊢ Faerie hills are hollow mounds of earth where the faeries live, though they have also been used as both burial mounds and safe havens to hide faerie gold. They are heavily guarded, and to loot a faerie hill brings certain death and frequently something even worse.

Fireball Pixie ⊢ Like most pixies of Faerie, the Fireball Pixies are most often described as beautiful adolescent girls with wings of gossamer and are no taller than a May leaf. They are known for their red hair and tempestuous passions. Fireball Pixies, however, are among the most dangerous members of their family tree, in that if their ire is stirred, they can wield fire and flame as explosively as any dragon. And they can fly twice as fast.

Garden Faerie ⊢ Garden Faeries are a unique species of the magical folk who are most often found tending to gardens and various fields of wildflowers. Diminutive and beautiful beyond compare, these tiny faeries have pointed ears and translucent wings, and wear petals and leaves for clothes. Often harmless, when riled, or particularly when their gardens are threatened, these faeries can be fierce protectors.

Gargoyle ⊢ Gruesome statues carved from stone, gargoyles stand guard upon cathedral rooftops, warding off evil spirits that would threaten both the church and the surrounding village. Legend claims gargoyles would come to life at night when the villagers were most vulnerable, only to return to their resting places before the sun rose.

Goblin ⊢ Twisted faeries, black of heart with sinister intentions, goblins make up the bulk of the dark armies of Oberon, the Shadow King. Though there are many subspecies of goblins, most are about the height of an average eleven-year-old, with long apelike arms, scaly hides, jagged teeth, and crooked noses that ooze with disgustingly slimy snoot. Limited in faerie magic, goblins rely on crude weapons and their overwhelming numbers to defeat their foes.

Hounds of Oberon ⊢ The Shadow King's vast armies are powerful and sinister — but few are as frightfully efficient as his Hounds, a contingent of the most horrible and wicked goblins ever to walk the Shadowlands. The king uses them to track down and find anything fortunate enough to have escaped from his dark grasp. There is nothing and no one they cannot find.

Kobold ⊢ The hired soldiers of the faerie underworld, Kobolds were originally miners. Unique skills, such as seeing through walls and being immune to iron, made them ideal candidates for the employ of the Black Witch, Morgan LaFey.

Jewel of Titania ⊢ The great Jewel of Titania was given to the Queen of Faerie as a gift, by the god of heaven. It is said to hold within it the power of life and death, and about it shines a light more brilliant than a thousand suns. While the Jewel was meant to bring light into the world, the desire for it, by Oberon and others, has brought with it a far more powerful darkness.

Morgan LaFey ⊢ Morgan LaFey is the half sister of King Arthur of Camelot. Sorceress. Immortal. Beautiful. Rich. Her dark motives are known only to herself.

Oberon's Gate ⊢ The Land of Faerie is separated from our world by a great Sea of Mist, impassable and desolate. In order to cross this great emptiness, Oberon requires the help of the greatest of portals, which he personally created and attended to every detail.

Order of the Grey Griffins ⊢ A secret society with four official members: Grayson Maximillian Sumner III; Natalia Felicia Anastasia Romanov; Harley Davidson Eisenstein; and Ernest Bartholomew Tweeny. The Order of the Grey Griffins formed shortly after the members banded together to rescue Ernie from the kindergarten class bully.

Portals ⊢ Like Oberon's Gate, portals are doorways that permit transportation from one place to another, usually in a very unpredictable and sometimes dangerous fashion.

Púka ⊢ The Púka is a terrifying shape shifter from the Shadowlands that most often takes on the frightening form of a dead man with spiraling horns rising from a goat's head. They have a ghastly reputation for waylaying unsuspecting victims deep in the recesses of night.

Round Table ⊢ An ancient game of high adventure, heart-thumping battles, and careful strategy, Round Table is played with a deck of oversized trading cards and a pair of ten-sided dice called knucklebones. The Grey Griffins are the only kids in Avalon to play the game, but these cards hold more secrets than Max and his friends had ever begun to guess.

Shadowlands of Faerie ⊢ With dark corners and dreamlike edges, the Land of Faerie holds glistening towers of goodness and kingdoms of light. But there are also places where evil dwells and attends to its dark purpose. It is here, within the Shadowlands of Faerie, that Oberon, the Shadow King, rules over a world of nightmares and horrors.

Sigurd the Slayer ⊢ Enigmatic mastermind behind the Black Wolf Society. Rich, charming, and gruesomely deadly.

Slayer Goblin ⊢ The assassins of the faerie underworld, Slayers are employed by the Shadow King for one reason: to kill his enemies.

Spriggan ⊢ Spriggans are small but surprisingly dangerous faeries left with the thankless task of guarding the treasures of faerie hills. Easily bored, Spriggans are notorious thieves and troublemakers. As shape-shifters, they can take the form of any living creature.

Templar Knights ⊢ An ancient order of knights, once the most beloved and respected soldiers in the Old World, the Templar Knights were betrayed and murdered on Friday, October 13, 1307, and those who survived went into hiding — taking with them their mysterious secrets and legendary gold.

Titania ⊢ Queen of the Land of Faerie, Titania is the wife of Oberon, the Shadow King. While she rules over the Kingdom of Light and has often come to war against her husband's evil, she is still a fearsome queen with almost limitless power. It is said that even looking upon her unsurpassed beauty could drive a human to insanity and despair.

Toadstool Ring ⊢ Lovers of both music and foolishness, faeries often join in an enchanting dance about a circle of toadstools that can be deadly to any human. Once both feet cross the path of toadstools, any human becomes a slave to the faeries for life, caught in a musical web of madness, never to return. Only a rescuer who manages to fend off the faerie enchantment while keeping one foot outside the ring of mushrooms can snatch the captive, freeing him from his doom.

Unicorn ⊢ Pure and good, unicorns are magical beasts that closely resemble horses, snowy white with flowing manes and a spiraled horn growing from their foreheads.

Werewolf ⊢ Not born of the faerie world, werewolves are cursed mortals who take the shape of giant wolves during a full moon. It is said that men strong of will have been able to master the art of morphing between man and wolf at their whim, even in the daylight, but such power is extremely rare. Though holy water may slow them down, the only way to kill a werewolf is to pierce its heart with a bullet of pure silver.

Witching Well ⊢ Its location is rumored to be somewhere in Scotland, and the Witching Well has a long and shrouded history, hinting at a strange power lurking in its waters.

Vampire ⊢ Vampires are classically described as undead shape-shifters, capable of flight, unnatural strength, and the terrible hunger for human blood. Their existence has never been substantiated.

Vlad Dracula ⊢ The historical Prince of Walachia (born 1431), Vlad "The Impaler" has been wrapped in a dark mythology, arguably linking him to the birth of vampires. A respected warlord and ruler, Vlad was one of the most powerful members of the knightly Order of the Dragon.

About the Authors

DEREK BENZ AND J. S. LEWIS grew up together in the American Midwest and were the best of friends. As children, they explored the sprawling forest behind Mr. Benz's family farm, which they secretly suspected was enchanted, and imagined they were on magical adventures. As they grew older, the lure of these stories continued to fascinate them, and it was these very woodland adventures that inspired Derek and J. S. to pen their first novel, *The Revenge of the Shadow King, Grey Griffins Book 1.*

Mr. Benz, always interested in archaeology, linguistics, mythology, and cosmology, currently works for a Fortune 100 company.

J. S. Lewis has worked in news reporting, radio producing, animation, speech writing, video game development, and now marketing.

Both Mr. Benz and Mr. Lewis live in Arizona with their families.

Danny Graham